---- ★ ----

MOM HAD A WAY WITH MURDER...

"Have you got any ideas who the new girlfriend is?"

"Ideas I've always got. But ideas I wouldn't be ashamed to say out loud, those don't come so easy. There's something this Connelly told you—but you should give me a day or so to think about it."

"All right, Mom, enough beating around the bush. Even Hitchcock has to get to the last reel eventually."

"Who's this Hitchcock? Somebody in the murder case you didn't tell me about yet?"

"Never mind that. What about the *witness,* the one who claims to have seen Roger Meyer go in and out of the Candy's house? You promised you'd tell me your theory about who it is."

"You didn't figure it out yet by yourself?"

---- ★ ----

Also available from Worldwide Mysteries by
JAMES YAFFE

A NICE MURDER FOR MOM

JAMES YAFFE

MOM MEETS HER MAKER

WORLDWIDE.

TORONTO · NEW YORK · LONDON · PARIS
AMSTERDAM · STOCKHOLM · HAMBURG
ATHENS · MILAN · TOKYO · SYDNEY

To Elaine, again.
And why not?
You're still the one who makes it all work.

MOM MEETS HER MAKER

A Worldwide Mystery/March 1991

First published by St. Martin's Press Incorporated.

ISBN 0-373-26067-9

PROLOGUE
Mom Praying

Dear God,

All right, You're probably surprised to see me here. I know I'm not the type that spends a lot of time in this place. The High Holidays, and occasionally on a Friday night, and that's about all You ever get from me. I realize there are women that come here whenever there's a minyan, and wail at You and sing-song at You, and I'm sure You appreciate them very much, but there's no possibility I'm ever going to be one of them. After seventy-five years, You don't teach a dog new tricks. Especially such foolish tricks.

Besides, I also know You don't hold it against me because I'm not one of those regular clients. Does God take attendance? Does God peek through the curtain and count how many seats are empty? If ticket sales were what You cared about, you'd go over to the Catholics, wouldn't You?

So if You're listening to me now—and why wouldn't You be? what else are You if not all ears?—You're understanding already that I wouldn't be here, sneaking into this place in the middle of a weekday when there's nobody else around, if it wasn't a matter of importance.

It's about this murder, naturally. All right, the murder is ancient history, it was all solved and wrapped up and put away in the closet a couple of months ago, on Christmas day. And since then everybody is telling my son Davie what a fine job he did and how smart he is, which I'm certainly not unhappy to hear. But what You know is that the whole truth and nothing but didn't come out yet. And You know that I know it too.

Which is why I'm here, talking to You now. Dear God, am I wrong to keep my mouth shut about this? Am I doing a terrible thing which forever into eternity You'll be angry at me for doing? I did it only because I thought it was for the best, I didn't mean to do something wrong. How could I lie to You about that? All these years You've been acquainted with me, how could I expect to fool You about my feelings and my motives and so on? But even so, maybe I was wrong and I should open my mouth and come out with the truth.

In other words, dear God, I'm full of doubts. I'll tell You the whole story—which naturally You know already, but I have to tell it anyway—and then I'm hoping You'll give me Your honest opinion . . .

Dave's Narrative

ONE

IN A TOWN like the one I live in, there's one thing you can always be sure about—when it's Christmas.

The reminders begin weeks, in fact months, ahead of time, and they quickly grow fruitful and multiply. Christmas music fills the airwaves just as the Halloween pumpkins are starting to turn rotten. Announcements for Christmas sales pop up in the stores before the last crumpled leaflets of Fall Clearance Sales have been swept away. The day after Thanksgiving, every cloth turkey, chocolate turkey, Kodachrome turkey, or any other form of turkey effigy has disappeared from every shop window, and been replaced by Santa Claus.

As I got back to my office after lunch that Wednesday afternoon, Christmas was still officially five days away, but there could hardly have been a local throat down which it hadn't already been thoroughly stuffed. I've made it clear by now, I hope, that it was putting me in a lousy mood.

My office is part of a suite that belongs to the public defender. Excuse me, "suite" is a euphemism. In fact, it's an outright lie. Ann Swenson, my boss, and her staff—her secretary-receptionist and her chief and only investigator, myself—are squeezed into three tiny rooms on the top floor of the courthouse, in the back. The district attorney and his staff occupy most of the second floor, with air conditioning, desks you could stretch out and take a nap on, and magnificent views of our local mountains, including the world-famous peak that sticks up above the rest, like some militant at a rally.

Our respective budgets are pretty much proportional to our office space. The public defender has one aging investigator, plodding along on his tired feet at all hours of the day and night; the district attorney has so many investigators that they're constantly tripping over one another. The district attorney's annual expenditure for coffee and doughnuts comes to pretty much the size of my whole salary.

I never got to my little cubicle to check my mail that morning. Ann's secretary, Mabel Gibson—a sweet little whitehaired lady who just became a grandmother, a role she had been rehearsing for all her life—leaned across her desk and gave me one of her loud whispers: "She's in there with some people. She wants you."

Mabel's eyes were gleaming. After all these years, she still finds excitement and romance in what we do. It's kind of touching, actually.

I knocked on Ann's door, and found her office full of people. That is, three people in addition to herself, but that's enough to make Ann's office look like a subway car in rush hour. There were no empty chairs, so I gently braced myself against a wall while Ann performed the introductions.

Closest to her desk were a couple who looked to be in their middle sixties—a tall broad-shouldered, heavy-featured man, with thick gray hair and immense bags under his eyes; a little woman, also gray-haired, who seemed to be half his height. Her eyes had no bags under them, but somebody had smudged dark charcoal rings around them. Neither of these people, or so it seemed to me, had been doing much sleeping for awhile.

"Mr. and Mrs. Meyer," Ann said. "Abe and Sarah."

Abe nodded at me with a grunt.

Sarah gave a little sigh. "I know your mother," she said. "We met once or twice at Friday night services at the synagogue. She isn't there too often. She has such an active social life, doesn't she?"

I couldn't disagree with that. When Mom finally moved to Mesa Grande last spring—after I'd been trying for over a year to persuade her that it was no life for her alone in a New York apartment—I was a little worried she might find time hanging heavy on her hands. But just the opposite was turning out to be true. Within a month, she seemed to have half a dozen circles of friends, none of them overlapping with any of the others. To me, twenty years her junior, her social life would have been exhausting.

"And this is Roger," Ann said, "Mr. and Mrs. Meyer's son."

He was tall and dark-haired, with a thin earnest face, black horn-rimmed glasses, and slightly unruly hair, which seems to be a requirement of his generation. He couldn't have been more than twenty-one or twenty-two. Abe and Sarah might have been his grandparents; he must be the child of their old age. Given what their own names were, how had they resisted the temptation to call him Isaac?

He stood up and shook my hand, and then he asked me if I'd like to take his chair. "I don't feel much like sitting anyway," he said. "I'm sort of fidgety."

My God, a kid with manners! I thought they'd all been rounded up years ago and sent off to rudeness camps, behind barbed wire, to be trained for modern society.

I thanked him and took the chair.

"The Meyers are here," Ann said, "because this office will be handling Roger's case."

"We were going to get a lawyer," Abe Meyer said, in his deep, guttural voice. "We couldn't afford it, it could use up all our savings, but we were going to get one. Then we went to the rabbi at the synagogue—Rabbi Loewenstein, you know him?—and he told us we should go to the public defender. It's free. I said to him, if it's so cheap, there must be something wrong with it—"

"Abe, Abe!" said his wife, rolling up her eyes a little.

"That's all right, Mr. Meyer," Ann said. "It's a natural reaction. Everybody has it."

"Exactly," Meyer said, giving his wife a look. "So the rabbi answered me, this is one case where free means the highest quality, where you'll be getting something for nothing. He said you've got a good record, he could give me the names of plenty of satisfied customers.

"He also told us you've got a genuine New York policeman working for you." Meyer turned his gaze on me. "And this, I admit, made me feel better about the whole proposition. I'm from New York myself. Born in Brooklyn—Bensonhurst—and didn't leave till I was twenty, when my uncle gave me a job in Detroit, which is where I met Sarah and where Roger was born and also our older child Jennifer, and it's less than four years since we left there and moved here."

Obviously he could have gone on forever telling us his autobiography, with details, but Ann interrupted him. "Roger is facing a serious situation," she said to me. "You probably read about it in the paper this morning."

"I didn't get a chance to look at the paper this morning," I said, not explaining that it's because I'm always in bed half an hour after my alarm goes off, so I'm always gulping my breakfast and rushing downtown to get to work on time. It's one of the penalties of having had a wife for twenty years and then being forced to live alone: you got used to an active personalized alarm clock who wouldn't take no for an answer, and now you have to adjust to the passive mechanical kind.

As this thought passed through my mind, I could almost hear Mom's voice in my ear. "So you know how to cure that problem, no? Do you think this town is populated only by people of the male sex?"

But maybe, before I go any further, I'd better explain about Mom and me, and what we're doing in this unlikely town, in the shadow of these improbable mountains.

I WAS BORN and brought up in New York City—God's country, or anyway the place He had the most fun creating—and for thirty years, until I moved out here, I worked for the New York City Police Department, in the Homicide Squad. I even made inspector before I was forty, which as far as I know is still a record.

Then my wife died, and New York lost its charm for me; waking up to its dreariness every morning, I could hardly believe that it ever had any charm in the first place. So I came out here to Mesa Grande, this middle-sized paradise in the foothills of the Rockies, to become the chief investigator for the public defender's office.

My only real regret about making this move was my mother. I didn't like the idea of leaving her back in New York. I urged her to come with me, but she was absolutely firm about refusing the offer. She liked her little apartment, she had her friends, the supermarkets would be terrible where I was going, and anyway she couldn't really believe that human beings actually lived and thrived west of the Hudson River.

It was a year or so before Mom changed her mind. I should have known all along, of course, that she'd change it. In the old days, back in New York, when Shirley and I came up to the Bronx for Friday night dinner, I always told Mom about my latest unsolved murder case, and between the chopped liver and the strudel she always managed to solve it for me. These exercises were among the greatest pleasures of her life, and she looked forward to them all week.

With my exodus from the city, her homicidal connection was cut. She became restless, dissatisfied, at loose ends. "It turns out I'm just like your Papa," she told me. "I took him once to the Catskills, for a vacation at this big resort. The food was delicious, the fresh air couldn't be healthier, but after the first day Papa spent all his time sitting on the porch, moving his fingers up and down, cutting imaginary pieces of cloth."

Then, last March, Mom came out to visit me, and experienced an amazing revelation. Out here in Mesa Grande, there were plenty of murders for me to investigate. "Isn't it wonderful!" Mom said. "People kill each other just as easy in the Southwest as they do in the Northeast! It gives you a nice feeling that human nature will never change!"

And so, she decided to settle here for good. Not such an easy decision for a woman in her seventies to make. After all, to put it in Mom's own words, "I've been a born New Yorker since I stepped off the boat at the age of seven."

For this reason, I always welcome interesting new cases that have unusual features in them. How else am I going to keep Mom from being bored?

And this brings me back to Roger Meyer's problem, which Ann was now describing to me.

ABE AND SARAH had come to Mesa Grande four years ago, when Abe retired from his job as a jeweler with a big Detroit manufacturing firm. Abe chose Mesa Grande because he had been stationed here briefly during the war. (We're a big military town, surrounded by an Army training post, an Air Force base, and something hush-hush that has to do with missile defense.) Abe was a kid in his twenties then, but he fell in love with the mountains and the clean air and the open space, and he determined, like a lot of other people have done before and since, that he would spend his retirement years here.

Thirty-five years later he did it. His daughter was grown and married, with children of her own, and his son, who had come along as a late surprise, was getting ready to go off to college: it was the perfect time to move.

So the Meyers used a large chunk of their savings to buy a one-story house in the east of town, the Fairhaven section which wasn't as densely built up yet as some other sections. Their house was on a street that had only one house next to it and none across from it. In their new house they had been living happily for nearly four years—growing some flowers in front and some vegetables in back, living simply but not uncomfortably on Social Security and Abe's pension from the jewelry firm, enjoying the fine evenings on their front porch, making friends and keeping busy through activities at the synagogue, and looking forward every year to vacation visits from their son Roger, who had a scholarship to Yale, and occasional appearances by their daughter and grandchildren, who ordinarily lived in Southern California.

Not a bad way to end your life, I thought, if you've been working hard for most of it and prefer not to go out in harness.

And then, a month or so ago, the Meyers' paradise turned into hell. A man named Chuck Candy—the Reverend Chuck Candy, the minister for a local church known as the Effulgent Apostles of Christ—had moved two years earlier into the house next to theirs. No problems arose at first. The Meyers didn't see much of Candy and his wife, but when they ran into each other, they exchanged the time of day in friendly enough fashion. The Candys had a grown son and grandchildren who came to visit every Sunday, and the kids were a little noisy occasionally, but not to the point of being really annoying.

As a matter of fact, the Meyers rather enjoyed the sounds of children's voices. "It took us back to the old days," said Sarah.

"And as long as they're not *our* kids," Abe said, "so if they cry *we* don't have to do anything about it!"

Late in November, there was a flurry of activity at the Candys—sounds of hammering, sawing wood, pickup trucks coming and going with the names of plumbers and electricians on them. This went on for three or four days, and one night, while the Meyers were washing up after dinner, a blast of music suddenly assaulted them, loud enough to rattle their windows. It was a Christmas carol, played by a brass band. "Little Town from Bethlehem," Abe said. "If that's how loud they play for a *little* town, I don't want to hear any songs about a *big* town."

More carols followed, and pretty soon the Meyers realized that the music was coming from the Candys' place down the street. They went out to look, and found themselves confronted by a house that had been turned into something resembling the Christmas display window of a metropolitan department store: lights, flickering on and off in five different colors, had been set up all across the roof, the front windows, and the porch; reindeer, elves, and Santa Clauses, making appropriate ho-ho noises, were gathered on the lawn, around a statue of the Virgin and Child, outlined in bright garish orange neon, also flickering on and off, with a small fountain of water shooting up from behind the Virgin's head. And surrounding it all was that music, coming out of loudspeakers on the roof, so thunderous that the Meyers, even halfway down the block, had to raise their voices to talk to each other.

"Shouldn't we ask them to turn it down a little?" Sarah yelled.

"They just put it up," Abe yelled back. "They don't have it adjusted yet. As soon as they realize it's so loud—"

"But if we point it out to them, they *will* realize."

"Come on, come on," Abe said. "They're celebrating Christmas. We don't want to spoil people's Christmas for them. Tomorrow it'll be better, believe me."

Tomorrow, though, and in the days that followed, it got progressively worse. Not only did the music remain at the same explosive level, but our local newspaper *The Republican-American,* ran an article, in its Lifestyle section, about the Candys' "spectacular and artistic display of Christmas spirit," as a result of which people started showing up from other parts of town to take a look at the show. And they brought their children and their mothers-in-law and their cars with them. The sound of honking horns mingled with brass renditions of "Come All Ye Faithful" from sunset to one in the morning.

Since only a few cars could park in front of the Candy house, the others lined up all along the street or simply cruised back and forth, blocking the Meyers' driveway, making it impossible for them to escape for an hour or two. Heavy feet used their front lawn as a shortcut, trampling down Sarah's beautiful delphiniums. Candy wrappers and soft drink cans were everywhere. So, every few days, were pools of vomit. The faithful were coming all right, and some of them brought their own Christmas spirits with them.

Abe Meyer complained to Candy, and the reverend just chuckled and told him he would feel better about it all if he'd only relax and get into the spirit of the season.

"Christmas is a time of joy and celebration," Candy said. "Celebrate, celebrate. What do you say you let these cares and cankers drop from your shoulders and join these good people in love and worship? Oh, my mistake, you practice a different form of worship, anyways so I've heard. Well, that's the greatness of this country. Religious freedom. We folks wouldn't think of interfering with your religion, so I figure you folks'll understand that ours is just as sacred to us.''

After a week of it, Abe Meyer called the police. He was told that nothing could be done. The Candys weren't breaking any laws—not even anti-noise regulations, which in fact applied only between one A.M. and seven A.M., and the Candys were always careful to turn off the music at one A.M. precisely. As for the lights and the ho-hoing figures and so on, a man was allowed to decorate his house any way he pleased. His neighbors might think he had lousy taste, but in a free country taste was up to the individual. And if people chose to come from miles around to gawk at his bad taste, that was up to them; no policeman could interfere with them. The constitution guaranteed them the right to gawk.

And then, four days ago, Roger Meyer came home from Yale for his Christmas vacation. He saw what was happening to his parents, their sleepless nights, their jumpy days. He called up Candy and pleaded with him to stop. He called the police, took his anger all the way up to one of the assistant district attorneys, and got the same runaround from everyone.

So yesterday around noon Roger stamped down the road to the Candy house and rang the doorbell. Candy opened the door for him, and the two of them harangued each other in the entrance hallway. After a few minutes, Candy pulled a gun out of a drawer in the hall table and ordered Roger out of the house. In another moment, Roger was grabbing Candy's arm, trying to take the gun away from him. It went off. Fortunately the bullet didn't hit anyone. Meanwhile, Candy's wife had phoned for the police, and right after Roger left the house a squad car pulled up. On Candy's complaint Roger was arrested for trespassing, disturbing the peace, and assault with a deadly weapon.

''Why did you start fighting with him?'' I asked. ''As soon as he pulled the gun on you, why didn't you get the hell out of there?''

"I don't know." Roger waved a hand helplessly. "That's what I should've done, I guess. But it seemed to me, if I turned my back on him, that crazy son-of-a-bitch—excuse me, Mother—was going to shoot me! I thought I *had* to take that gun away from him. It was like something out of an old movie. You know, Peter Lorre pulls a gun on Humphrey Bogart, and Bogart grabs it. I'm a big fan of old movies. Okay, it was crazy, but it all happened so fast, I guess I just wasn't thinking straight."

"Nobody thinks straight when they're looking into a gun barrel," Ann said. She turned to me. "You have to finish up your reports on the Raminez case. But maybe you could get over to Candy's house first thing tomorrow. See if you can get some other account of what happened. It would be nice if there were an impartial witness."

"I don't think anybody was there except Mr. and Mrs. Candy and me," Roger said.

"So what happens now?" Abe Meyer said.

"Well, early next week," Ann said, "they'll be bringing Roger in front of a judge. Probably not till Tuesday or Wednesday, because Sunday is Christmas and Monday is still a holiday. It won't be a trial yet—just a preliminary hearing, to determine if there's enough evidence to go ahead with a trial. If the judge thinks there is, a trial date will be set. Probably not for a few months, depending on how crowded the calendar is."

"But I have to go back to New Haven in January," Roger said. "I'm finishing up my senior year."

"I''m sure the judge will take that into consideration. We'll ask him to give you special permission to leave the state, as long as it's school you're going to. But you'll have to come back for the trial, of course."

"Please—Mrs. Swenson." Sarah Meyer hadn't been doing much of the talking, and she spoke up now in a low timid voice.

"Yes, Mrs. Meyer?"

"It's going to be all right, isn't it? They wouldn't send him to jail?"

"We'll be doing everything we can for him. Dave is a first-rate investigator, he'll dig up all the pertinent facts if there *are* any to dig up. And with the kind of persecution the Candys have been subjecting you to, I'm sure we can establish that Roger's state of mind—"

"But you didn't answer me yet. Is it going to be all right?"

Ann was careful not to lower her eyes. "I'm no prophet, Mrs. Meyer."

Sarah gave a little groan. "I knew it. All along, didn't I know it? This is the big mistake we've been making since we came here to this town. Thinking we could be sure about the future. Thinking we could finally not worry."

Her husband went to her and took her arm, and then looked at us over her shoulder which wasn't hard for him, the way he towered above her. "We'll go now," he said. "You've got your work to do."

Abe and Sarah left the room, his hand still holding tight to her arm. Roger started after them, but in the doorway he suddenly turned and spoke to me, in an eager voice, like an excited kid. "I was wondering—is there anything I can do to help you out with your investigation?"

"Like how?" I said.

"Well, if there's any legwork you want done. Looking up things, running errands, just to leave you free for the important stuff. I've got four more weeks of vacation, and nothing much to do, and I know public defenders are always shorthanded. You'd be doing *me* a favor, actually. The fact is, I'm very interested in detective work. It's what I've been most interested in all my life. My major at school is sociology, with an emphasis on criminology. I'm writing my thesis on the unreliability of fingerprint evidence."

"That's terrific," Ann said. "I wish more young people had a serious interest in criminology. If Dave finds he needs any help from you, I'm sure he'll let you know."

She had done it as neatly and elegantly as only Ann could, and the boy left the office with a vague smile on his face. Not quite sure, I suppose, if he had just received a word of encouragement or a brush-off.

When the door had shut behind him, I turned to Ann and said, "So what *are* his chances, do you think?"

She gave a little shrug. "You know what I think as well as I do. A Jewish kid from an Eastern college shoots a Christian minister in his own house, because the kid's parents object to the minister playing Christmas carols and putting a statue of the Virgin and Child on his front lawn. And this takes place in a town that has a hundred churches for every bookstore! Dave, my love, we've got our work cut out for us!"

THERE WAS NO WAY for me to get started on the Roger Meyer thing in what was left of the afternoon. I had too much work to do in connection with our latest client, a Mexican-American hash-slinger who had wiped out his wife and three kids with a shotgun, which then had jammed when he turned it on himself: a very expensive accident for the state, which had to support him in jail and put him on trial, and a tragedy for himself, because all he wanted was the chance to finish the job he had botched. Ann had just talked a jury into convicting him of manslaughter rather than first-degree murder, and now I had to write a report and fill out a dozen forms.

Standing orders from that alcoholic little prick Marvin McBride, our district attorney: any move the public defender makes has to be reported downstairs in quadruplicate. McBride doesn't like us much, and who can blame him, considering how many apparently airtight convictions Ann has snatched away from him in recent years? His strategy seems to be, if he can't beat us in court, maybe he can bury us in paperwork.

So it was nearly five-thirty when I finally got out of the office, walked through the first-floor rotunda, and went down the front steps of the courthouse.

It's a huge building recently put up at great expense, though probably it wouldn't have been so great if the contractor hadn't been the mayor's nephew. You could describe its style of architecture as Greco-Pueblo—columns and arches reminiscent of the Acropolis, mixed in with pink adobe courtyards and belltowers reminiscent of old Zorro movies. When I got to the sidewalk, I turned around to look, and saw with exasperation and disgust that the topmost belltower of all was festooned with silver confetti, like some giant penis masquerading as a Christmas tree.

In the parking lot two blocks from the courthouse, colored lights—red and green, what else?—had been strung up from the poles that marked the parking lot boundaries. I tried my hardest to ignore them as I drove my car from its usual parking place.

A block away, a red light pulled me up next to the Methodist Church. The sign, planted on the grass plot in front of it, proclaimed in large black letters:

CHRISTMAS MORNING SERVICES
DR. POTTLE WILL SPEAK ON
"HOW FAR HAVE WE STRAYED
FROM THE MANGER?"

I switched on my car radio, and the strains of the Hallelujah Chorus came blasting out, apparently sung by the entire population of St. Louis, Missouri, accompanied by every symphony orchestra in the United States of America. I switched it off again fast.

The light turned green, and in the next four blocks—comprising pretty much the entire downtown section of town—I counted five streetcorner Santa Clauses ringing bells and holding out receptacles to collect money. Yesterday I had counted only three of them. They were multiplying like rabbits.

As a matter of fact, the only Christmassy reminder that was missing was snow. Popular ignorance has it that we spend the winters in this section of the country up to our noses in snow, but it isn't true. We get our share of the stuff, only it seldom comes our way before November and sometimes not until after the first of the year, and even then there's a lot more of it in New York City and other points way east of the Rockies. The citizens of Mesa Grande may dream of a white Christmas, but what they can be sure of getting is an infinite number of White Christmas Bargain Sales.

I stopped for another red light and heard a voice quavering shrilly from the curb:

"Beware and repent, o ye sinners! Cast out thy iniquities before it's too late!"

The voice belonged to an old man whose knotted and disheveled whiskers seemed to have come from the same rag-bag as what passed for his clothing. The stick-like arms and scarecrow neck and scrawny ankles that thrust out from these rags were as grimy as the rags themselves, and the voice sounded as if it had gone through the same wringer and been trampled in the same mud.

Nobody around him paid much attention, except for a few amused side-long glances. To all of us he was a familiar sight; he'd been preaching his brand of hellfire on various downtown corners since long before my arrival in Mesa Grande. Every once in awhile the cops, for lack of anything better to do, picked him up and brought him before a judge. But there wasn't much the judge could hold him for. He did a little bit of occasional begging, but he never blocked anybody's way, or even touched anybody with his loathsome fingers.

And he pursued his mission only in the daytime. At night he sat quietly in various local bars, filling himself up with cheap liquor until he was on the verge of oblivion; then he crawled back to his crummy downtown hotel and presumably collapsed into bed.

"Repent, repent!" he was shouting, loud enough to make himself heard above the traffic noises. "Heed the words of the Prophet! 'They have defiled the egg, and they shall choke on the wild yolk!'"

A young couple standing next to him on the curb snickered. Exactly what I had done once or twice when I first encountered the old man. In those days, I wasn't used to his peculiar but basically simple religious vision: the world is a preview of hell, because we are being punished for our brutal and sadistic treatment of God's favorite and most hallowed creation, the egg. Redemption, happiness, freedom from suffering, and eternal life will be possible for us only when we stop frying, boiling, poaching, mixing into batters, and otherwise desecrating the holy eggs around us, and start living with them in peace and harmony.

During the last few years, I didn't snicker anymore. It made about as much sense, I decided, as any other prescription for the millenium that I had run across.

I HAD A DATE THAT NIGHT. Not a "hot" date exactly—because at my time of life that would be more than wishful thinking, it would be sheer fantasy—but at least pleasantly warm. I didn't drive straight home, though. I went to Mom's house, which is only a five-minute drive from my own, so that I could check to see if she was all right or needed any help.

Mom had moved into this house only a month or so ago, and to tell the truth I hadn't been enthusiastic about that move. I didn't see why she couldn't go on living with me. My house has two or three more rooms than I need, there's a large extra bathroom and a good kitchen, and after all, Mom *was* in her seventies and all alone.

But she had turned down that offer flat. "It wouldn't be a good idea," she had said. "You'll drive me crazy with all your fussing. I wouldn't feel like I had any freedom."

"Freedom for what, Mom? You're planning to throw wild parties? You're planning to have men stay the night?"

"I wouldn't say I was *planning*. But suppose for the sake of an argument such a possibility came up, how would you react? You know I'd never hear the end of it. So better we should live in separate houses."

"But it *isn't* a possibility!"

"With you around it certainly isn't."

Nobody ever succeeded in winning an argument with Mom. So I gave in more or less gracefully, and I admit the house she found for herself could have been a lot worse. It had only one story, which saved her walking up and down stairs; it was small but with all the modern conveniences; and it was on a nice tree-lined street in one of the new sections of town, not too far from the supermarket.

No sooner did I get used to the house than Mom hit me with a new anxiety. She bought a car, a sporty new two-door Toyota, colored bright red.

"For God's sake, Mom, in New York you never even knew how to drive!"

"Build a subway here, like any civilized city, and I wouldn't *have* to know."

"But it could be dangerous. At your time of life."

"Don't you read the statistics? The danger is for teen-agers. Practically nobody over seventy ever gets into a car accident."

Very reassuring.

Nevertheless, between the house and the car, I made a point of dropping in on her for a few minutes before dinner three or four times a week.

"What a surprise!" she said, opening the door for me. "Step in, look around, make your inspection. The house is clean. I hung up my clothes. No junk food in the icebox. No marijuana cigarettes in the ashtrays."

"All right, Mom, very funny," I said, as I kissed her.

"Don't get me wrong," she said. "It's nice to have a son who worries about me. It drives me crazy, but it's also nice."

We went into her small living room, where the TV set was on. "So tell me, any interesting murders today?"

I settled onto her sofa, which she had picked up second-hand at Good Will and transformed, after a little cleaning and sewing, into an exact replica of the thick, soft faded sofas she used to have in her apartment in the Bronx. Leaning back in it made me feel like a schoolboy again.

"No murders," I said. "But we've got an interesting as-sault-with-a-deadly-weapon."

I couldn't tell her about it just yet though. We were distracted momentarily by the TV. It was the local news, and the mayor of Mesa Grande, the honorable Willard A. Butterfield, suddenly filled the screen: short, skinny, fifty-ish, with a dry grating voice that was made for grinding out platitudes. He had a flourishing real estate business and had been chairman of the Board of Realtors before he became mayor, but he gave up that job after election, "in order to avoid any conflict of interest," he said. Since then he had supported every single real estate boondoggle, every proposal for annexation, tax relief, water rights, or other special privilege that had come before the Council. Which led some people—unfortunately not a majority—to say that he still had his old job; he had simply changed titles.

But here he was now, on the TV screen, sitting in a big armchair, surrounded by unhappy-looking children of both sexes, with a book open in his lap. The newscaster's voice accompanied this peculiar spectacle: "Mayor Butterfield, in what has become an annual Christmas tradition, appeared at the city-operated halfway house for children earlier today to read Charles Dickens' classic tale *A Christmas Carol*. The children were delighted and enthralled—"

Close-up of His Honor, his face contorted in a broad politician's smile, his voice quavering with emotion, or maybe he was just having trouble with the long words.

Close-up of a small boy expressing his delight and enthrallment by inserting a grubby finger into his nose.

Mom switched off the TV. "You'll stay for dinner?" she said. "I've got a beef stew, I'm heating it up from my dinner party last Sunday."

"I didn't know you gave a dinner party last Sunday."

"Don't be hurt, you would've been insulted if I invited you. It was my afternoon canasta ladies and their husbands. We were celebrating how we got second place in the statewide tournament."

Mom had been in town about three months now, and already she was playing in canasta tournaments. I had been living here for three years, and until this minute my offhand opinion would have been that canasta was a game nobody ever heard of outside of New York City, Miami Beach, and Beverly Hills.

"How about dinner?" she said. "There's plenty stew, and it tastes better the older it gets."

I had to refuse the invitation. I told Mom I was meeting somebody for dinner tonight, and though her expression didn't change I could feel her inside radar switching on and humming. "So? It's somebody I know?"

I knew the question she was dying to ask, and I didn't prolong her misery. "It's a woman I just met. She's got a job at the courthouse, she's a paralegal assistant to one of the judges."

"Educated then? And intelligent, I hope? Your last two or three—"

"She's a nice bright person, Mom. She's just been divorced, and there's nothing serious going on with us. It's the first time I'll be taking her out, all we'll be doing is having dinner and going to a movie."

I broke off, exasperated with myself. Why was I apologizing for myself and justifying myself to Mom, the way I used to do when I was a dating teenager?

"And naturally," Mom said, "it would be too much to expect if she happened to be Jewish?"

"I haven't got any idea if she's Jewish. That's not the big thing on my mind when I meet a woman. 'Hello. How are you? Are you Jewish?'"

All right, I knew this answer was slightly dishonest. The woman's name was Virginia Christenson, and I was damned sure she wasn't Jewish.

"I don't know why it matters to you so much anyway. Shirley was Jewish, and you never liked her very much."

"This isn't true," Mom said. "I was fond of Shirley. She was a lovely girl. It was only her crazy ideas and the snotty things she said that I didn't like. So, if you can't stay for dinner, why don't you tell me quick about your assault-with-a-deadly-weapon?"

I was as glad as she was of the chance to change the subject. Already, since her settling in out here, she had been useful to me in one or two cases; the thin mountain air, I was happy to see, didn't slow up her mind any.

So I now filled her in with everything I knew about Roger Meyer and the Reverend Chuck Candy's Christmas decorations and the conversation in Ann's office with Roger and his parents.

As I talked, Mom's face grew more and more serious, and her chin sank into her hand. When I was finished, she gave a little sigh and said, "It don't look too wonderful for this boy, your client, does it?"

I repeated what Ann had said about our chances, and Mom nodded. "And already it's happening, what she predicted. Did you see the paper this morning?"

"No, I didn't. I was in a hurry when I left the house."

"Because you overslept yourself, and you didn't even get a decent breakfast, am I wrong or am I right? The paper's out in the kitchen, I'll get it for you. Read what it says on the editorial page."

We have only one newspaper in Mesa Grande, *The Republican-American,* and its editorial position is somewhat to the right of Attila the Hun. A year or so ago it came out in favor of mandatory life sentences for third-time convictions for welfare fraud. It also came out, believe it or not, *against* aid to the contras in Nicaragua; its position was that the United States should stop pussyfooting with incompetent foreign troops and send in the Marines "to kick those atheistic Marxists out of our hemisphere once and for all."

Roger Meyer's arrest got big headlines on the middle of the front page.

Minister Shot in Anti-Christmas Assault;
Harvard Student Held for Attempted Murder

A box underneath a picture of the Reverend Chuck Candy—fat face, big nose, ten-gallon cowboy hat, wide smile, apparently waving to a crowd—urged readers to "See editorial on Page 12."

The editorial on page 12 was also framed in a box, so that nobody could possibly ignore it. And another unprecedented thing: it was signed by the publisher of the paper himself, Arthur T. Hatfield.

I won't depress myself by quoting that editorial word for word. Hatfield dwelt at length, and with plenty of repetition, on the sinister attack on religion, morality, and "Christian values" which was undermining the fabric of society in our times, jeopardizing the strength of America, corrupting our children, and striving to establish the Kingdom of Satan in the fair city of Mesa Grande, just as it was already established in other cities across the land, notably New York and Los Angeles.

He referred to the Reverend Candy as "a God-fearing and law-abiding pillar of the local religious community" who, simply because he wanted to decorate his house during this holiday season and thus bring the message of Christ's birth to his fellow townspeople and especially to the children of Mesa Grande, had been intimidated, threatened, and ultimately shot at with a deadly weapon by those whose interest it was to prevent that message from being delivered.

Then Hatfield referred to Roger Meyer as "this young radical from Harvard College coming here from the East to disturb the piety and faith of our city." And in another paragraph Roger was linked with "practitioners of the religion—or should we say, anti-religion?—of secular humanism who, feeling no commitment to Christianity themselves, seek to undermine or destroy all traces of Christianity wherever they may be found."

The word "Christ-killer" wasn't actually used in this editorial, but even an idiot would have had no trouble finding it between the lines.

After awhile, Mom said, "You'll be talking to this Candy tomorrow, this minister?"

"First thing in the morning."

"I'm sure you're planning to ask him all the obvious questions. And I'm sure he's got his answers all ready for you. So here's a question to ask him that maybe he isn't expecting. How late do he and his wife usually stay up at night? What time is their usual bedtime?"

"But why should I care?"

"Am I asking you to care? I'm only asking you to ask. And when you find out, give me a call—I'll be here all day tomorrow, I'm giving the house its big weekly cleaning—and maybe I'll have some other suggestions for you."

Her question made no sense to me, but I promised her I'd ask it anyway. Knowing, of course, that she wouldn't tell me the reason for it until she was good and ready. Mom dearly loves a mystery.

I WENT HOME, shaved and showered, and put on a suit and tie in preparation for my date.

Actually you don't have to do that out here in the foothills of the Rockies. Most people dress up only on the most formal occasions, weddings and funerals usually. But let's face it, I'm a New Yorker, at least in my guts, and it will never seem natural to me to go out on a date without a suit and tie. If God meant us to wear open shirts and jeans, why did he create Brooks Brothers?

All right, the less said about this date, the better. Virginia Christenson had seemed like a nice, good-natured woman every time I passed the time of day with her outside her judge's chambers, so my reaction was perfectly normal last week when she let me know that her divorce decree had just become final.

"It's really a relief," she said. "Would you believe it, I haven't *dared* go out with any men for almost a year. But now, thank heaven, I can start having a social life again."

When a hint like that practically walks up to you and smacks you in the face, you don't ignore it, do you?

But the fact is, you have to spend a whole evening alone with somebody if you want to be sure of finding out what she's really like.

Consider, for instance, the commercials they show before the main feature in our local movie houses. This particular set was full of Christmas cheer: Volvos bouncing along mountain roads, accompanied by "Jingle Bells"; boys slipping cut-rate diamond rings onto girls' fingers, while "Joy to the World" was being caroled in the background; Santa Claus, in the form of a beautifully stacked young woman with a white beard, a floppy red hat, and a miniskirt lined with white pom-poms, jumping out of a giant can of Seven-Up.

I started to whisper to Virginia some sarcastic comment about this obscene display, but I never got it out. She was too busy laughing and crying out, "Now that's just too cute for words!"

After the movie, I told her I'd better take her home, because I had a terrible migraine headache. Another two or three hours of her sighing and gasping at every Christmas wreath and every snatch of "Silent Night"—"Isn't it beautiful? Don't you just love Christmas?"—and I'd be ready to make Ebenezer Scrooge look like the Pope.

I wasn't a bit tired once I had dropped her off at her house. I decided I might as well keep the evening from being a total loss.

I drove east, into the Fairhaven section, and I had no trouble finding the street where the Meyers and the Candys lived. Blocks away the traffic was already getting thick, and pretty soon it was moving bumper to bumper, with a lot of horns doing a lot of honking. It took me more than fifteen minutes to approach the shrine. About half a block away— as I drove by a small house with a few lights in its windows; the Meyer house, I supposed—I could hear the strains of "Little Town of Bethlehem" blasting out in full brass.

Then I was moving past the Candy house. My original idea had been to stop the car, get out, and take a close look, even though there was a definite chill in the air. But it was clear that I'd have to give up this plan. All I could do was inch past the place; if I stopped, I'd arouse the wrath of the long line of cars behind me. Plenty of time, though, to stare at what there was to see.

Even the Meyers' description hadn't fully prepared me for this neon monstrosity. Explosions of tinsel and flickering lights, an obscene crowd of head-shaking, arm-waving dummies letting out shrieks and giggles on the grass. And over it all, "Deck the Halls with Boughs of Holly" thundering out like a marching song at a pep rally.

Soon my car came to a large empty lot at the end of the street. Cars were using this space to turn, screeching and grinding in the effort to maneuver without banging into other cars. My own ancient Ford is small enough so that I managed to turn without problems, then I started down the street again, moving in the other direction.

This brought me closer to the street across from the Candys' house. Nothing but trees on this side of the street. Then my lights picked out a figure I hadn't noticed on the way in. He was standing on the curb, staring at the Candys' house.

His clothes, as usual, were not much more than rags, and his face was blotchy and unshaven; his wrists and ankles, thin as matchsticks, seemed to flare up in the glare of my headlights. Maybe it was that glare that made his eyes look as if they were on fire too; a kind of crazy excitement glittered out of them as he stared at that house which was a caricature of a Christmas tree.

Was his mind, or what passed for it, taking him way back to some Christmas tree of his childhood? Dimly, in disjointed flashes, was he remembering, or almost but not quite remembering, what he had been before he became the mad prophet of downtown Mesa Grande, preaching the gospel of the Sacred Egg to sniggering unbelievers?

My headlights swept past that ragged figure, and he clicked into darkness again, like some actor on the stage when the spotlight moves away from him. I went on driving, and at last I was in the clear.

TWO

AS SOON AS I GOT to my office next morning, I called the Reverend Chuck Candy's house to set up an appointment. No answer, so I tried the number of the Church of the Effulgent Apostles of Christ. A business-like female voice told me the reverend would talk to me, and a moment later a thick Western drawl came oozing into my ear.

"Reverend Chuck here, how you doing, having a nice day?"

I didn't answer the question. People are always asking you that question in this part of the world, but nobody really expects you to answer it. So I started to tell him who I was and why I wanted to see him, but the voice spoke up again, interrupting me, and I realized I was listening to a recording.

"I'm not available for conversation just right now," it said, "but that don't mean I'm not hankering to hear what you got to say. Come on down here to the church, and take a look around at our beautiful new sanctuary and the altar made out of genuine Colorado marble and the game room for young people in the basement, with three ping-pong tables, and the chances are I'll be giving you my personal greetings before you can shake a stick. But if you got more questions you need to ask right now, you just hold on a bit and my secretary'll come on the line and take care of you."

The voice cut off, and so did I. I decided to bypass the secretary and go right out there to take advantage of the Reverend Chuck's hospitable offer.

ON THE WAY I made a short detour. I wanted to have a quick talk with my friend Francesca Fleming, and took a chance

I'd find her at the restaurant she owned, Fleming's Flake. It wouldn't be open for business this early, but Francesca spent a lot of time there, keeping her eye on the help and the cash flow.

Fleming's Flake, located near the campus of Mesa Grande College, was a popular hangout for the students. It specialized in with-it food—bean sprouts sprinkled all over everything—but it also served steaks and had a pretty fair wine cellar.

Francesca herself was a little like that. She had flaming red hair, wore Indian shawls and beads and headbands, had three ex-husbands though she couldn't have been more than forty, and plunged headlong into every advanced cause that might be going, from feminism to anti-nuke protests to clean air to picketing the college because it wouldn't get rid of its holdings in companies that did business with South Africa. But she also had her hair done regularly at the beauty salon of the Richelieu Hotel, our fancy resort on the outskirts of town.

The restaurant was in a small white house on a side street. It had frosted-glass doors and pseudo-stained glass windows, all with the same insignia worked into the design: FF, the two F's intertwined so they vaguely looked like lovers in an embrace. This was the restaurant's mildly raunchy monogram, and Francesca was obviously fond of it, because she had it stamped on everything—the menus, the napkins, the tablecloths, even the little white doggie bags that the waiters gave you when you wanted to take some food home with you.

The place wasn't open yet, and I had to ring the front bell for awhile. Then I heard Francesca's voice from inside, yelling, "Coming, coming! Don't get your ass in an uproar!" Francesca always yelled or barked, she never spoke in a normal moderate tone of voice.

She pulled open the door and greeted me with a hug and a loud laugh. Her outfit, even at this early hour, was outlandish; a lot of strings and lace streaming from her like tinsel on a Christmas tree. "How's the servant of the people?" she shouted. "I heard you served somebody pretty interesting the other day. A mass murderer, wasn't it? Typical American man in the street!''

"He's a member of an oppressed minority," I said. "Surely you don't believe that oppressed minorities should be deprived of their constitutional right to kill each other?"

She roared with laughter; she loved it when people insulted her. Then she led me across the restaurant—tables piled on top of tables, a few waitresses bustling around, a busboy using a broom to smooth out the sawdust on the floor—to her office in back. It was small and plain, equipped for business not for show.

She waved me to a chair and offered me a drink. I told her it was a little early for me. I noticed she didn't take any herself either. She leaned back in the swivel chair at her desk and clasped her hands behind her head. "I'm at your disposal," she said.

"I need some information from you," I said.

"In my capacity as this town's chief source of juicy gossip?"

"In your capacity as resident expert of this town's religious life." Francesca got this expertise from her work with the local chapter of the ACLU. (The American Civil Liberties Union, if there's anyone whose heart doesn't beat faster at the sight of those initials.) "What do you know about a local minister named Chuck Candy? He's connected with something that calls itself the Church of the Effulgent Apostles of Christ. I never heard of it before."

"Your office is going to be defending this kid that took a shot at Candy?" she said. "Good for you. Actually, it's no wonder you never heard of this outfit. Do you know how many churches there are in Mesa Grande? Eight hundred ninety-six—that's about one for every three hundred people—and those are just the ones that are listed in the Yellow Pages. Count them, if you won't take my word for it. And how many distinct and individual sects, including a whole lot that hardly anybody has ever heard of anywhere else? Fifty-three, believe it or not. And most of them don't have any affiliation with the big well-known sects. They're not Baptists, they're not Methodists, they just growed.''

"Where do Candy and his church fit in?"

"That's another reason why you never heard of him before. The Effulgent Apostles of Christ are comparatively new in town. Just opened up four years ago. For the first year, while his church was being built, he operated out of one of those downtown movie theatres that went out of business and the owners couldn't find any buyers. He's another one of the unaffiliated, of course, and there's no way I can tell you the exact size of his membership. Size is the big secret for all these fly-by-night outfits. Let's put Candy's congregation at two hundred families, the upper limit—definitely not the most successful around, some of the older ones manage to pull in thousands. Still, the Effulgent Apostles *are* keeping up the payments on the building loan."

"Where'd he come from originally?"

"Somewhere south of here—Arizona, New Mexico maybe—some small desert town. He went to one of those Bible colleges, there's one to every square foot in certain sections of the country. He didn't learn much grammar or logic there, but he picked up the jargon. He used it to found a church that had the same name as this one here. Did a fair business in prayer meetings and so on, but I suppose the pickings weren't good enough for him in those low-population areas. So now we're the lucky town that's got him."

"Anything shady about Candy's operation financially?"

"I never heard tell of it if there is. He looks to be honest enough, unless you take the view *I* take, namely that enterprises of this sort are con games by their very nature. Otherwise, the only crimes he's ever committed are his sermons."

"What are they like?"

"Ah, now I get to give you one of my little lectures. There are two types of evangelicals, sermon-wise. There's the hellfire-and-damnation type, scaring the pants off their people, and don't those poor slobs love it! And there's the sweetness-and-light type, promising you success, health, happiness, and a Volkswagen dealership if you'll believe in

Jesus and put your money in the plate. Candy's the second type. From his sermons strong men get diabetes."

She looked at her watch. "Oh, sorry, Dave, I'll have to cut this off now. Today's the day when I take my regular weekly drive out to the country to buy fresh vegetables. And I have to start out right away, because unless you get to these yokels while they're on the farm, you can't talk them into selling to you cheap."

I had to smile to myself. Mesa Grande's most prominent bleeding-heart, it seemed, could be a tough cookie when it came to maximizing the profits.

Francesca stood up and reached out for my hand. While she was holding it, her sardonic tone got a little more serious. "Here's a piece of advice, Dave. Don't underestimate that Chuck Candy character. And pass that on to Ann, okay? He may look like a clown, but he isn't kidding about wanting to eat your client alive. And if you saw the paper this morning, you probably figured out that our great newspaper tycoon, Mesa Grande's answer to Citizen Kane, the esteemed Arthur T.—for Turd—Hatfield, wants to join in on the feast. And Hatfield's used to getting what he wants in this town. So watch your step, both of you."

TEN MINUTES LATER I left Fleming's Flake and was back on the track for the Church of the Effulgent Apostles. To distract myself from the lousy Mesa Grande drivers I scanned the various local radio stations, but the disc jockeys seemed to have nothing in their files but "Rudolph the Red-Nosed Reindeer".

My drive took me to a fairly crummy section of town: trailers, motor homes, and rundown clapboard houses, huddled together like bums in line at a soup kitchen. These houses were occupied by blue-collar whites and were identical in decrepitude to the houses in similar neighborhoods for blacks and Chicanos.

The Church of the Effulgent Apostles of Christ presented a strong contrast to the architecture around it. While the rest of the houses were crumbling with age and neglect, the church had obviously been put up just a few years ago;

it was a modern ranch-style building, made of sleek, shiny hardwood, sitting on top of a small hill so the silver-plated cross that stood up from its roof would be visible for blocks around. I wondered how many old ladies had lived on yogurt for a year or two so that some local contractor could take his family to Disney World on the profits from this job.

There was a huge parking lot in back of the church. I had my choice of places now; it wouldn't be so easy on Sundays, I supposed. I went up the wooden front steps, which were just beginning to need a new coat of paint, and paused at the tall double doors with crosses carved into each of them. A cardboard notice was tacked to one of these doors:

COME ONE, COME ALL
IM INVITING YOU TO SUNDAE SERVICE
SUBJECT OF MY SERMEN:
"LETS WISH OUR LORD MERRY CHRISTMAS!"

All this was written out in large block letters, with a black crayon, and at the bottom was a signature, "Reverend Chuck," in a handwriting that put a flamboyant curlicue under the capital R and the capital C.

Going through the entrance doors, I found myself in a long reception room, like a barracks, only instead of bunk beds there was a receptionist's desk and switchboard at one end of it and some leather chairs and sofas along the way.

A blonde in her thirties, wearing practically no makeup but still with possibilities, was pounding away at a typewriter at the reception desk. A wooden placard on the desk told me she was "Mrs. Connelly."

She stopped to take my name, plugged into the switchboard, and then announced that Mr. Candy would be with me as soon as he was free. "He can't talk to you too long, though. Today's Thursday. On Thursday mornings he has to squeeze in a lot of people, because he leaves right before lunch and won't come in again 'til tomorrow."

"What does he do on Thursdays?"

"He goes home, and he doesn't see anybody or answer the phone. He just communes."

"What does that mean, he communes?"

"He communes with his thoughts. He meditates. He looks inside himself. You know, like he thinks."

"And he keeps on doing that all afternoon?"

"You got it. 'Til he's got his sermon for Sunday all finished."

"And he's willing to see me on a Thursday without an appointment?" I let my voice fill up with awe. "I feel honored."

"Oh, that's just how the Reverend Chuck is. What he always says is, 'I'm not one of your big business tycoons that nobody ever gets a look at. If the Lord can take time out to notice the fall of a sparrow, I can sure say hello to folks that go to the trouble of coming by to say hello to me.'"

As she laughed, I realized something about her that had been stirring around in my head below the surface. "That accent of yours," I said. "You're not from around here, are you? Wait a second, it'll come to me—sounds like New Jersey."

"Newark," she said. "You're from that part of the world yourself?"

"Right across the river. To be exact, the Bronx. What are you doing all the way out here anyway, in the wide-open spaces?"

She gave a little shrug. "You know how it is. Things happen. You got to light somewhere. I could ask you the same question."

"I can't answer it any better than you can. Well, it looks to me like you've lighted in a pretty nice place. This church, I mean."

"It sure is. And would you believe it, before it got built there was nothing here but a garbage dump."

"Must've cost a pretty penny to put up a beautiful building like this."

"You can say *that* again! But it's like the Reverend Chuck says, 'It wasn't any high-falutin' bankers or businessmen that did it, it was the nickels and dimes of little people, and God loves those nickels and dimes more than He loves all the credit cards and stock certificates of the rich and powerful.' "

"Doesn't your boss have to tap *some* rich people to keep the church going?"

"If he does, you never see them around here. And there's one thing I have to correct you about. We don't call the Reverend 'boss.' He doesn't approve of that word, because nobody has the right to be anybody else's boss. There's only one boss for us all, that Big Boss up in the sky."

There wasn't much I could say to *that,* so I went over to one of the leather chairs and sat down. I glanced at the magazines on the end table next to it. I don't know what sort of inspirational reading I was expecting, but what I got was a month-old copy of *Newsweek* and something called *Your Church,* which featured a cluster of dollar signs on the cover and a blurb for a story inside, "Making Christmas Pay Off for the Lord."

Then I became aware of the music seeping through the walls—piped-in organ music, slow and boring in keeping with its religious nature. Apostolic Muzak.

And then I noticed the large TV screen that was fastened to the wall above the reception desk. Filling this screen, grinning out at me, was a fat long-nosed face with a cowboy hat set on top of it. Out of this face was coming the Reverend Chuck Candy's voice—I recognized it from the telephone recording a little while ago—delivering, in a friendly easygoing style, pregnant observations about life.

For example:

"You can bring a horse to water, but you can't make him drink. Well, *God* can sure make him drink. Bring yourself, bring your friends, your family, your kiddies, to the waters of Christ, and he'll make the whole bunch of you drink. And the lift that drink will give you will be better than any old Coca-Cola, classic *or* modern, that you ever tasted in your whole life."

Having delivered itself of these words of wisdom, the voice would take a brief rest, the video screen would fade to black, and the organ music would drone on for a minute or so. Then the fat face would rematerialize, like some door-to-door salesman you just couldn't seem to get rid of, and the voice would come out with another gem.

I sat there for twenty minutes, while face and voice delivered eight or nine messages. Then the screen went to black, and the blonde at the desk stopped her typing and said, "Hold on a minute while I rewind." She pressed something under her desk, there was a whirring noise from the TV, and a minute or so later Candy's face filled the screen, starting in again with the horse and the Coca-Cola.

Ten minutes or so later the secretary called out to me: "Reverend Chuck just buzzed. He's ready to see you now."

I WENT WHERE SHE POINTED, through a door and down a corridor and through another door. And I was in the Reverend Chuck Candy's office. Mostly a big desk and a wall full of pictures—Jesus' face alternating with his own.

The man at the desk, fat-faced and large-nosed, with a red-and-yellow checkered sports shirt, looked about the same as he had just looked on TV. Only he wasn't wearing his cowboy hat, so I could see there was very little hair left on his head. He rose up to greet me as I entered, but not as far up as I'd expected. On the TV screen, you couldn't see how short he was.

His handshake was strong and hearty, and his voice was full of good-humored energy. "I sure am pleased to meet you," he said, waving me to a chair across the desk from him. "From what you told my secretary, you're investigating this here assault case, you're representing the Meyer kid?"

"That's right. And you ought to know, the public defender's staff has the same legal right to question witnesses as—"

"Hold your horses," Candy broke in, laughing. "Nobody's challenging your right. Not a bit of it. Matter of fact, I'm happy to answer all your questions and give you any cooperation you need. Bringing out the truth and seeing justice done, that's pretty much all *I'm* out for."

He leaned back, folding his hands over his stomach and grinning at me like I was his longlost brother. He was running true to form so far, I thought. A glib glad-handing hypocrite. Like the evangelists I had seen on TV, he reminded me less of Moses or Jesus than of the fat little fellow who tries to sell you used cars or bargain furniture on the local commercials.

"Reverend Candy," I started in, "could you tell me what happened between you and Roger Meyer on Tuesday?"

"I told the police all that four or five times already. Well, I don't mind going through it again for you. Only thing is, you got to cut out this 'reverend' stuff. I'm Chuck to my friends, and I'll take it as a privilege if I can call you—what is it?—Dave."

"Maybe we won't turn out to be friends."

"That sure won't be any fault of mine. Every man's my friend. Brothers in Christ, that's what we all are."

"About Tuesday?"

"Sure enough. Well, I opened the door to this kid— around lunchtime it was—and he started ranting and raving, right there in the hallway of my house. Very excitable, no self-control, waving his arms—comes from New York City, don't he?"

"Actually, he comes from Detroit."

"But the way I hear it, the father's from New York City? Well, anyways, I tried to calm the kid down, talk some sense into him, but it didn't do no good. Pretty soon I began to worry he'd get violent, so I took the gun out of the hall table and told him to get out of the house."

"In that order?"

"How do you mean?"

"First you pulled the gun, and then you told him to get out of the house?"

"I sure did. But that kid wouldn't take no for an answer, he started grabbing for the gun and it sure enough went off."

"While you were holding onto it?"

"That's right. The noise scared the sh—the pants off him. He hotfooted it out the front door, and a couple minutes later the police got there—my wife called them on the phone while the kid was sounding off to me—and they went next door and ran him in. Now that's the whole story, just the way I told it to the people from the district attorney's office."

"I wonder if you realize what my boss, Mrs. Swenson, is going to make of that story in front of a jury, Mr. Candy."

"Chuck, Chuck."

"You invited the Meyer boy into your house—which means he wasn't trespassing. You can't say he pulled the gun on you, because it was *your* gun, and *you* took it out of *your* hall table. You can't say his refusal to leave the house provoked you into pointing it at him, because you did that *before* you ordered him out. In fact, you can't even say Roger Meyer deliberately shot at you, because he never actually got his hands on the gun, you were holding onto it when it went off. Looks to me like the DA's going to have a hard time making any of the charges stick if he's counting on your testimony."

He frowned for a moment, thinking that over, then he grinned again. "Well, sir, if I was you, I'd advise your boss not to try *that* in court. Don't she know about this town? This is a town where nine out of ten families keeps a gun in the house, and there's a general belief that a man has a right to use it if some smart aleck hoodlum from out of state comes busting in and gives him a hard time. So where you going to find a jury that'll blame me for doing just that?"

I knew how much truth there was in this, so I switched direction. "Are you in the habit, normally, of keeping guns in your hall table?"

"Why not? I'm vigorous and zealous in spreading the Lord's word. There's plenty out there, minions of Satan, who wouldn't stop at violence to silence me and nip the Lord's word in the bud. I've been threatened plenty of times."

"Who's threatened you?"

"Minions of Satan, I just told you. Finally I had to take the necessary steps to protect myself. I went to the police, they'll tell you I've got a legal permit to carry a weapon."

He refolded his hands over his stomach.

At that moment there was a knock on his door, soft and hesitant.

"Come!" he yelled.

The door opened, and a young man took a few steps into the room. He was short and had a pale pudgy face which bore a strong resemblance to Chuck Candy's, a kind of smudged unfinished copy by an amateur. The young man wore a jacket, a tie, and a vest. You don't see many vests in this section of the world.

"Well, what?" Candy barked at him.

"I just had a question, Daddy," the young man said. "On your message to the congregation for this Christmas newsletter, I can't make out your handwriting. Especially this one word—"

"Figure it out for yourself," Candy said. "Don't I always tell you, use the brains the good Lord give you. This here's my son Gabriel," Candy gave a wave in my direction. "Gabe's my assistant in the church." He said my name to Gabe and went on, "Dave here's doing some investigating for the public defender. They're going to court for that hot-headed Meyer kid."

"Oh yes?" The young man fidgeted and didn't meet my eye.

"All right, all right," Candy said, "let me look at that word, give it here!"

He looked at the piece of yellow paper Gabe held out to him, gave a snort, and said, " 'Holiness,' that's what it is! What'd you *think* it was?"

"Well, it sort of looked like 'hopscotch'—"

"Hopscotch! Will you tell me how in the name of Satan I'm going to fit *hopscotch* into my Christmas newsletter? Get out, get out of here, get back to work!"

The pudgy young man retreated in disarray. Candy leaned back in his chair and chuckled, "Notice how he gave a flinch when I called him my 'assistant'? He don't like that one bit. He likes to call himself the 'associate pastor.' On account of he went to college and theology school and got himself one of them doctor's degrees. Assistant's too good for him."

Candy let his chuckle die out, then he put on a business-like voice. "Maybe Connelly told you out there this is a busy day for me. So if there's no more questions—"

"Just a few more," I said. "You've been living next door to the Meyers for four years now. You've managed to get through three other Christmases without putting any special decorations on your house. How come you're doing it this year?"

Candy's grin spread. "For those first three years God didn't tell me to do it. This year He told me. And when He gives a command, believe you me I always hop to it."

"Doesn't it bother you at all, with the noise and the lights and the crowds outside your house, that you're making life miserable for those two old people?"

His grin faded, he looked positively solemn. "That sure does bother me. Way I see it, though, they're making life miserable for themselves. Why don't they join in on the Christmas spirit, come on over to my house at night and enjoy the lights and the music and those cute little talking statues? They'd sure be welcome. All they got to do is stop being so stiff-necked, stop looking down their noses at the simple pleasures of simple people."

He laughed, then he cocked his head to the side with a shrewd gleam in his eye. "You know what, Dave? I'm getting this strong feeling *you're* looking down your nose at me too."

I saw no point in saying anything to that.

"Yes, sir, I sure am getting that feeling," he went on. "What's your background, Dave? You come from somewhere in the east, I'd say, round about New York City. You're a peculiar people, you New York people. I don't guess I'll *ever* figure you out. Lots of brains, you go to fancy Eastern schools, you end up being big moneymakers. But you don't look like you've got any *God* in your life. Sorta look down your nose at *Him* too, now don't you? And at the kind of people Him and me serve in my church."

"Do you *serve* them? Or—" I didn't go on.

"Or do I con them? Swindle them out of their hard-earned pennies? That's what you're meaning to say, or am I wrong?" A tightness came into his voice, and he wasn't smiling so genially anymore. "Well, why don't you ask *them* what they think about that? Why don't you find out *their* opinion of me? Trouble is, you're not really much *interested* in their opinion, are you? When's the last time you ever went out of your way to exchange a word with the kind of folks I've got in my congregation?''

I fidgeted in spite of myself. The son of a bitch made me sick, but there *was* a certain truth in what he had just said.

"You know what their lives are like?" he said. "You know what it is to have some kind of dead-end job you'll never get out of for the rest of your life? Unless you get laid off, and then you can't feed your kids. And them kids'll never go to any fancy Eastern colleges, or any colleges at all more likely. And when you get to be old and sick, what've you got saved up that'll keep life from being a burden on you? You got nothing.

"Except you got Jesus Christ. You got the comfort of coming to His church and praying to Him, and knowing He's looking out for you and is going to make everything up to you one of these days when He gives you your eternal reward.

"That's what I'm bringing to these people. And your kind, with your high-toned attitude and manners, what're you bringing them that's better? All you want to do is take away the comfort and hope and glory that they're holding onto. So what call you got to look down on *me*?''

Before I could respond to this, his voice became genial again. "Don't you get me wrong though. I don't hold it against you. You been brought up with this prejudice against people in my line of work, on account of those big-time preachers on TV—those Bakkers and Swaggarts and all. You see them people on TV, and you read in the papers about all the money they're pulling in and all the bad things they're doing, and you get me mixed up with them. You call me 'Hypocrite!' same as you call them. Now don't you tell me not.''

I couldn't tell him, because in fact I had applied just that word to him a few minutes ago.

"Hypocrite!" He laughed heartily. "It's kind of a joke you come right down to it. You see any of that big TV money coming *my* way? I minister to the poor, and I'm one of them!''

He stopped laughing and put on the serious look again. ''That's all right though, I don't hanker after any of them materialistic things. Those are the false idols of the modern world. Family and kiddies, that's where the *real* riches come. I got Gabe, my only child, and his lovely wife, Patti Mae, and their five beautiful kiddies—they're always up to something, them grandkids of mine. And my lovely wife Ruthie of thirty-three years, that's my whole life, outside of the Lord. Here, this is my little family, you take a look now!''

He waved at a couple of framed photographs on his desk. In one of them he had his arm around the waist of a thin pale woman, taller than he; he was grinning at her from ear to ear, and she was trying to grin back but not making a good job of it. In the other photograph, pudgy Gabe Candy and an overweight young woman were surrounded by kids; Gabe looked as if he wished he could escape from the picture.

''Now you can't deny that's some family!'' Candy said. ''You got any family of your own, Dave?'' He didn't wait for an answer. ''Anyways, you can see how I'm brimming over with sympathy for that old couple, them Meyers. It's terrible what it does to a family when one of the kids is in trouble.''

''You could help the old couple by withdrawing your charges against their son.''

Candy gave a sigh. ''Don't I wish I could do that! But that's a matter of the law now. It's right there in the Good Book. Render unto God what is God's and unto Caesar what is Caesar's. Billy Graham and Pat Robertson and them others that're on TV, you wouldn't catch *them* going against the Good Book.''

I looked into his smile for awhile, then I got to my feet. ''I won't take up any more of your time,'' I said.

''You take care now,'' he said. ''I worry about you people.''

I tightened up. ''What people?''

"You Jewish people. You're the most spiritual God-fearing people that ever lived. You started it all. You're forever blessed. Why do you want to curse yourselves and head straight into damnation by turning your face away from His truth?"

"Now listen—"

"Now, now, no call for you to get hot under the collar, hear? I wasn't meaning to offend you. What I always say is, God's been patient with you for two thousand years, and He'll go on being patient for as long as it takes. So I reckon *I* can be patient too." He laughed and held out his hand. "Thanks again for dropping by."

I didn't shake his hand. I nodded and muttered my goodbyes and went to the door. And then, suddenly, Mom's voice was echoing in my ears, and I turned and said, "One last question. What time do you and Mrs. Candy ordinarily go to bed at night?"

The sheer asininity of this question shocked him into answering it. "We go to bed at nine-thirty, been doing it for thirty-three years. When you're doing the Lord's work, you want to get an early start. Now you just wait a second, what's the point of—"

I went through the door fast, shutting it behind me.

As I crossed the long reception room, heading for the fresh air outside, the Reverend Chuck Candy's voice throbbed after me from the TV screen: "Brothers and sisters, you know why you should read your Bible? Because that's where God gives you His previews of the Paradise that's waiting for you in the Eternal World. Like them previews you see in the movie theatre, telling you what the next show is going to be like. Only *all* the shows Jesus is planning for you, if you only believe in Him, is Academy Award winners—"

THE OFFICE CLOCK read a few minutes after ten when I got back, but I still had an urge for something strong to drink.

This doesn't happen to me often. The bottle of Scotch in my desk had been there for two years and was still almost half full. I gulped down a finger of the stuff like medicine.

That's what whiskey tastes like to me, the kind of medicine that's so obnoxious you know it must be good for you.

It did the job, and I got down to work. My first duty was to report on my morning to Ann, but Mabel Gibson told me she was in court and probably wouldn't be back in the office for the rest of the afternoon. So I moved on to my second duty. I called Mom at her house.

There was a lot of noise on the line. "Maybe I better try again," I yelled. "Something's wrong with this connection!"

"It isn't the connection," I heard her yelling back at me. "It's my soap opera, it keeps my mind busy while I'm polishing the silver. Give me a minute so I can find out if that nice young doctor is the father of her baby or he isn't."

After the noise cleared up, I told Mom about my morning, trying as always to leave out absolutely nothing, no matter how inconsequential it seemed. I had learned on plenty of occasions in the past that for Mom inconsequential didn't exist.

When I got to Candy's answer to Mom's mysterious question—the information that he and his wife went to bed by half past nine at night—Mom gave a sigh of satisfaction. "It's always nice, isn't it, when what you expected turns out to be true?"

"What's turned out to be true?"

"You should look for the real estate agent, that's what. Call up Abe and Sarah Meyer and ask them. But this you naturally figured out already for yourself."

This is one of Mom's favorite little games. Whenever she says, in her offhand voice, that I naturally figured out something for myself, what she means is that I couldn't have figured it out in a million years and she'll have to explain it to me.

"What are you talking about?" I said.

"It's exactly like the Birnbaums that lived upstairs from us in the Bronx. A couple of know-it-alls! They read a psychology book, they told everybody in the building how to bring up their babies. When your baby starts crying in the middle of the night, they told us, it's bad for its psychology you should lie there and hope it'll go to sleep again. Get up right away, no matter how late it is, and put the baby in your lap and stick food in its mouth. And then this Mrs. Birnbaum finally has a baby of her own, and the first time it wakes up crying at night she and her husband lie in bed 'til it finally shuts up."

"What's the point, Mom?"

"The point is, you can tell people how they should make sacrifices for their high ideals, but maybe you feel different when you're the one has to do the sacrificing."

"But what's that got to do with Mr. and Mrs. Candy?"

"This Candy and his wife are early go-to-bedders, their usual time is nine-thirty. Suddenly, a month ago, they put music on loudspeakers, and that music plays as loud as it can 'til one o'clock every morning. You follow me? It isn't only Abe and Sarah Meyer that are losing their sleep from that music. It's Candy and his wife too."

"Yes, I follow that. But what—"

"What I'm asking is, why? That these people should suddenly change their sleeping habits, which are always the hardest habits for people to change, on account of they love Christmas so much—this you'll get me to believe on the day you introduce me to the toothpaste fairy! The explanation that pops right away into my head is, they're deliberately making a *megillah* next door so they can drive the Meyers crazy. For some reason they want the Meyers should sell their house and move out."

"How does a real estate agent come into this?"

"I'm saying to myself, there must be easier ways to get people to sell their house—like, for instance, making them an offer to buy it from them. What the Candys are doing is only what you do when you tried the easy way already and it didn't work. So that's why I'm suggesting to you, call up Abe and Sarah and ask them has there been some real estate agent, a month ago maybe, that made them an offer on their house? And if there was, you should find out from this agent who's behind the offer. And afterwards call me back. I'm curious."

I promised her I'd do that and started thanking her for the lead, but she interrupted me.

"You'll excuse me," she said, "I have to get back to that nice young doctor and this no-good girl she's trying to blackmail him into marrying her. Between you and me, it's obvious the baby isn't his. Already I've noticed three logical clues—"

As soon as Mom hung up, I called the Meyers. Abe was home, and I put my question to him.

"Now you mention it," he said, "some real estate fellow called me last month, he said a buyer was interested. His offer was pretty good, and he called me back three or four times, and every time it got better. I had a lot of trouble making him understand we didn't want to sell this place at any price. We bought it for retiring into, and we love it, and we've been hoping some day we could pass it down to our boy. Our girl has a house for herself already, and a husband that can afford it, but Roger has no place he can call his own."

"What's the real estate agent's name?"

"I hope I can remember. All the names out here, to tell you the truth, they sound the same to me. It was one of those Mac names. You know what I mean? MacMahon, MacArthur. Douglas MacArthur? No, that it couldn't be, could it? MacDonald? Wait a second, it's coming to me. McKee. Dwayne McKee.

"I remember it clearly now, because back in New York did you ever run across anybody with a name like Dwayne?"

As soon as Abe was off the line, I looked up Dwayne McKee in the phone book. He was there, identified as a realtor, which by some in this section of the country is considered to be the highest calling a human being can aspire to. I thought about getting him on the phone and making an appointment for after lunch, but then I decided to drop in on him right away, without any warning; sometimes you can accomplish a lot that way.

McKee's offices were in a little white house wedged between a five-story office building and a warehouse. Mesa Grande is full of blocks like that, where half a dozen different levels of history push and jostle against each other. Nobody ever wins, as far as I can tell, but through the years all the combatants are showing the wear and tear.

A Christmas wreath was hanging from a nail on the front door, leading to McKee's waiting room, and another wreath was on the door to his private office. They were small genteel wreaths; they didn't shout out "Merry Christmas!" at you in loud vulgar tones, they whispered it discreetly.

That's how Dwayne McKee operated too. In Mesa Grande male real estate agents run to loudness and heartiness (female agents run to loudness and gushiness); they emphasize their points with their fists, and they do a good deal of clumping around. But McKee was soft-voiced and pussyfooting, with a habit of weighing every word before he let go of it. He could have been an accountant, or a college professor.

"Mr. McKee," I began, "you recently made an offer to Mr. Abraham Meyer to buy his house in the Fairhaven district. On whose behalf were you acting?"

McKee fiddled with a paperweight on his desk blotter and gave his throat a few gentle clearings. "I'm not sure it would be ethical for me to give you that information. It's always been my policy to respect my clients' wishes for confidentiality."

"I'm no lawyer," I said, "but I think I know what my boss would say to you about that. Under the law a defendant in a criminal case is entitled to bring out in open court all facts which might be relevant to his defense. People in possession of such facts have to testify to them under oath, unless the law allows them some specially privileged status. That means psychiatrists and priests, and lawyers whose clients have conferred with them on a professional basis. I've never heard that real estate agents are included on the list. The confidentiality between a real estate agent and his client may be sacred in the eyes of the Board of Realtors, but not in the eyes of the law."

"But if I feel a certain moral obligation—"

"My boss' advice, I think, would be to suppress it. Tell us what you know right now, and sign a deposition, because maybe you'll have to testify at the trial or maybe you won't. But if you *don't* tell us what you know, I guarantee you my boss will slap you with a subpoena and you'll stand up in court and tell the whole world what you're now refusing to tell to me only. Or if you don't, you'll go to jail."

I said all this in a nice, easy friendly tone of voice, not trying to pressure him or argue with him but simply giving him information.

It was enough for McKee. He came out with the whole story. Yes, he had been commissioned by a client to make an offer for the Meyers' house, and that client was the Reverend Chuck Candy himself. Furthermore, this wasn't the only such job he'd ever done for Candy. At the same time as he was making an offer to the Meyers, he made offers to five other families in the neighborhood. The rest of them all agreed to sell. As of a month ago Chuck Candy was the owner of their houses.

That, he added, was a matter of public record, in the Office of Deeds and Titles, but Candy had made a point of it with the people he bought from that they shouldn't tell anybody about the transaction.

The Meyers wouldn't sell, though. McKee went as high as he was empowered to go, without success, so finally, in the middle of November, Candy told him to forget the whole thing. "I'll take care of it myself," he said. "There's more than one way to skin a cat."

He didn't explain to McKee what he meant by that. All he said was that he didn't think it would be more than a few weeks before old Meyer was calling McKee up and asking if his client still wanted to buy the house. At which point McKee was instructed to offer exactly half of what the very first offer had been.

Then I asked McKee the obvious question. "Why did Candy want the Meyer house and all that other property in the neighborhood?"

"Well, he's never taken me into his confidence. But if I were going to make an educated guess—in the course of practicing this profession, one occasionally hears rumors, bits and pieces of real estate news about various deals that might be developing behind the scenes or under the table. Well, a recent rumor I've heard is that a large corporation from the East is planning to build a string of shopping centers in the Southwest, one of which is to be located here in Mesa Grande. In the Fairhaven section, as a matter of fact, where the Reverend Candy and the Meyers live. Now if the Reverend Candy managed to hear that rumor too—and if it occurred to him to buy up property in that area before this Eastern corporation got started— Nothing really wrong about it, of course. I'm sure he intends to use the money for his church, not for himself personally. He's a sincere man of God—"

"You belong to his church, Mr. McKee?"

"Oh no. I'm First Presbyterian. Same as my father and his father before him. The Reverend Candy's church is more appealing to people with less stable, less solid— Well, it takes all kinds, and we're all equal in the eyes of our Father, aren't we?"

I dictated an official deposition, with all this information in it, to McKee's secretary, and McKee signed it, and the secretary and I signed it as witnesses.

I left McKee's office an hour after I had arrived. The front door wreath seemed to be gazing at me reproachfully: how could I behave myself so boorishly at this time of year, while the whole world is praying for peace and good will to men? Pushy and aggressive, just like all of them.

I HAD PROMISED TO CALL Mom back, to satisfy her curiosity, so as soon as I was in my office again I did.

And I couldn't keep the self-satisfaction out of my voice. "Do you realize what a terrific break this is?" I said. "Candy himself made an offer to buy the Meyers' place! Wait till Ann throws that at him on the witness stand. It not only proves he's been trying to provoke the Meyers so they'd move out of the neighborhood, it also makes the whole business with the gun look fishy. I'll bet the assault charge never gets past the preliminary hearing.''

A long silence on the other end of the line.

"Mom? What's the matter? Is there something wrong with my reasoning?''

"What's wrong," Mom said, "is that this Candy is the one who tried to buy the Meyer house.''

"But that's the luckiest thing that's happened to us so far!"

"Fine, it's lucky. But also it's peculiar, it raises a question you have to clear up. Candy has been buying up houses in his neighborhood, five houses he's already bought. How can he afford it? Houses aren't ice cream sodas, it takes a lot of money to buy one, even more to buy five. Even if you borrow from a bank. And this Candy's church is full of poor people, he isn't one of the big-business ministers in town—would you expect him to have so much money at hand or such good credit at the bank?''

"Maybe not, but he *has* been doing it.''

"Exactly. So *how* has he been doing it? There's somebody else behind him. Somebody who *has* got money on hand is using this Candy to buy up those houses. Somebody who's so worried his name should come into it that he don't even dare to make the offer himself. He doesn't hide behind a real estate agent, he hides behind an agent who hides behind the real estate agent. Believe me, Davie, you shouldn't be finished with this case of yours till you find out who's the somebody.''

"All right, Mom, I promise you I'll look into it.''

But I was humoring her. I was perfectly happy with what I'd just found out, and Ann would be happy with it too. It was enough to get our client off the hook: what else should we care about? We weren't in the business of digging up Absolute Truth; we were in the business of getting acquittals.

I looked at my watch after I hung up the phone. I was surprised to see that it wasn't quite noon yet. The morning had been a full one.

So I grabbed a sandwich at the coffee shop in the court-house, and then, for the rest of the afternoon, I put Roger Meyer and Chuck Candy and Christmas on the back burner, while I finished up a lot of neglected paperwork. Then I had a drink at an outlying saloon with one of my under-the-table information sources. I pumped him in connection with a drunk-driving case—in which, in our opinion, our client wasn't drunk and wasn't driving—and the results were more than satisfactory.

I didn't get home till six o'clock, when I opened my door to a ringing phone.

It was Ann. I started to tell her the good news that had come out of my meeting with Dwayne McKee, but I never got out a word. "Meet me down at the Meyers' house, will you?" she asked. "You know the address?"

I told her I did and asked her what was up.

"Somebody shot the Reverend Chuck Candy," she said. "He's dead, and the cops are looking for Roger."

ON THE WAY TO the Meyers' house, the downtown traffic slowed me considerably. Mesa Grande is one of the fastest-growing towns in the west, according to the statistics, so we're naturally acquiring traffic jams, parking problems, an increased crime rate, and smog: all the refinements of big-city culture. What we *haven't* acquired yet is a movie house that shows anything with subtitles, a restaurant where they serve you the salad *after* the main course, and a nightclub or coffee shop that's open after eleven and doesn't cater exclusively to teenagers.

During this entire downtown trip, I crawled along behind a Plymouth station-wagon with a "Honk If You Love Jesus" sign attached to the rear bumper. Then I left downtown behind and started through some of the city's nicer residential districts. Hanging across nearly every doorway were wreaths, large ones dripping with pine cones, small ones punctuated by red artificial cherries.

I had got a glimpse of the Meyers' house two nights ago, in the dark. Now it was twilight, and I could see it more clearly. Though it didn't display any wreaths, it looked in

every other respect like an old *Saturday Evening Post* cover:
red-and-white shutters, neatly-trimmed hedges, puffs of
smoke rising lazily from the chimney on the roof. I figured
Abe and Sarah Meyer had been attracted to it for just that
reason: for people of their generation what could the
American dream look like except a painting by Norman
Rockwell?

Inside the house the atmosphere was more Old Testament than *Saturday Evening Post*. In the living room Sarah
Meyer was on the sofa, clasping and unclasping a rolled-up
wet handkerchief; tears smeared her red cheeks. Abe sat
next to her, tightly holding onto her free hand, blinking in
bewilderment at the opposite wall. Standing next to the sofa
was Ann, with a grim look on her face.

Perched on the edge of a chair was a little man—very little, scarcely taller than five feet. He was in his thirties, with
a clean-shaven pinkish face, and he was wearing a light-gray
suit and a black yarmulke.

(A yarmulke, for the uninstructed, is one of those small
round caps that a pious Jewish male wears indoors and out,
because at all times he's supposed to keep a covering between the top of his head and God. A Jewish female doesn't
have to follow this rule: God, apparently, doesn't have anything against the top of *her* head.)

This dapper delicate little man was our local rabbi, Eli
Loewenstein. We had met before at various public occasions: the rabbi was a popular guest of honor at Rotary
lunches, Chamber of Commerce dinners, and other affairs
where the gentile establishment wants to display some official representative of the Jewish community. It's a pretty
small Jewish community in Mesa Grande; the synagogue
has less than a hundred families in it, and the rabbi is
obliged to conduct services that are a mixture of Orthodox,
Conservative, and Reform. But small as the Jewish community is, its members are all conscientious voters, and from
time to time the powers-that-be feel impelled to acknowl-
edge its existence officially.

I nodded at the rabbi, and he got to his feet, bustled
across the room, and shook my hand, with a tactful mix-

ture of heartiness (to show he was glad to see me) and restraint (to show he was aware of the solemnity of the occasion).

"How's your mother?" the rabbi said, with that throb in his voice that I've noticed in all the clergymen of my acquaintance, regardless of sect, creed, or denomination; as if their most trifling remark is being delivered from a pulpit. The ministerial tendency to imitate God's rhetorical style seems to be perfectly ecumenical. "We're expecting to see her at Oneg Shabbat tomorrow night. I think she's supplying the potato pancakes."

"I wouldn't be surprised," I said. "It's something she enjoys supplying."

"I was hoping to see her last Friday too," the rabbi said. "Too bad she couldn't make it. A woman like her who could contribute so much. Well, we should be thankful for what we *do* get of her, shouldn't we?"

The rabbi didn't expect me to make any response to that. Long ago he had recognized the pointlessness of lecturing *me* about coming to synagogue. Now he conveyed the same message in the guise of talking to me about Mom.

"We haven't got much time," Ann cut in. "You should be filled in, Dave."

"Oh, I'm sorry," the rabbi said. "If you want me to go to another room until you're finished—"

Ann told him it was fine with her if he stayed. Then she turned to Abe Meyer and asked him to tell me what had happened.

The weary mechanical way in which the old man ground out his story made it clear that he had been over it half a dozen times already, with Ann and various representatives of the law. "It was a couple of hours ago, maybe four-thirty, Sarah and I were sitting here in the living room. Roger was here too, looking at the basketball game on TV—"

"Roger is a basketball fan?" I put in.

"Between you and me, not much. He watches the games when *I* watch them. He knows it gives me pleasure so he pretends to care about them like I do."

"He's a good boy," said Sarah, and suddenly she started sobbing.

"All right, all right," Abe said, almost in exasperation. "Crying isn't going to help. Facts. Only facts are going to help. Four-thirty, the basketball on TV. All of a sudden the phone rang. We were expecting long distance from our daughter who lives with her husband in Los Angeles—"

"He's in the insurance business," said Sarah, between sniffles. "He's doing very nicely, a lot of those Hollywood stars are his clients."

"And what's that got to do with the price of beans?" Abe said.

"I'm only explaining—"

"Explain when it's something important, all right?"

"It isn't important that Jennifer's husband is a successful man? It's important to *me*. It's important to *her* and to the children. And I can imagine how unimportant it would be to *you* if she happened to be married to a bum that couldn't earn a decent living—"

"All right, all right!" Abe raised his fists in the air, as if he were calling on God for mercy. "Now if you'll give your permission, I'll get back to the matter in hand. The phone rang, but it wasn't our daughter from Los Angeles, it was somebody asking for Roger. A voice—"

"Male or female?"

"I couldn't tell. The voice was whispering, you know like a low whisper, like somebody with a bad cold or too weak to speak up. To me it didn't say much more than Roger's name. I put him on, he listened in the receiver for only a couple seconds, then he hung up and said to us, 'I'm going out. I'll be back soon.' Then he ran out of the house, throwing his coat on from the hall closet, and that's the last we saw of him. After an hour he still didn't come back, and all of a sudden a police car was pulling up in front of the house, and a man from the district attorney came in and asked us where Roger is. And when I told him we don't know, he acted like we're liars, he told a couple of other men to look through the house—"

"Without a warrant," Ann said. "Typical."

"They didn't find him, naturally, because I don't tell lies to the police. Or anybody else." Abe's bewildered look was overshadowed for a moment by a glitter of anger. "So then they told me there's been a murder—somebody shot the minister, that no-good from down the street. And they told me Roger went into that house and did it, and now he's running away. So first I called Mrs. Swenson, and then I called the rabbi—"

A sob from Sarah cut Abe off for a moment. Then his voice rose, as if he were trying to drown her out. "Our boy Roger, he shot a man? Never! He never used a gun in his life! What do they think he is, one of these animal-hunters from this section of the country that pull out a gun and start shooting whenever the idea happens to come into their heads?"

"He didn't tell you where he was going, though, after he got that phone call?"

"Not a word. We asked him, and he said some funny things—not where he was going or who he'd been talking to though. And to tell you the truth, it got put out of my mind, because the phone rang again right after he left, and this time it *was* long distance, our daughter from Los Angeles, so for the next hour or so we talked to her—"

"Her baby has the flu," Sarah said, "the doctor's giving an antibiotic."

"Big deal!" Abe exploded. "Our son disappears, they're saying he killed a man with a gun, and we got to listen to antibiotics!"

"What funny things?" I said.

"What?"

"You just told us Roger said some funny things before he left the house. Can you remember what they were?"

"I didn't understand them, to tell you the truth. They were about Christmas. Let me make sure I got this straight. He said, 'Christmas is the time for brotherly love and forgiveness. If the Christians can do it at this time of year, why can't the Jews do it too?' And then he ran out of the house."

There was a silence, then I said, "Did he take your car when he left?"

"He's got his own car," Abe said. "An old piece of junk. He parks it in front of the house because our garage is big enough only for one. His piece of junk isn't in front now, so I suppose he took it."

Ann moved up to me. "The Assistant DA is waiting for us in Candy's house. He says we can look over the scene of the crime, as long as he stays with us. And he won't be there for long, so I think we'd better get going."

We left quickly, assuring the Meyers we'd do what we could and urging them to get in touch with us immediately if they heard from Roger. We both tried putting on reassuring smiles, but if mine was as convincing as Ann's, poor Abe and Sarah weren't very reassured.

Rabbi Loewenstein followed us out to the hall and spoke in a low voice. "The boy didn't do it. It's important you should believe that."

"How do you know?" Ann said.

The rabbi smiled, a little sadly. "I'm supposed to believe that a boy like that would throw away his life and his parents' happiness for a man like that? Sometimes God acts as if He's cruel or unjust, but you'll never convince me He's capable of making stupid jokes!"

THE CANDY HOUSE, half a block's walk down the street, looked very different this evening than it had looked last night, when I went driving by with all the other rubbernecks. The Christmas lights were out now, and you could see the front of the house covered with a web of wires and dead bulbs, like the debris scattered around a room the morning after a party. The reindeer on the front lawn weren't gleaming and sparkling anymore; the Christ-child wasn't giving out any childish squeals; these figures, still and shadowy in the twilight, were like leftover party guests, collapsed on the floor, sleeping it off. And no music blared from the loudspeakers on the roof.

The rubbernecks were still out in force, though. Attracted, I supposed, by the first reports of the murder on the TV news. A few dozen of them, in cars or lined up, could be seen across the street, because the police weren't letting them on the sidewalk that passed in front of the Candy house. Even the high-echelon well-paid rubbernecks—the TV crews, that is—were being kept at a distance.

A uniformed guard let Ann and me up to the front door, and it was opened by Assistant District Attorney George Wolkowicz, one of Marvin McBride's bright, nasty young henchmen. Rumors were that Wolkowicz was on the verge of getting an offer from the State's Attorney's Office in Pennsylvania, where he could hobnob with a higher and finer type of criminal, but at the moment he was forced to go on slumming in Mesa Grande. That didn't improve his temper; with his thick black eyebrows, low forehead, and jutting jaw, he always reminded me of a pug dog about to bite.

"So here you are," said Wolkowicz. "Glad you could make it. What murder would be complete in this town without the two of you? Okay, you've got ten minutes, after that I'm pulling out. My wife's got my dinner on the table, and Marvin's expecting a report on his desk first thing tomorrow morning."

That was a joke. It's been many years since our esteemed district attorney was in any condition to read reports, or even keep upright at his desk, first thing in the morning.

"Thanks for your consideration, George," Ann said. "It isn't often the public defender gets a chance to look at the evidence this early in the case."

She knew damn well, of course, that the law required the DA to call her right away if one of her clients was involved. Or his case could get thrown out of court, which in fact had happened to him a few months ago.

Wolkowicz grunted. "Hell of a lot of good it's going to do that punk kid," he said. "I'll take you to the room where the body was found. It's the family living room, right down the hall. The fingerprint people and the photographers have been over it already, and the body's been removed for autopsy, of course, but otherwise it's in the exact same condition as it was before we got here."

In other words, several herds of flatfooted buffalo had trampled all over the scene of the murder, efficiently wiping out any evidence they didn't happen to notice themselves. Still, it never hurts to look. Sometimes, by accident, the vandals miss something.

We didn't get to the murder scene just yet though, because two figures suddenly appeared on the stairs at the end of the hallway. One of them was Chuck Candy's son Gabe, the other was Gabe's mother, "Ruthie." I recognized her from the framed photograph I'd seen this morning on Chuck Candy's desk—a skinny woman in her fifties, disheveled hair. Her face was even paler and gaunter than in the photograph. Her eyes were red and bulging.

The pudgy young man, holding onto her arm, was still wearing the suit and vest he'd been wearing this morning. But it was rumpled now, it looked as if he'd been sleeping in it.

Wolkowicz introduced us, and as soon as he heard who Ann and I were Gabe Candy's face got red. "These are the people defending that *killer*? You get them out of this house! This is a holy time of grief. Don't you see my mother's here, prostrate? How can you do this, Mr. Wolkowicz, bringing these minions of my Daddy's bitter enemies into my mother's house?"

"I'm the public defender, my name is Ann Swenson," said Ann, in her coolest voice. The more somebody tries to intimidate her, the cooler she always gets: it's what makes her such a terror in the courtroom. "This gentleman is my chief investigator. Mr. Wolkowicz here will tell you that the law gives official recognition to our status as Roger Meyer's legal representatives. We have the same authority to examine the scene of the crime as the police have."

"It's not right, it just isn't right!" Gabe Candy's voice was rising to a squeak. He sounded like a desperate little kid. "Is that true, Mr. Wolkowicz, they can come into this house any time they please? It just isn't right." He shook his head a few times, and then a long low sigh came out of him and he passed his hand over his eyes.

"We'll be as quick as we can," I said, for a moment feeling sorry for the guy. After all, he *had* just lost his father.

He took his hand away from his eyes and put it on his mother's arm. "Come along, Mama. We'll sit upstairs awhile." And he led her, not too steadily, up the stairs.

Wolkowicz gave a grin. Anything amused him if it made us uncomfortable.

THEN HE TOOK US through an archway into the living room. A large room, with a picture window looking out on the front street. This must have been where the late Reverend Candy stood at night, watching the crowds as they gawked at his Christmas display. And maybe thinking with satisfaction about the infidels who were tossing and turning in their beds next door.

The living room also had a large number of photographs cluttering the walls: mostly they were close shots of the late Reverend Candy, sometimes looking pious as he communed with his God, sometimes angry as he shook his fist at the Devil, sometimes laughing it up, no doubt as he beat the Devil ignominiously back to hell. A fireplace dominated the opposite wall from the picture window, and a Christmas tree, fully decorated for the season, stood in front of it, almost reaching to the ceiling. Nothing was burning in the fireplace—maybe it was just for show, which is often the case in new houses—and the lights were out on the Christmas tree.

Then my eye was caught by the strips of white tape on the carpet a couple of feet in front of the Christmas tree. They formed the crude outline of a human body, with the legs slightly bent, one arm sticking up over the head, the other arm sticking out from the chest at a right angle.

"That's pretty much the position we found him in," said Wolkowicz. "More or less on his side, with his right cheek against the carpet."

"What killed him?" I asked.

Wolkowicz pointed to a spot six feet or so away from the "body," close to the archway. On the floor there, in the wooden area between the end of the carpet and the archway, was another arrangement of white tape, much smaller than the first. "That's where we found the gun. Your boy must've dropped it after he shot the victim."

"The killer must've dropped it," Ann put in.

"That's what I said."

"How long did it take him to die?" I asked.

"Two shots were fired from the gun, and there are two bullets in Candy's body—one in the chest, to the left of the heart and a little below, one in his right hip. Neither of them killed him instantly, but there was a lot of internal bleeding, and some external—you can see it on the carpet, around the body—so our estimate at the moment is that he didn't last more than half an hour."

"Nobody in the house heard the shots?"

"The house was empty, except for the victim. His wife was out doing Christmas shopping, his son and his son's family don't live here, and there are no fulltime servants. His wife got home around an hour ago, and by that time he was dead."

"Did he have time to call for help?"

"He tried to. Look at the phone." I saw it now, resting on the floor next to the sofa, three or four feet away from the body. "We figure he crawled over to it and managed to get it off its table and down to the floor. But he ran out of strength, and either he couldn't manage to dial or he didn't have enough voice to talk into the receiver. Anyway, he put the phone back on the hook and tried to communicate in a different way."

"What way?"

"Right over here," Wolkowicz said. "Now walk carefully, and for God's sake don't step on them or Marvin'll give me hell. As it is, he doesn't much like the idea of letting you two loose at the scene of the crime."

"Must make it tough for him," Ann said, "since the law says he has to do it."

But we lost interest in baiting Wolkowicz when we saw what he was pointing to. On the carpet just a few inches from the body's outstretched arm were a series of crayon marks. A moment later I realized they were fully formed capital letters, pretty crude and shaky in spots, but since the color of the carpet was beige and the crayon marks were bright red, it was easy to make out what these letters spelled out.

GOLD, FRANKINCENSE AND MYRRH

The first three words stretched from the lefthand edge of the carpet, and the last word had been scrawled directly under the first one.

"Oh, there's no doubt Candy did this," Wolkowicz was saying. "We found the piece of red crayon between the fingers of his right hand. And he *was* righthanded, we've checked that with his family. And over here, this is where he got the crayons from."

A few feet away from the scrawled message was a package of drawing crayons for kids. Its Christmas wrapping had been torn off it, it had been pulled open hastily, several of the crayons had spilled onto the carpet around it. I picked up the box and glanced at it, "Infant Jesus Drawing Set," it read. "Caution: Crayon marks must be scrubbed out with turpentine and cold water."

"You have any theories," I said, "as to *why* he used up the last of his strength to write this?"

"Not really," Wolkowicz said. "'Gold, frankincense and myrrh.' I'm a little rusty on my Bible, but those are the three gifts that the Magi bring to the Christ child, aren't they? Well, maybe he was trying to call attention to Christmas— to the fight he had with the Meyer kid over the Christmas display in front of this house."

"If he wanted to accuse Roger Meyer," I said, "it would've been a hell of a lot easier for him to do it directly. He could've written 'Roger Meyer killed me'—something like that."

Wolkowicz shrugged. "He was a dying man. People don't always think clearly when they're dying. Anyway, what does it matter? We don't have to explain this message, we've got plenty of evidence against your boy without it."

"Oh yes," said Ann, turning to face him squarely, "I've been waiting for this. *What* evidence do you have against him?"

Wolkowicz's pug dog jaw pushed forward. "To begin with, he's got a motive, which even you can't get around. Candy was making life miserable for the old Meyer couple, and the son's already lost his temper once and assaulted the man with a deadly weapon."

"That's what the hearing next week was supposed to determine," Ann said. "Our contention is that the boy acted in self-defense."

"Your contention is now irrelevant," Wolkowicz said. "Candy's dead, he can't testify against anybody in the assault case—which gives your client another good motive for the murder."

"Why kill Candy for that? He was sure to be exonerated in court." On the way here from the Meyer house I had filled Ann in on my talk with Dwayne McKee.

"That's your opinion, counselor. Maybe your client didn't share it. Maybe he wanted a guarantee that he wouldn't go to jail. Juries are undependable, you never know how they're going to jump. Dead witnesses are very dependable."

"You're making the boy out to be a moron."

"All murderers are morons, you know that. Otherwise we'd never be able to catch them." He stopped, frowned for a second, then gave a shake of his head and went on, "Next piece of evidence. Your client was at the scene of the crime during the time when the murder could've been committed. He left his parents' house just before four-thirty, went straight down the street to the Candy house—"

"You've got absolutely no proof of that. The boy got a phone call, and *that's* why he left his parents' house."

"We'll argue that the call was from Candy. He wanted to discuss the Christmas decoration issue with your client—who went to see him, lost his temper like he'd already done once before, and grabbed the gun—"

"Roger Meyer's never owned a gun in his life."

"He used Candy's own gun, the same one he tried to shoot him with a few days ago. It was in a drawer in the hallway, the Meyer kid saw Candy take it out of there last week. This time he simply beat Candy to it. And incidentally, we'll have conclusive proof of that tomorrow or the next day at the latest."

"What proof?" Ann said with scorn in her voice. Only somebody with long experience at reading the lines around her eyes would have known that her confidence was being shaken.

"There were smudged fingerprints on the handle of that gun," Wolkowicz said. "The experts are examining it right now, we'll have their report soon. But I'm willing to bet at least one of those smudges will turn out to belong to Roger Meyer."

"Of course it will. He struggled with Candy over that gun last week. He admits it freely."

"The experts will decide if his prints are last week's smudges or new ones. Anyway, that problem won't even come up for the footprints."

"What footprints?"

"Shoeprints, to be exact. Didn't you notice them out in the hallway? There are half a dozen on the carpet out there, moving away from this living room in the direction of the front door. The killer got blood on his shoes, and left a nice trail of it as he hotfooted it out of here. We've got photographs of those shoeprints, and we've already taken away half a dozen pairs of Roger Meyer's shoes from his parents' house."

"Did you have a warrant to do that?" Ann asked, very quietly.

Wolkowicz almost allowed himself a laugh. "Would I do such a thing without a warrant? Do I want this whole case to go out the window on the grounds of illegal search and seizure? Well, those photographs of bloody shoeprints are being compared to Meyer's shoes right now, and I'll make another bet—they'll turn out to be made by shoes of the same size and style."

"Still, I gather you didn't find any bloodstains on the boy's shoes."

"Of course not. He got the bloodstains on the shoes he's wearing right now, the ones he was wearing when he killed Candy. If he's still wearing that pair when we pick him up, our case will be airtight. By the way, there's another little point that might keep you awake tonight. If he isn't guilty, why did he run out of Candy's house, and why is he hiding out?"

"Because he never went into Candy's house in the first place," Ann said. "And he isn't hiding out either. He got a phone call that sent him off on some errand, it has nothing to do with the murder—maybe it's a girl he's been trying to make it with, and suddenly she's in town with only the evening to spare. He'll show up again late tonight or early tomorrow, and you and your boss will feel like a couple of damn fools."

"He was being pretty secretive about that girl, wasn't he? Why wouldn't he even tell his parents where he was going?"

Ann grinned. "Come on, George, you were young once. In spite of appearances, I'm sure you were. Did you fill your parents in on the details whenever you went out with a girl?"

"Damn right I didn't. It would've killed them before their time. But that's got nothing to do with the Meyer kid. He was in that house at the time of the murder, you can take it from me. It's not only the fingerprints and the shoeprints. There's a witness."

Wolkowicz smiled, one of those gloating smiles that he specialized in.

"You said nobody else was in the house."

"This witness was outside the house. Standing across the street, with a perfect view of the front door. He saw everybody who came in and out from three o'clock or so until the squad cars got to the scene. And he'll testify that Roger Meyer went through the front door around four-thirty, stayed inside for five minutes or so, and came running out again, looking very agitated. Then he jumped into his car that was parked on the curb close to the Meyer house, a green two-door 1979 Volkswagen Jetta—and he drove off,

going a lot faster than the legal limit in this neighborhood."

"Who's your witness?" Ann said.

"Oh no. *That* I don't have to tell you yet. Not 'til we've
got his deposition, sworn to, signed, and notarized. Then
we'll give you his name, all fair and square."

"It *is* a man though?"

"Did I say so? Oh yes, I said 'he.' That was the generic
'he,' standing for male or female. I'm usually careful not to
use it, knowing that many women nowadays take offense at
it. But sometimes old habits just make it slip out. I beg your
pardon."

"Is it a 'he' or isn't it?"

Wolkowicz looked at his watch. "It's after seven, my
wife'll just about kill me if the dinner is ruined. Not that her
dinners *can* be ruined—"

"Wait a second, George," Ann said, "we still need a lot
of information from you. Was Candy expecting any visitors today?"

"He never has visitors on Thursday afternoons. He stays
in the house by himself and writes his sermons. Or waits
maybe for God to dictate them to him. And he didn't tell his
wife or his son or anybody else that today was going to be
different."

"Was he alone in the house from lunchtime on?"

"That's what is wife says."

"What time was that?"

"Around noon. But she left the house a lot earlier. She
went to the church to do some errands, then she went out to
the mall to do some Christmas shopping. That's where she
grabbed a bite herself."

"Leaving him to fix his own lunch in the house?"

"That's the arrangement they have on Thursdays."

"What about enemies?" I spoke up. "A lot of nuts get
attracted to these fundamentalist preachers. And he told me
himself, when I talked to him this morning, that he kept a
gun in his house because people had threatened him."

"The only nut we know about who threatened him is your
client, the Meyer kid. And he's the nut who killed him."

He put a hand on Ann's arm and another on mine, and moved us firmly towards the living room archway. But then, for the first time, I noticed something that made me stop short, in spite of his hand. "What's going on up there?"

Over the fireplace, where I was pointing, a small picture was hanging. But all you could see was the back of it, because its face was turned towards the wall.

Wolkowicz went up to it and turned it around. It was a picture of Jesus in closeup, with a crown of thorns on his head, a beatific smile on his face, and a halo glittering above him.

"Now why do you suppose—?" Wolkowicz said. "The killer felt guilty maybe? He didn't want Our Lord looking down at him while he committed murder?"

"Roger Meyer is Jewish," Ann said gently. "Jews don't believe that Jesus *is* Our Lord."

Wolkowicz shot her a furious look, but he didn't have anything to say.

IT WAS ALMOST EIGHT-THIRTY before I got to Mom's house. I had called her earlier, right after Ann gave me the news about the murder, to ask if I could drop by later. Mom said I could and she'd give me a bite to eat no matter how late I was.

True to her word, she had dinner ready for me. I told her about the murder between mouthfuls of vegetable beef soup, and she asked me questions while I dug into the lamb chops and mashed potatoes. And the peas too. After all these years, Mom still won't let me leave a dinner table until I've consumed my quota of green vegetables.

"So tell me please," she said, when I had finally got to the end of my story, "did he finish the sermon?"

"What do you mean, Mom?"

"Did the police find it anywhere, this sermon he's supposed to have spent the whole afternoon writing?"

"I just don't know. I'll ask the assistant DA."

"Also ask him to let you read it, so you can tell me what's in it."

"Okay, but I doubt if he wrote the name of his killer in it or anything like that. What he wrote on the carpet with the crayon—*that* was his attempt to say who the killer was."

There were deep creases in Mom's forehead. "Those words he wrote on the carpet—those are the things that the three wise kings brought to the baby Jesus, as a birthday present. In your opinion, how do they say who the killer is?"

"Maybe he wanted to get across that the killer was a wise man of some kind? A professor maybe? Somebody who works at Mesa Grande College?"

"Why not write his name? It would be quicker and easier, especially for a man who's bleeding to death from a gunshot."

"Maybe there were *three* murderers, and he didn't have time to write all their names. Or maybe the murderer was in disguise, with a long white beard, *looking* like one of the wise men—" I broke off, all too aware of the feebleness of my speculations.

"So do you want some dessert?" Mom said. "I've got something nice for you, I made it special. I'll give it to you as soon as you finish your peas."

I obeyed orders, then Mom whisked away my plate and brought in the dessert, one of her strawberry shortcakes. She doesn't buy them from the bakery either, she creates them herself from scratch. She brought coffee along with it, strong, black and hot, just the way I like it. All through my childhood I had been smelling Mom's coffee and yearning for it, but it was only on my fifteenth birthday that she finally allowed me to taste it—bringing a cup to my place at the head of the table, right after I blew out the candles on my birthday cake.

I enjoyed this treat just as much now, years later. But I noticed that Mom wasn't looking as pleased as she usually looks when I'm wolfing down her food.

"What's wrong?" I asked her.

Shaking her head, she answered, "It's only that I've got a funny feeling about this murder of yours."

"What feeling, Mom?"

"I'm smelling something in it—behind it, underneath it, who knows where? I'm smelling—what's the word? What do you call somebody that has an idea and believes in it so strong he'll do anything for it, including he don't care how many people get hurt or even killed for it?"

"A fanatic."

"Fanatic, that's it. Somewhere behind all this business with the Christmas lights and the real estate deals and the three wise kings, I'm smelling a fanatic. They're the only type people that scare me."

"Robbers and murderers don't scare you?"

"Not the ones that do it for ordinary everyday reasons. Like they're greedy for money, or they're jealous because they lost their girlfriend, or they're mad at somebody for calling them a dirty name. I don't *like* such people, I wouldn't invite them into my house, I'd be upset if somebody in my family married one of them. But they don't scare me, because the reasons they do things are human beings' reasons."

"Fanatics are human beings too."

"They don't *act* human. A little greed, a little lust, a little anger, that's all I'm asking from them. But for them it's strictly, what do they call it, idealism. It's some cause that's going to make the world a perfect place to live in, some idea that's above such minor feelings like lust and greed and anger. For them it's no problem to kill somebody or rob somebody, because they're right, they *know* they're right, and anything you do for what's right has got to be right also."

"If you ask me, Mom, you're being influenced by all this religious rhetoric. You just can't take it at face value. People like Chuck Candy aren't fanatics. They're businessmen. They don't believe their own line for a minute. They've got more than their share of those human motives you're talking about."

"Sure, sure, I understand this. Even so, somewhere this fanatic is hiding. Curled up in a dark corner somewhere, like an animal that's waiting to jump out."

She broke off, and I suddenly didn't feel like having any more strawberry shortcake.

THREE

Friday, December 23

OUR LOCAL RAG, *The Mesa Grande Republican-American,* devoted most of its front page Friday morning to the murder. The President had just delivered a blast at the Congress, and terrorists had bombed a restaurant in Paris, but these events were relegated to the bottom of the page, under small headlines. They were stale stuff, after all; they happened all the time. How often did an upstanding, God-fearing representative of the Christian community get himself shot to death by a Jewish youth from New York City?

Not that the *Republican-American* put it in just those words. All it did was make a lot of references to the Christmas decoration fracas, refer to Roger at every opportunity as "accused assaulter Meyer," and never mention his parents without adding that they were "former residents of New York City."

On one of the inside pages was an editorial, boxed by thick black lines and signed, like the one the day before, by Arthur T. Hatfield. In it he deplored the infiltration into our city of "elements who have no understanding of, and often are viciously hostile to, the deepest and most hallowed traditions of our Christian community." He alluded to the fact that "the fugitive has, of course, not yet been proven guilty in court," then he went on to declare, "If and when that verdict is delivered, this newspaper hopes he will receive the full penalty the law allows. The regrettable tendency, in recent years, of certain local public officials, mostly judges and so-called public defenders, to be soft on crime, to let their hearts bleed for the lawbreaker at the expense of his victims, must not be permitted to enter into this case."

Right next to this editorial was an ad for the upcoming local production of Tchaikovsky's Nutcracker Ballet, to be performed on Christmas afternoon. The ad urged us to "bring the kids for an entertainment full of the joy and beauty and warmheartedness of the holiday season."

I gulped down my coffee and drove downtown. A few blocks from the courthouse I was delayed by a small traffic jam, because a banner was being put up, stretching from the top floor of the Mesa Grande United Bank building on one side of Kit Carson Avenue to the top floor of the Southwestern Savings and Loan at the other side. The banner announced, in blazing red-and-green letters, that the annual Municipal Christmas Tree Lighting ceremony would take place in this very block at seven o'clock on Christmas Eve.

This local custom had been going on for a long time before I arrived at Mesa Grande. A giant tree would be put in place in the middle of the block, its branches loaded with colored lights, and the mayor himself would turn on the switch, after saying a few appropriate words about the spirit of the season. This giant tree would remain in the same spot, an inspiration to all our citizens and a cause of endless traffic jams, until it was taken down on New Year's Day.

Twenty minutes later I slid into the cubbyhole I jokingly refer to as my office. The first thing I did was to put in a call to Candy's house. A female voice told me that Mrs. Candy was at home for condolence calls. I asked if her son, the Reverend Gabriel Candy, was there too, and the voice told me he was at the church, taking care of all the problems that had come up as a result of the tragedy.

That decided me. I'd better get to Candy's house right away. Who could tell when I'd get another crack at the widow out of her son's hearing?

But I had to postpone the visit, because Ann buzzed me at that moment.

"Can you come in here right away, Dave?" she asked. "A couple of people just rang up to make an appointment with me. I think you better sit in."

THE PEOPLE Ann was expecting got to her office two minutes after I did.

One of them was Francesca Fleming, wearing something
that looked like a cross between a Japanese kimono and an
Apache squaw's housekeeping dress. Her red hair blazed
out, as usual, like a fire that was out of control. She acknowledged my presence with a laugh and a handshake, but
even so, she seemed to be holding herself in, almost trying
for a serious expression on her face.

Maybe it was the restraining influence of the second visitor. This was the Reverend Eugene Grant Morgan, the
minister of Mesa Grande's Unitarian Church and president
of the local chapter of the ACLU. He was taller than anybody else in the room. Through the years this had caused
him to walk with a pronounced stoop which, along with his
thick black-rimmed glasses, his deep earnest voice, his
thinning hair, and his slightly horse-like face, tended to
make him look a lot older than his forty years.

I knew people who found Gene Morgan an unbearable
bore. Awfully noble and idealistic, there certainly ought to
be more like him, but it was pure punishment to be forced
to spend an evening with him, while he droned on about
human rights and race prejudice and his other favorite top-
ics of light social chitchat. But the fact is, I kind of liked the
guy. He occasionally said things I was glad to hear, and as
for the vast stretches in between—a long time ago I learned
the fine art of shutting off my ears when I don't want to listen. Without this talent police investigators, like psychiatrists, couldn't possibly get their work done.

The visitors sat down, and no time was wasted on small
talk. "We're here with a proposition, Ann," Francesca
started in. "Frankly I don't think you can turn it down."

"Now I don't think I'd call it a proposition," Morgan
said. "More like a gesture, in the common cause of seeing
justice done, fighting together for—"

"We've got business to do in this office, Gene," Ann cut
in. "Christmas is a busy season for the criminal classes.
Even if it's the slack season for you church people."

Francesca gave a sharp laugh and a wink in my direction.

"Very well then." Morgan cleared his throat. "It's this case you're involved in now, the boy who's accused of killing the minister—the ACLU is offering to take it off your hands. We want to hire our own lawyer to defend the boy at the pre-trial hearing next week. And for any court proceedings that might follow. And entirely, of course, at our expense."

He paused. Maybe he was waiting for Ann to jump up and shout "Hallelujah!" and throw her arms around him. She just sat there, with no expression on her face at all, and finally said, "Why is the ACLU making this generous offer?"

"Because whether or not the boy is guilty, he's entitled to a fair trial, all the protections of the law. And we're afraid he isn't going to get them."

"What makes you think so?"

"Religious bigotry has raised its ugly head in this case. For a long time we've been concerned about the increasing militancy with which certain groups in town are trying to impose their religious beliefs on others—"

"Did you see our local yellow sheet this morning?" Francesca said. "Did you read that poison on the editorial page? Damn near made me throw up my soft-boiled egg!"

"What particularly disturbs us at the ACLU," Morgan said, "is the distinct possibility that this case may become a rallying point for forces of reaction in this city. It's happened before. In the thirties, Mesa Grande had a larger Ku Klux Klan membership than any other city outside of the South."

"I warned you the other night, Dave," said Francesca. "Arthur T. Hatfield signed his own name to that garbage this morning. That means he's taking a personal interest in your client. Every few years he likes to pick out somebody, preferably somebody from some minority group, and railroad him into the pokey. In this case maybe even the gas chamber."

Morgan leaned forward, with even more urgency on his face than before. "You're a good lawyer, Ann—nobody says you aren't—and you've got a fine investigative staff."

Brief complimentary nodding in my direction. "But everybody knows how understaffed you are. You don't have the time, the personnel, the resources in terms of money and manpower that this boy needs for the best possible defense. I can understand you might feel a certain resentment for my saying this, but let's face it, what are your feelings or my feelings compared to the Meyer boy's life and freedom?"

"Dave," Ann turned to me so quietly and smoothly that I knew she was mad as hell, "how's the investigation going so far? You feel you're letting Roger's interests down, on account of not having enough money or manpower?"

"The investigation's moving along just fine," I said. "Actually I've got all the manpower I need."

I didn't mention that the manpower I referred to was actually womanpower—a seventy-five year old lady who at that moment was probably beating a rug to death in her backyard.

"So there you are," Ann turned back to Morgan. "We'll put your offer up to the client, of course—"

Francesca interrupted, shoving her chin forward, "Have you talked to him? Do you know where he is?"

"—but I'm bound to tell you," Ann sailed on, smiling softly, "our professional advice to him will be that he should turn it down."

"He can't *afford* to turn it down!" Francesca's chin started stabbing the air. "Goddamn it, Ann, you don't realize what we can do for him! We're on the verge, practically a hundred percent certain, of getting Victor Kincaid to handle this case!"

The name brought us to a sharp silence for a moment. Victor Kincaid might not have been as much of a household word—or curse, depending on your household—as he had been back in the late sixties and the early seventies. Back then he had defended every radical and war protestor and activist in sight. But even a decade or so later plenty of people remembered him, and if he mixed himself up in the Meyer case Mesa Grande could count on being mentioned in *Time* and *Newsweek*.

"You know Kincaid?" I said to Francesca.

"He's an old buddy of mine. From when we were both on the barricades in the anti-Vietnam movement—more years ago than I care to remember. He's in town this week, representing some Eastern firm that's looking for investments out here. Didn't you see his picture in the paper yesterday morning?"

I had to admit it wasn't my habit to pore through *The Republican-American* with a fine-tooth comb.

"Mr. Kincaid is staying at the Richelieu," Morgan said. "Francesca's already sounded him out, and he's definitely interested."

"I'll be lunching with him tomorrow, at my restaurant. I'll be softening him up with a good wine, and I expect him to tell me he'll handle the case."

"I must confess, I'm puzzled," Ann said. "Since when does Victor Kincaid take piddling little cases that get themselves dismissed for lack of evidence before they can turn into national news?"

Francesca swung on Ann. "This *isn't* some piddling little case! That's just the attitude that's going to sink your client!"

"Maybe the case isn't piddling, but it *is* going to be dismissed for lack of evidence."

"You're bluffing," Francesca said. "There isn't a chance in a million the charges will be dismissed. The kid's fingerprints are on the murder weapon, his bloody shoeprints are all over the house, there's a witness who puts him on the spot at the right time, he took a shot at the victim once before—"

"You're doing a good job of making the DA's case," Ann said. "I don't know what Victor Kincaid might have in mind, but *I'm* going to make *our* case when we get into court."

"Bullshit!" Francesca's favorite word exploded out of her, then her mouth opened and shut a few times. I had seen her mad before; she was a woman who prided herself on the care, discipline, and effectiveness with which she lost control of her emotions. The tactic worked very well in bulldozing committee members who disagreed with her.

But then she surprised me. Suddenly she stopped opening and shutting her mouth, and she laughed. A loud
amused-sarcastic laugh, just like her usual self. "Well, you
can't shoot us for trying, can you? And I don't blame you
for a minute, believe me. I mean, whether this Meyer kid
gets off or not, there's going to be a lot of good publicity for
whoever defends him. So why shouldn't the public defender get it instead of the ACLU?"

She started laughing again, but there was no sign of mirth
on the face of the Reverend Eugene Grant Morgan. "You're
speaking for yourself, Francesca, not for the organization.
The ACLU is never activated by self-serving motives. Justice
and individual rights are our *only* priorities. Let me assure
you, Ann, the whole chapter met on this last night, and we
came to the unanimous decision—"

"That's right," said Francesca, "all five of us." She got
to her feet, easily, almost lazily. Not for the first time I
found I had no trouble believing the stories that circulated
about her sexual conquests. "I've got to be off, it isn't good
for the help if I'm out of the restaurant too long. You know
what happens when the cat's away." She tossed a smile at
Ann and one of her winks at me, and then she was out of the
room.

"Reconsider our offer, won't you, Ann," said Morgan,
rising slowly to his full height. A pretty impressive sight, like
some sort of large snake unwinding itself and rearing up
from the ground. "Please—for that poor boy's sake."

"We're grateful for the moral support," Ann said,
standing up too. "It's the legal support we don't need. But
thanks anyway, Gene, I know you mean it for the best."

As soon as Morgan was gone, Ann sighed and said,
"Have you ever noticed how the people on your side so
often make you want to change sides?"

BUT I HAD NO TIME to consider that profound bit of wisdom. I had to get to the late Chuck Candy's house and pay
my condolence call on his widow.

As I got into my car, I noticed for the first time that the
sky was looking sinister. A black-and-blue smudge, like a

bad bruise, was rising up from behind the mountains. Could it be, I wondered, that we were going to have a white Christmas after all? But I wouldn't take bets on it. In Mesa Grande the weather always looks as if it's going to do something and then does just the opposite. Like a lot of people I know.

Fifteen minutes later I drove past the Meyer house—it looked shut up, no cars were parked in front—and pulled up at the Candy house. There were still a dozen or so rubber-necks staring from across the street.

I rang the doorbell, and a dried-up little woman in black opened the door for me. She ushered me into the living room. In it were a lot of other people dressed in black, male and female, middle-aged to elderly. The fact that a murder had happened in this room yesterday wasn't discouraging any of them from sipping coffee and munching cookies.

In the midst of them was Mrs. Candy. She was in a long black dress, with a high black collar, and her face, sticking up from all this blackness, looked as white as death. This effect was enhanced by the redness of her eyes and the dark smudges underneath them.

Though she'd been introduced to me yesterday, I don't think she had any idea who I was. I told her, and apologized for intruding on her in her grief but it was necessary for my official investigation.

The other callers gave me dirty looks and muttered darkly among themselves, and I was sure Mrs. Candy would order me out of the house. I wouldn't really have blamed her. In all my years as a cop, I've never quite got used to the part of it where you stick your nose into people's lives and pry at them and badger them just at the moment when they're suffering the most. Still, I go on doing it; suffering people are more likely to come out with things than people who are thinking clearly.

But Mrs. Candy stood up and said, "There's a room we can talk in, across the hall." Ignoring the mutters around her, she led me across the hall to a small room with a desk, a sofa, and a few chairs in it. She told me to sit down on the sofa, a faded old-fashioned piece that looked as if it had been through the wars. So did the gray upholstered chair she took for herself, and so did the rest of the furniture in the room.

Mrs. Candy offered to get me a cup of coffee. I said no thank you. "I hate to bother you," I said, telling the lie I always tell on such occasion. "I have to ask you some questions, and they may be questions you've answered already for the district attorney. But it's my job to carry on my own investigation. I'll try and be as quick as possible."

She didn't say anything, just stared at me out of those red eyes.

"First, could you please go over it one more time, what you did yesterday—how you found—"

Very clearly, even methodically, she said, "I went out right after breakfast. There were things I had to do over at the church, and then around twelve o'clock or so I went to do my Christmas shopping. For my grandchildren mostly."

As I listened to her talk, I grew more and more puzzled. She sounded, unmistakably, like an educated woman. Her vocabulary, her way of pronouncing words, even her grammar couldn't have been more different from the down-home, folksy aggressive ignorance of her husband.

"What things did you have to do at the church?" I asked.

"I was bringing over the New Year's Day poster. Where it says the time of the service and the title of the sermon, and a special message of Happy New Year from Chuck. He wrote down what he wanted it to say, and I copied it off on the poster board, the way I always do—"

"New Year's Day is a week from Sunday. I thought he never wrote his sermons till the Thursday before services?"

"Oh, he never writes his *sermon* till then. But he usually has the *title* a lot sooner. He thinks up a catchy title that'll bring people in for the service, and later on he writes down a sermon to fit it."

"Your husband went home at lunchtime, Mrs. Candy, but you didn't?"

"I never fix his lunch for him on Thursdays," she said. "On Thursdays he has to be in the house alone. He spends the afternoon communing, and when the light comes to him he writes his Sunday sermon.''

"And you finished your Christmas shopping at what time?''

"It was five-thirty when I got back to the house.''

"You left the church around noon, and spent more than five hours shopping?''

"I'm afraid I dawdled around a bit. I had lunch at the cafeteria in the shopping mall. I sat awhile over my coffee. And after I bought what I was looking for, I went back to the cafeteria and had some more coffee. You see, I couldn't get back to the house before five-thirty. Chuck doesn't like it if I get home earlier than that, when he's communing.''

"You didn't happen to run into anybody you knew at the shopping mall, did you, Mrs. Candy? Especially later, when you had your second cup of coffee?''

"No. I didn't run into a soul. Maybe the salesgirls will remember me. But nobody's going to remember me in the cafeteria, because it's self-service.''

"When you got back to the house, did you ring the doorbell?''

"Why should I? I just used my key and went in.''

"Did you notice anybody outside the house? Hanging around the street?''

"I didn't see anybody on the street. The crowds don't show up for the Christmas lights till it starts getting dark.''

"And then, once you were inside?''

We were coming to the tough part, and I fully expected her to break down at the memory of it. But she didn't, she kept her voice very calm. "I called out for Chuck to help me with my Christmas packages. But he didn't answer, so I took the packages into the living room. I found him there. By the Christmas tree.''

"And then you called the police?''

"I went up to him first. I thought maybe he fainted, got sick or something. But then I saw the blood. And then I called the police.''

"Did you also see what was written on the carpet next to him? Those words he wrote in red crayon?''

"Gold, frankincense, and myrrh. Yes, I saw."

"What do you make out of them?"

"They're the gifts of the magi."

"Yes, but have you any idea why your husband would've written them there?"

She shook her head. "I don't know. Maybe he wasn't thinking clearly. Because he was in pain maybe—" She broke off, biting her lip.

"Did you touch anything in the living room when you found him? Move anything, change its position?"

"No. I didn't even sit there, I couldn't. I went across the hall, to this room. I waited for the police here."

A sudden thought occurred to me. "What happened to the packages?"

"Packages?"

"The Christmas shopping you did. You just said you brought it into the living room. Then you saw your husband, and you went over to him. You must've put the packages down somewhere. But I didn't see them yesterday, when I examined that room."

"What did I do with them?" She shook her head. "Oh yes. Before I came in here to wait for the police, I took the packages up to my own room, our bedroom."

"Why did you do that?"

"Well, I don't know exactly. I just thought— They were for my grandchildren, Christmas presents. They didn't have anything to do with Chuck's death. I didn't want them mixed up in it."

My curiosity had been growing all this time, and now I couldn't ignore it any longer. "Mrs. Candy, how did you and your husband first meet?"

A vague smile flickered across her face. "It was in Santa Fe, New Mexico. I was just a girl. I was still living with my mother and father on the ranch. I was planning to go off to college in the fall."

"College?" I'm afraid I couldn't keep the surprise out of my voice. "It's kind of strange, isn't it? You and Mr. Candy, that is—" I stopped talking, wishing I hadn't started in the first place.

Her smile, as she turned it on me, grew gentle, and maybe there was even a touch of wryness in it. "You're thinking, what could she ever have seen in him—an educated girl and this ignorant, lower-class oaf?"

"No, I wasn't—"

"It's all right. You're not the first person who's said that to me. My parents didn't like Chuck at all. They said a girl like me, who was well brought up and her family had some money, could do a lot better than some wandering preacher without a penny to his name. But you see—" Her smile wasn't directed at me anymore. She seemed to be smiling off into space. "I wasn't happy as a young girl. I didn't want to go to college. I didn't want— I didn't know what I wanted. And then I met Chuck."

"He came to your parents' ranch?"

"No, no." She shook her head. "He came to town to do a prayer meeting. He was doing them even in those days. I went to it, and I got saved. I walked right up to the front, and this young handsome boy put his hands on me and saved me. He wasn't any older than I was, but he saved me. And one thing led to another— My parents got very angry at me. But I was saved, so I didn't have to do what they told me anymore."

She went on smiling. Off in a world of her own. I hated to do it, but I had to pull her back into the real one.

"What happened to your husband's sermon, Mrs. Candy? He did spend the afternoon writing his sermon, didn't he?"

"Let me think. This room is his study, it's where he does his writing. His sermon was over there, on that desk."

"I wonder if I could look at it."

"I don't have it. I gave it to Gabe. That's my son. Gabriel."

"Could you tell me what was in it?"

"Oh, I never read his sermons. It was three pages—on yellow paper, he always uses those big pads of yellow paper. His handwriting is so hard to make out. He brings it over to the church Friday morning to get it typed up—" She winced slightly, as if a disturbing thought had just come to her. "No, he won't be doing that this week—" All of a sudden, her face seemed to crumple, like paper crumpled up in somebody's fist, and a low moan was coming out of her.

I wished I could've got out of there, but I still had one more question to ask.

"Mrs. Candy, do you know of anybody, anybody at all, who might have had a reason for killing your husband?"

She looked up. The moaning stopped, and I saw that her cheeks were dry, no tears had come.

"Gabe says it's that boy. The one from next door."

Something in her voice put me on the alert. "You don't agree with that?"

"Gabe wants them to put that boy in jail. He'll do his best to make him the guilty party."

"Why?"

"Maybe because— He's got to believe he's doing something for his father, standing up for him, something like that. When Chuck was alive, he was always telling Gabe he couldn't do anything right. Well, I suppose Gabe feels he has to do *this* right."

"But you think the guilty party might be somebody else?"

A strange intense glitter was suddenly in Mrs. Candy's eyes. "It was *her,* that's who it was." She leaned forward, putting a bony hand on my knee. Her grip was surprisingly tight. "Winding her web around him, day after day. With her evil symbols and incantations and witch language. The language of witches comes from the devil—that's what it says in the good book."

"You'll have to be a little clearer, Mrs. Candy. Who're you talking about?"

"The woman of evil. Stealing his soul away—that pure white soul that came straight from the hand of God. But *she* took hold of it, squeezed it in her iron fist—oh, they're strong, those fingers of hers, she *keeps* them strong, doesn't she? But they couldn't hold onto him forever, could they? He saw he was trodding the ways of darkness and sin, and he repented and turned back to the paths of light. She couldn't stand that. That's why she killed him. The children of the Lord can endure suffering, they can turn the other cheek. But not the children of the Devil, there's no meekness in them, they sow the wind and will reap the wild wind."

"Who are you accusing? What I need from you is the name—"

"Names! No!" Her head swiveled to the right and left, as if she heard enemies closing in on her from every direction. "I will not say names. I will not cast the first stone. I've been a good Christian since Chuck came for me on the ranch. Good Christians don't cast the first stone."

"If you won't tell me who you're accusing, how can you expect me—"

"God will find a way," she said, lowering her voice to a hoarse whisper. "Vengeance is *mine,* saith the Lord!"

She broke off, breathing hard awhile longer, and then she got to her feet. "Please excuse me now. I must be getting back to my callers."

I didn't need any more invitation. I left that house as fast as I could.

I GOT OUT of the neighborhood, then I stopped at the first drugstore and used the pay phone.

Luckily Mom was home. I filled her in on what had happened since our last talk, and especially about my crazy talk with Mrs. Candy.

Mom didn't say anything for a long time. I began to wonder if we'd been disconnected, but then her voice came through. "It's one of the big mysteries of life, isn't it?"

"What is?"

"You said this Reverend Candy was a little man with a bald head and a big nose?"

"That's right."

"Positively not the Great Lover type. Only have you ever noticed how many times the great lovers don't look like great lovers? You see them on the street, in restaurants, in theatre lobbies, funny-looking little fellows with bald heads and big noses—but always, on their arm, are the most beautiful girls. That's the big mystery."

"But what's it got to do with the Reverend Chuck Candy?"

"It's what his wife just told you about him."

"I couldn't make out what she told me. She sounded completely hysterical to me."

"Hysterical people don't necessarily have nothing to say. The secret is in the translation. Now first of all, this Mrs. Candy talks about 'her'—some woman in her husband's life, who, she says is 'stealing his soul away.' It's a love affair she's talking about—can you have any doubts about that?"

"No, I guess not. Though when a man's having an affair, he doesn't usually let his wife know all about it."

"Who says so? Did I ever mention to you my second cousin Seymour? He was always having affairs, a different woman every year. And he was always dropping hints about them to his wife, Lucille. The truth is, he got a bigger kick from telling Lucille about the other women than he got from the other women.

"Even so, I'm not saying this Candy was another cousin Seymour. There's plenty ways a wife can find out about her husband's hanky-panky. Sooner or later, believe me, a woman knows what's going on. And then she gets mad, like this Mrs. Candy, and blurts it out to people."

"If she's so mad, why didn't she blurt out her rival's name?"

"Because inside her is two people. The first person is the jealous wife that's married to a no-good—so she takes you into a private room and gives you information. The second person is the loyal wife that's married to a saint—so she makes a mishmash of the information so you wouldn't understand what it's all about."

"Maybe you're right. But that means Mrs. Candy's deepest feelings are tied up with her refusal to tell me who her rival is. She'll *never* give us the name."

"She don't have to."

"Mom! Do you really think you can guess—"

"Who guesses? After all these years, you're accusing me of being a guesser? She told us who's the woman, Candy's love affair, without meaning to tell us. You only have to pay attention to her words.''

"I thought I did."

"You remember what she said about this woman? 'Winding her web around him day after day.' So it's someone Candy saw practically every day. 'With her evil symbols and incantations and witch language.' So it's somebody who used peculiar symbols in her relationship with Candy, a language his wife couldn't understand. How far do you have to look, in a man's everyday life, for such symbols and such a language? What about shorthand? 'She squeezed his soul in her iron fist—oh, they're strong, those fingers of hers, she *keeps* them strong doesn't she?' How does she keep her fingers strong? By exercising them every day in some kind of strenuous activity. Like pounding a typewriter.''

"You're saying that Candy had an affair with his secretary? With Mrs. Connelly?''

"Why not? Plenty of men do it and always did, the idea wasn't original with him. And you met her, this Mrs. Connelly, when you went to speak to him this morning. You said she was an attractive girl. So at least you should talk to her and make up your mind if there's any truth to the story.''

"You're right, Mom. I'll get to it right away.''

"You're coming for dinner tonight, before I go to the synagogue. So you'll let me know what you find out. Maybe you'll even come to the services with me after we eat?''

I told her quickly that I couldn't make it, I had a previous engagement.

I heard her grunt. Then she said, "By the way, I've been thinking about that witness. The one that saw the Meyer boy go into the victim's house yesterday, you remember?''

"Of course I remember.''

"I've got it figured out, I think, who this witness has to be.''

"And who is it?''

"You'll find out tonight when you come for dinner.''

That wasn't unusual for Mom, dangling a tidbit under my nose and then pulling it away just as I was about to snap at it. I knew better by this time than to try and coax it out of her. That only made her enjoy the game even more.

AFTER MOM HUNG UP, I used the drugstore phone to call Candy's church. I recognized the voice of his secretary, Mrs. Connelly. She started right in with a speech about the church being closed today because of the Reverend Chuck Candy's tragic death, but if I would leave my name and number the Reverend Gabriel Candy would return my call as soon as possible. She reeled off all this quickly and almost expressionlessly—obviously she had made this speech a hundred times already this morning—but underneath I thought I could hear her voice shaking and a sob struggling to break through. She was upset, maybe even grieved, over the death of her boss. Excuse me, her brother in Christ.

I cut her off, telling her she was the one I wanted to talk to. Then I identified myself, and there was a long pause at the other end of the line.

Finally she spoke more slowly, as if she were choosing her words with great care. "I don't think they'll appreciate it if I talk to you."

"We could arrange it so they wouldn't find out. We'll meet for lunch—do you get off at noon? There's a nice Italian place, Pasquale's, in the mall right near your church."

"Pasquale's!" I could hear the sudden eager jump in her voice, but a moment later I could hear her pushing the eagerness away, remembering the solemnity of the day. "I don't think I should. The Reverend Gabe says you're trying to destroy everything the Reverend Chuck stood for."

"I'm only trying to bring out the truth. The truth can't hurt what the Reverend Chuck stood for, can it?"

"Well—"

"Look, so your conscience won't bother you about this, you're being forced into it. The public defender has the same right to investigate crimes as the district attorney. So if you refuse to talk to me, you could go to jail."

"You wouldn't—"

"Not if you talk to me," I said. "And as long as you've got no choice, you might as well get a nice lunch out of it."

"Well, all right. I guess you twisted my arm."

"I certainly did. One thing though. I have some questions I've got to ask Gabe Candy today, which means I'll be coming over to the church in a few minutes. But I'll look right through you, nobody'll know we're getting together later."

She agreed to that, and I hung up.

I LEFT THE DRUGSTORE and headed north to the Church of the Effulgent Apostles.

It was in its mourning clothes. Black crepe covered the front doors and hung in the windows. A sign in front, in printed capital letters, said: "Memorial Services Sunday morning, Christmas Day. To send our dear Reverend to Glory. All are welcome."

The parking lot, I noticed, was a lot fuller than it had been when I was there yesterday morning. The body couldn't be out of the morgue yet, the autopsy was scheduled for this morning. How big would the crowds be when the devout and the curious actually had a body to stare at?

I went inside to the reception room. People were milling around, pointing at the blown-up photographs of Candy that lined the walls. Strips of black cloth had been hung on top of each of those photographs, but not so low as to cover any part of the martyr's face. The TV screen, over the reception desk, was completely covered by black cloth. Just like the coffin would be, I thought.

Connelly was at her desk, trying to talk on the phone and fend off questions at the same time. I made my way over to her. "I'd like to talk to Mr. Gabriel Candy," I said. "I'm from the public defender's office."

As soon as these words were out of my mouth, I began to wish I'd kept my voice a little lower. A couple of people in the crowd had copies of *The Republican-American* in their hands, and it seemed to me they were giving me very unfriendly looks.

"Reverend Gabe's not seeing people this morning," Connelly said. "He's in the sanctuary, engaged in silent prayer."

"Which way is the sanctuary?"

"I'm sorry, he left orders—"

I saw her give a desperate look at the crepe-covered door that Chuck Candy had come out of yesterday, so I marched across to it and pushed through. I found myself in the corridor outside the office where Candy and I had talked. The door at the end led to the sanctuary, I supposed, and I started over to it.

Then I noticed that the office door was slightly ajar, and I saw Gabe Candy's pudgy figure inside. I gave a rap on the partly opened door and walked in without waiting to be asked.

Gabe Candy was sitting behind his father's big mahogany desk. His coat was off, his collar was open; he wasn't wearing his vest. His hands were clasped together on the desk blotter, as if he were holding something in the palms of his hands and contemplating it. The expression on his face was awfully close to despair.

He looked up sharply as soon as I stepped in, and pulled his hands down to his lap. A kind of wavering annoyance crossed his face. As if he'd like to rise up to anger but was just too tired. "I told them out there I don't want to be disturbed."

"Sorry about that," I said. "When you're carrying on an investigation, you have to act fast, before the trail turns cold. You can't wait around 'til people are ready for you."

"What's so hard about following *this* trail? I'd say it was paved in concrete."

"Maybe so. But I've still got my job to do. The sooner you answer my questions the quicker I'll be out of here."

His hand brushed his eyes quickly, and he said, "All right, all right, what can I do about it anyway? Ask what you want. But don't take too much time at it."

I took a seat across from him. "That's nice of you, Mr. Candy."

"Dr. Candy," he said.

"Oh, you've got a doctorate?"

"Of divinity."

"What seminary did you graduate from?"

"University of Kansas, if you want to know. I've been out two years. I started older than most—I was having a family, and that delayed me."

Or maybe it had taken awhile before his father was doing well enough in the preacher business to send his son off to theological school.

"What did you do between college and the seminary? Besides have babies, I mean."

"I worked for Daddy in the church. When it was down in Arizona. Just outside Tucson." His face darkened a little. "That's just as important as any studying and getting degrees and all. I was laboring in the vineyards. That's what Daddy did, and I learned more from him than any of those professors of divinity could teach me."

"Is that what your father used to tell you?"

Gabe flushed. Then he lifted his chin, trying to make his voice firm and dignified. "You didn't come in today to hear the story of my life. You came to ask questions about Daddy's murder. Go ahead and ask them."

I took him through everything he had done yesterday, and everything he had seen his father do. There wasn't much to it. His father had left the church a little before noon, as was his custom on Thursdays, going home to ask the Lord's help for his Sunday sermon. Gabe had stayed on in the church, where he had a lot of administrative business to take care of. Mostly to do with finances, he said.

There was so much to do that he hadn't gone out for lunch. His wife had given him a sandwich and an apple in a paper bag when he left the house that morning, and he had eaten these at his desk while he was going over the books. Then, from roughly two o'clock to four o'clock, he had discussed the books with the church's business manager, a local accountant who was a member of the congregation and volunteered his services "for the benefit of his salvation." After Mr. Perkins left, Gabe had stayed on at his desk for another hour or so, then he had gone home, to find his household in an uproar, his wife weeping, his five children screaming, and a policeman in his hallway. His mother had called a few minutes before to break the news.

"How come she didn't get in touch with you, here at the church?"

"Maybe she tried. The switchboard here was closed down. I let Mrs. Connelly off early yesterday. At four, when Perkins the accountant left."

"Why'd you do that?"

"She had to work late a couple days this week, so I figured to make it up to her."

"Wouldn't incoming calls go directly to your office phone?"

"Only if I connected it up. I didn't, on account of I wanted to get my desk work done without being disturbed."

"You say you spent the afternoon going over the church's finances? So how are they?"

His eyes shifted a little for a moment. "That's not the kind of thing I really have a head for. But Perkins says we're keeping our heads above water. What Daddy always said was, 'Religion is no profit-making business, and it was never meant to be, and thank the Lord for it. But as long as we've got a God-fearing flock that feels close to Jesus Christ when the collection plate goes 'round—'"

"My boss might want to send somebody down to look at your books in the next day or two."

"You have to do that, I suppose. All right, all right. Give us a few hours' notice, I'll have Perkins open everything up for you."

"Now you were saying you stayed on in your office yesterday afternoon, after your accountant left at four o'clock. For about an hour, was it?"

"It must've been closer to an hour and a half. It was quarter of six when I got back to my house, and that's a ten minute drive from here, even if the traffic's light."

"Say you were here for an hour and a half then. You weren't all alone in the building, were you? There must be a janitor or a cleaning woman."

"The night janitor doesn't come on 'til seven. And we haven't got a full-time day janitor, or cleaning women either. We can't afford them, we use volunteers from the congregation."

"The collections won't stretch to a daytime janitor?"

"Daddy would never allow it. He didn't like the idea of siphoning money from something more important. One of our good works maybe, or our annual contribution to the Central Baptist Missionary Society."

"You're affiliated with the Baptist Church? You don't say anything about it on any of your posters or ads."

"We *contributed* to the Baptist Missionaries. We'll contribute to any cause that does the work of the Lord. But we don't care to be *affiliated* with anybody. What Daddy always said was, 'We meet Jesus face to face, we don't need any bureaucracy to stand between us.'"

"Your father wrote a sermon yesterday afternoon, while he was alone in his house. I understand you've got that sermon."

"Do I?" He blinked a little. "Yes, I guess I do. Right here in my briefcase." His eyes narrowed. "How do you know I've got it? Have you been talking to—" He broke off with another sigh, the thread of indignation just wasn't worth pursuing. He reached down to the floor for his briefcase, an old brown one with the leather fairly battered, and pulled a few sheets of yellow lined paper out of it. "You can look it over, but don't ask me to give it to you. I'm delivering this sermon at the memorial service Sunday morning."

"Isn't it unusual to hold a funeral on Christmas day?"

"It won't be a funeral. Actually the funeral won't be 'til Monday. It's a *memorial* service we'll be holding on Sunday. Daddy always said he wanted it that way. Whatever day he died, he said, he wanted a memorial service on Sunday, because that's the day Christ rejoined His Father in Heaven. Of course it's even better the way it's actually worked out. Daddy died on Thursday, and Christ was born on this coming Sunday. Four days. It's the exact same time as there was between the crucifixion and the resurrection. I'm going to mention that coincidence in my remarks at the service."

"You're going to deliver a sermon too, along with your father's?"

"The dead will speak, and then the living will speak. It shows the continuity. Christ died but His mission to humanity lives on forever." His eyes lowered, and he was holding on tight to the edge of the desk. "Daddy never let me—I never gave any of the sermons while Daddy was alive. But if I'm going to continue his work, I have to start showing right away—" He couldn't finish the sentence. The knuckles had turned white on the hand that was gripping his desk.

Was "continuity" the key word, I wondered. Would Gabe Candy have committed a murder so he could inherit the church?

"You *will* be taking over for your father then?" I asked. "You'll become the chief minister of the church?"

"The Board of Vestrymen had a quick emergency meeting first thing this morning, and they offered me the appointment. They'll announce it officially this afternoon, we already sent a notice to the TV news."

"You accepted the appointment, did you?"

"I was proud to accept." Another dignified lift of the chin, but the look on his face made me turn my eyes away; I had never seen such a look of misery on anybody's face before.

"That's what I'm doing here in Daddy's office," he said, obviously pushing himself hard to go on talking. "I'm looking over his papers, seeing if there's any business that can't wait. Letters he was getting off that he never finished, for instance."

"*Was* there any business that can't wait?"

"I didn't find any yet. There's a lot to do though, Daddy wasn't a very methodical type of man. He didn't go in for paperwork. Or for reading, as a matter of fact, or for thinking about theological points, and all. He was a *people* kind of minister. That's the big difference between him and me. I always loved the reading, I thought awhile about going off some day and joining a monastery—there are monasteries that aren't Roman Catholic, maybe you didn't know that. But I was a dumb kid then, and Daddy made me see what a crazy idea that was, how I'd be giving up on my duty to the Lord and His children—"

Gabe broke off, and for a moment a tear appeared in his right eye. It never had a chance to run down his face though. It bulged out, but then it receded again, sucked back in by his eyelid.

I ducked my head and got busy reading the sermon.

The handwriting, as Mrs. Candy had warned me, was pretty hard to decipher. And half the time what was scrawled there weren't complete sentences, just fragments, reminders for lines that no doubt he intended to flesh out from the pulpit.

It would've been a highly emotional sermon, that much I could tell. It began with long passages from the story of the prodigal son in the Gospels, and reached its climax with this thundering sentence: "Pray then, my dear fellow warshipers, for the Prodigle Son, who traveled the path of Sin, sedused by the Scarlett Woman. But now, with travail and suffering, he frees himself from the Scarlett Womans Evil Influense and returns, a broken and humilyated man, to the fold of the Rightious."

Well, if you've got an inside track to God's ear, what do you need with correct spelling?

"He was a powerful speaker," Gabe Candy said, as I looked up. "He would've done a terrific job with that one."

"It isn't much like his usual sermon, is it? I get the impression he was usually more positive. Lots of joy and comfort, and if you believe in Jesus your ills will be cured and you'll achieve success."

"That's so, I guess. But the fact is, Daddy couldn't ever be sure *how* his sermon was going to turn out. The Lord gave him the words, and he just wrote them down."

Suddenly he smiled. It was a faint smile, a little sad too, but it was the first less than wretched expression I had seen on his face since coming into the room. "I'm glad we had this talk. I was a little sharp with you when I ran into you in my house yesterday, and I want to say I'm sorry for that. At a time like this, a man's under a strain. I guess you can appreciate that."

I told him I could. And the thought came into my mind that Gabe Candy was frightened and bewildered, and worst of all alone and lonely, and he badly needed a friendly word.

The only words I had to give him were "Goodbye, and thanks," but I put as much friendliness into them as I could.

IT WAS a little before noon when I got to Pasquale's at the mall. Connelly wouldn't get off work till noon, so I had about fifteen minutes before she'd arrive. I used it to commandeer a table for myself—pretty soon this little place would be full of lunchtime customers—and then to order a glass of wine.

Connelly got to the restaurant a few minutes later. She was wearing a dark blue coat which was probably meant to be indicative of mourning; it looked a little threadbare. In spite of the tragic occasion, though, she had put on some lipstick and powder—which she was evidently forbidden to wear inside the church—and they made her look younger and a lot more attractive. I was also surprised by her hefty bust and her long classic legs: those assets hadn't been visible from the other side of her reception room desk.

I got up and held her coat for her as she took it off.

"Thanks, that's nice," she said, slinging it across the back of her chair. "People don't do that for you like they used to do. I'm in favor of Women's Lib, but I'm getting tired of these guys that race you to see who gets through the door first."

She sat down and looked around. She was obviously pleased by what she saw, but her strategy was to be blasé about it. "Nice place. I don't recall I was ever here before. The Reverend Chuck used to have lunch here every day. When he got back to the church, you could smell the garlic on his breath—"

She cut herself off. Her lips began to tremble a little. "Listen—do you think I could order something to drink? Something a little strong? I won't pick the most expensive—"

"You order whatever you want." I signaled for the waitress, and pretty soon Connelly was sipping a margarita, which is the only cocktail ever invented that you have to put salt on. I had a second glass of wine.

"Well, I guess you don't want me drinking like this," Connelly said, "unless I tell you what I know about the Reverend Chuck getting killed."

"*Do* you know anything about it?"

"Best of all would be if I knew something that could do the Meyer kid some good? That right?"

Just then the waitress came, and gave us the menus. Connelly began timidly, asking if this or that was too steep for me, but I encouraged her and she ended up ordering the works—minestrone soup, antipasto tray, spaghetti and meatballs, and a side order of garlic bread. Her figure suggested to me that she didn't eat like this ordinarily, when she was paying for it herself.

"Working for a church doesn't exactly make you rich, does it?" I asked.

"That's a fact. But I'm not complaining, it's a good place to work, nice people. They believe in God, and that means they mostly don't shout at you and curse at you, and the men mostly keep their hands off you. Some of the places I've worked! I could tell you stories, you better believe it!" Her smile faded a bit. "But they *don't* pay you too good in a church, I won't kid you about that. They don't have any money, that's because they're non-profit and tax-free. Some weeks it's just a goddamned drag to— Oh, sorry about that. There I go again, taking His name in vain. The Reverend Chuck told me what a lousy habit that was, and mostly I try and be careful. Only sometimes you just have to—well, the way the grocery prices are going up these days—"

"Isn't it easier with two salaries coming in?"

"What two salaries?"

"Yours and your husband's."

"Who's got a husband?"

"The sign on your desk says Mrs."

"Plenty of Mrs. nowadays don't have any husbands. Connelly walked out on me five years ago. I got a divorce, and he's supposed to send me the alimony every month. Do you think I ever saw any of it? Meanwhile, that new wife of his, that hooker that got him drunk and married him, is walking around in a fur coat and driving a Japanese four-door. A friend of mine saw her on the street only last month.''

"Why don't you go to the cops? The judge could order him—''

"What does *he* care about any judge? They're living down in Texas, him and this hooker. Nobody ever got a dime out of an ex who's in Texas. They don't have any courts down there, I'll bet you didn't know that.''

"You're still using your ex-husband's name though.''

"Sure I am. What the hell else did he leave behind for me? At my age you better be a missus. If you're a miss, everybody thinks there's something wrong with you. You're either a lesbian or you're a whore. I don't have anything against either of those things, but I don't happen to be one, so I don't want anybody thinking I am.''

The waitress showed up with our lunches. My own was a salad—I prefer to use my calorie quota at Mom's dinner table—but Connelly lit into hers as if food were going out of style.

A little later, with her mouth full of antipasto, she said, "There's no way you can send any of this back, is there? Okay, I'm going to level with you. I don't know a god-damn-darn thing about this killing. I can't help your client at all.''

"Maybe you can without knowing it. Tell me about the late Reverend Candy. What was your job for him exactly?''

"Mostly answering the phone in the reception hall and doing the church typing and taking dictation for his letters. I did that an hour every day, in the middle of the afternoon.''

"Who looked after the reception desk during that hour?''

"One of the volunteers mostly. There's always a bunch of them around. Widows or maiden ladies who don't have any husbands or boyfriends to go home to.''

"What sort of letters did the Reverend Chuck dictate?"

"Most of them were to people in the congregation. The people who were too shy to see him in person, they wrote him and asked him questions—how they could be at peace with God, how they could pay off the mortgage, that sort of question."

"And he was able to answer them?"

"He'd pretty much say the same thing to all of them. If they'd make their peace with God, the mortgage would get itself paid off. Material things weren't important."

"And in order to make their peace with God, what did he advise them to do?"

"They had to pray harder and believe better. That's what Jesus wants us to do. That's how we get to be saved."

"Were any of the letters he got unfriendly or angry or anything like that? People threatening him maybe?"

"I never saw any letters like that. Not since I've been around. But I only started working for him a little more than a year ago."

"And how was the Reverend Chuck to work for?"

"Not bad. I've had worse. Always polite, and he had a cheerful word for you at all times of the day. And forever making jokes. Sometimes they weren't so funny, but some of them were pretty good. And *he* thought they were *all* good. And he never tried to sneak extra work out of me, by dumping a big job on me just before closing time. That's a trick I've seen plenty of, but he never tried it."

"What about the other people working for him? Did he treat them all pretty well? Any of them feel any resentment or anger?"

"Why should they? Most of them are these religious types. He made them feel like they were working for Jesus Himself."

"Did the Reverend Candy ever save *you*?"

She lowered her eyes. The blasé tone deserted her for a moment. "Well, not officially. Like I never got up at the meeting or anything. I'm a pretty hard case. Where I grew up, my folks didn't go in much for praying and all. Have you been to Newark? Okay, you know what I mean. But I've

been listening to the Reverend Chuck. I don't say I buy it all.
Or even most of it. But I'm thinking it over. What's the
harm in thinking?''

"And the Reverend's family? How did they get along
with him?''

"He never asked me to his house."

"His wife and son both work at the church. You must see
a good deal of them there.''

"Not too much. I keep out of their way." There was no
way of reading her expression; her face might have been
frozen.

"Why don't you tell me what you think of them," I kept
pushing. "Just a quick impression. Start with his wife.''

"I've got nothing against any of them. None of them ever
did me any harm. They're real nice people.''

"But what *kind* of people?''

Connelly couldn't answer; her mouth was filled with the
last of her meatballs. Then, when that was done, she filled
it over again with wine. And then she looked at her watch.
"We're sitting here pretty near an hour. My lunchtime is
over, I have to get back—''

The chance was slipping away from me. I had to be crude,
or I'd miss out completely. "Why are you afraid to say
anything bad about Candy's family? What are you feeling
guilty about?''

"Who's feeling guilty?''

"Whose idea was it, his or yours?''

"What idea?''

"The affair you had with Chuck Candy.''

She opened her mouth, but no sound came out of it. She
looked as if I had hit her across the face, which in a way I
had. When she spoke, her voice was hoarse. "That was over
with a long time ago. If you don't know *that,* you don't
know a goddamned *thing*.''

I didn't let my face show any sign that this was news to
me. "How did it get started in the first place?''

"Nothing got started. What'd we do that was wrong?''
She lifted her hands in a what-the-hell gesture. "All right,
we *did* things. But with the Reverend Chuck, it wasn't like

with anybody else. I've done plenty in my life—I guess you already figured that out for yourself—but with Chuck it was always, I don't know, it was beautiful. It was like praying or something."

"Were you in love with him?"

"Love!" The word burst out of her with contempt. "Why is everybody always talking about love? What the hell has *that* got to do with anything? Can't two people have a great time with each other—"

"But what was there about him that you found attractive? He must've been twenty years older than you. And it isn't as if he was—"

"Robert Redford? No, he sure wasn't. And he wasn't young either. Don't you think I knew all that? But I had all that stuff before—young and Robert Redford, I had them with Connelly, and look what good they did me! You want to know what there was about Chuck? He showed an interest in me, that's what."

"Come on, plenty of men must show an interest in you, it must happen to you all the time."

"Plenty of men look me over, they tell me a lot of horse manure about how beautiful and sexy I am. I'm no genius, but it doesn't take one to know what they're showing an interest in—it's not *me,* it's how I can make it come up for them. The Reverend Chuck—he was different."

"You're telling me he was genuinely in love with you?"

"Did I say that? God, you can't let go of that word, can you? I'm telling you he genuinely took an interest. You knew, when he talked to you, you were the most important thing he had on his mind. He wanted you. He didn't just want a quick lay, and who cares who with, he wanted *you*." For a moment something almost like a smile was on her face. "And it wasn't so convenient for him either, when you get right down to it. His wife was with him every night and on weekends, and he worked in the church all day."

"So when did the two of you—?"

"In the afternoons mostly. When things at the church got slow. When I went into his office to take dictation."

"While the volunteers were manning the desk in the reception room?"

"Why not? That way we were sure nobody would bust in on us."

"It's amazing you managed to keep up with his mail."

"I *never* got behind with his mail!" She raised her chin, as if this was a point of pride with her. "On the days when there was too much of it, I took the extra ones home with me. I didn't mind doing it. I was glad to."

"One thing you said before—it's been over between you and him for a long time. Could you explain that to me?"

"What's there to explain? I never kidded myself about that. I knew right off, right from the start, it wouldn't last long. A man like Chuck, with all the love he's got to give, he wasn't about to keep giving it to only one person. He told me that right off. He said we'd find our spiritual delight, and we'd be made better by it, and then we'd move on."

"So when did he move on?"

"About three months ago. About last fall, right after Labor Day. He didn't do any bullshitting with me, he told me straight out there was somebody new."

"Who did he say it was?" I could feel my curiosity rising, though I kept it out of my voice.

"How should *I* know? He never told me, and I sure as hell never asked him, figuring it was none of my business. All I know is, he buttoned up that afternoon and told me this was it."

She put her spaghetti-filled fork down on her plate, and tears came from her eyes.

I sat and waited, and it wasn't long before the tears stopped coming. Then she wiped her face with a napkin, and then she gave her sarcastic grunt again. "Did you see that rum cake that just passed by? If you wanted to make it up to me, for the emotional pain and suffering you just put me through—"

I ordered the rum cake for her, and it gave me pleasure to watch her as she polished it off to the last crumb.

AFTER LEAVING PASQUALE'S, I made my way across most of Mesa Grande, to my office. Christmas music assaulted me from the radio, including one disc jockey who specialized in rock arrangements of traditional carols. You've never really heard "Adeste Fideles" until you've heard it done by the Rolling Stones.

I spent the rest of the afternoon doing as much of the routine work, the sheer drudgery, on the case as I possibly could.

I trotted down to the DA's office and picked up a copy of the autopsy report and slogged my way through it. There was nothing in it that everybody hadn't figured out already.

I spent half an hour on the phone with Perkins, the local accountant who handled the finances of the Church of the Effulgent Apostles. He sounded scared as hell and evasive as hell, but people often do when they're talking to investigators in a homicide case; nothing in our conversation gave me evidence that he had something to hide. Just to double-check though, I got a court order for somebody from the City Accountancy office to take a look at the church's books.

I called Connelly to send me over a file of Chuck Candy's mail, and to my horror it arrived in less than half an hour. Which meant I had to start reading my way through it. After a few hours, I had disposed of it all. Plenty of nut cases whom I had no trouble imagining as murderers or worse. But no indications that any of them had a reason to kill Chuck Candy. Still, I'd have to do some checking into the most promising ones—if they had alibis, etc.

I called the police lab and asked if they had reports yet about the fingerprints on the murder gun and the bloody shoeprints in the hallway. Nothing yet, they told me. I didn't think they were lying to me on Wolkowicz's orders, either. It was the day before the Christmas weekend; nobody was in any hurry to get anything done.

Then it was five-thirty, and I left the office and drove out to Mom's house for dinner. My arms and shoulders were stiff, my head ached, I couldn't stop myself from yawning.

What else could I expect, spending the last four hours doing the work of three men?

Mom was serving earlier than usual tonight, because she was planning to go to the synagogue for Sabbath services. As the rabbi had gently pointed out to me, she didn't do this every Friday, or even particularly often, but once in a while all that childhood brainwashing got to her.

"So who is it, Mom?" were the first words out of my mouth as I walked through the door. "Who's this witness the DA's so proud of?"

"You don't kiss your mother any more?" she said.

I kissed her, but she still wouldn't let me talk about the case. She started putting food on the table, and we settled down to her pot roast; Mom's pot roast has been one of my favorites since childhood, maybe because it used to make me feel grown-up to eat something with wine in it.

"I'm leaving for synagogue at seven sharp," she said. "I don't like to get there after the services begin. The rabbi gives me dirty looks."

"Come on, Mom. I doubt if he even notices."

"You doubt it, do you? An eye like an X-ray machine that man's got. He can have his nose in the Torah, all wound up in some long Hebrew chant, but at the same time he's watching every door. And he lets you know about it afterwards too. You're munching a nice piece apple pancake at the Oneg Shabbat, and suddenly he's pushing up next to you and telling you how sorry he is you had to rush through your dinner to get here tonight."

"He's always seemed like a nice man to me. People around here like him and respect him, he's a good representative for the Jewish community."

Mom gave a shrug. "He's got one big problem he can't get over, though."

"Which is?"

"He's a rabbi. So can you eat two roast potatoes?"

I told her I could, and set to work proving it, and at last Mom let me know she was ready to talk about the case.

"About this witness then—"

"We'll discuss witnesses after you tell me what happened with this secretary at lunch."

Mom loves to put people in suspense. (Was Alfred Hitchcock really a Jewish mother?) But when she's in that mood, there's nothing you can do except go along with it. So between bites and chews, I somehow negotiated the details of my meeting this morning with Gabe Candy and my lunch with Connelly.

I got to the end of my story, and Mom was looking pleased.

"Very interesting, what this secretary told you. You believe her when she says she stopped being the minister's girlfriend three months ago? There's another one that took her place?"

"I don't see why she'd lie about that. By admitting that Candy dumped her, she's giving herself a perfect motive for killing him."

Mom nodded. "That's a nice piece of logical reasoning. I agree with you, she isn't lying. She could still be the one that killed him though. She could be telling us the truth about her affair with him because she figures you're bound to find it out eventually, the new girlfriend could come forward and make herself known, and then wouldn't it look bad for the old girlfriend that she kept her mouth shut?"

"Have you got any ideas about who the new girlfriend is?"

"Ideas I've always got. But ideas I wouldn't be ashamed to say out loud, those don't come so easy. There's something this Connelly told you—but you should give me a day or so to think about it."

"All right, Mom, enough beating around the bush. Even Hitchcock has to get to the last reel eventually."

"Who's this Hitchcock? Somebody in the murder case you didn't tell me about yet?"

"Never mind that. What about the *witness,* the one who claims to have seen Roger Meyer go in and out of Candy's house? You promised you'd tell me your theory about who it is."

"You didn't figure it out yet by yourself?"

"Would I be asking you if I had?"

"There's only one person this witness can be. The assistant district attorney told you the witness saw Roger Meyer go inside the Candy house by the front door, and come out again five minutes later by the same door. The witness said also that nobody else went in or out before or after. So what does this mean except that the witness was watching that door steady for a long time? In other words, it wasn't somebody with business to do in the neighborhood—the newsboy delivering the paper, the postman delivering the mail, a visitor calling on somebody that lived nearby, a driver that just happened to be driving by the house. None of those types would stop for a long time and keep their eyes on the front door of that house. So who *would* do such a thing?"

"One of the neighbors maybe. Somebody in the house across the street."

"But you told me there *is* no house across the street, it's only a field with some trees and bushes in it."

"All right, somebody in one of the houses next door."

"Davie, you're not concentrating. On one side of the Candy house, you told me, is a big empty lot, the nearest house on that side is over a block away. From such a distance, who could keep an eye on the Candy front door and recognize people coming in and out? And on the other side of the Candy house is where the Meyers live. You're not telling me that the secret witness against the Meyer boy is his mother or father."

"I guess not." I shook my head. "But all you're proving is that *nobody* could be that witness."

"Nobody except one person. And you saw him yourself. You saw him the night before the murder, standing across the street watching the Candy house."

"The Prophet!"

"Exactly. That crazy *alter cocker* that hangs around downtown and tells people the end of the world is coming so they should stop eating eggs. Who else could spare ten minutes, in fact a lot more than ten minutes, to do nothing but stand on a curb and watch the front door of a house?

Who else hasn't got better things to do with his time? It appealed to his imagination, something about that big Christmas show that Candy was putting on, and every chance he got he came to stare at it. So yesterday late in the afternoon he was staring and he saw the Meyer boy go in and out.''

I don't let myself feel optimistic very often, but this had to be one of the times for it. "If you're right about this, it's great news. I have to call Ann—''

"What's so great about it?''

"What kind of a witness do you suppose the Prophet is going to make? Everybody in town knows he's nuts. Not to mention half-drunk most of the time. Whatever he thinks he saw, nobody's going to take his word for it.''

"Even so,'' Mom said, "I hope you're going to talk to this Mr. Abernathy and find out from his own words what he saw.''

"Abernathy? Who's he?''

"This crazy old man, the one you call the Prophet. His name is Luke Abernathy. He used to be some kind of teacher, in a high school somewhere, but that was a long time ago. He's got a room in that dirty little hotel downtown, it looks like it was here before the town got settled, it was abandoned by the Indians—''

"The Hotel Cochran. But for God's sake, Mom, how do you know this old nut's name? And where he lives?''

"And also he's got a married daughter that lives in New Orleans, Louisiana. She sends him fifty dollars a week, on condition he never calls her or tries to see her. Actually she sends the fifty dollars to the hotel, it's the rent for his room. She's afraid, if she sent it straight to him, he'd spend it all on liquor. And he himself admits she's got a point. As for his eating, he does it at the Salvation Army soup kitchen.''

I knew I was gaping at her throughout this recital. She knew it too, and enjoyed every minute of it. "All right, all right,'' I finally got my voice back, "what's the magical explanation? How did you manage this Sherlock Holmes bit?''

"I'd like it you should think I did some magic trick like Sherlock Holmes. But I wouldn't lie to you—the way I got all this information about the old man, I talked to him and he told me about himself.''

"When did you talk to him?"

"Plenty times. I'm shopping downtown, I'm standing next to him on the corner, the light turns red so I can't cross the street—him and me pass the time with a little conversation.''

I should have known it, of course. People talk to Mom. Probably because she actually does what most of us have trouble doing: she listens. She nods her head every once in awhile, she says "Yes" or "You don't say!" or "Then what happened?" and in no time at all she's got their life stories out of them. I could live next door to people for twenty years, and never find out as much about them as Mom finds out after going to their door to borrow a cup of sugar and chatting with them for twenty minutes.

Don't think it's because she's so warmhearted and sympathetic, though, and "loves people" or anything sloppy and sentimental like that. Actually she seldom has much good to say about the people who are so eager to open up to her. What she uses those conversations for is to file them away in her mind, in some big folder marked "The Weaknesses and Foolishnesses of Human Nature."

Fifteen minutes later she was ready to leave for synagogue. She locked up her house, making sure the porch lights were on, and then I walked her to her little red Toyota which was parked at the curb. "So am I ever going to see you again?" she said, through the car window.

"I'll take you out for dinner tomorrow night," I said, "There's a new Japanese steakhouse downtown. Rashomon's.''

"You haven't got a date on Christmas Eve?"

I looked her straight in the eye. "With you. That's my date.''

She made one of her humphing sounds, then she went tootling off to worship God, and I went home to watch a movie on TV.

THE MOVIE, naturally, had Christmas in it. At this time of year you can't get anything on TV, at least not in our area, which isn't Christmas-related. So this was that old one, which I saw when it first came out, about the little old man who works as a department store Santa Claus and starts thinking he's the real thing.

It's a funny movie, but tonight it succeeded only in depressing me. I wasn't in the mood for stories about aging, balding geezers who lose their marbles because their wives are dead and they're all alone in the world. I know the people who made this movie had no such intention, but what it did to me tonight was fill me with wild sexual fantasies. I saw myself as Santa Claus coming down the chimney of some big-busted, passionately inclined female, not too young to be out of my reach by legal means but not too old to be unappetizing.

I was toying with the idea of calling up Virginia Christenson. She was far from ideal, as my last date with her had amply proved. Let's face it, she had the brain of a Barbie doll, and the personality to match, but there *was* a genuine bust there—

Luckily, my phone rang.

I just had time to say hello, and identify myself, when I was interrupted by a low urgent voice, talking almost in a whisper. "Mrs. Swenson is my lawyer, isn't she? So that means you've got to help me, don't you?"

"Who is this?"

"It's Roger Meyer. I want—"

"Where are you, for God's sake?"

"I'm sorry, I just can't tell you where I am. I know the police are looking for me, I want to give myself up."

"That's smart of you. But if you don't tell me where—"

"I don't want to get anybody else in trouble. I want to give myself up to *you,* to you and Mrs. Swenson. I want to go to the police station with the two of you. I don't trust the police—they could shoot at me, and say they cornered me and I wasn't giving myself up at all. They always do it in those old gangster pictures."

I decided it was no time to remind him that real life wasn't an old movie. Besides, he almost had a point. It might very well slip the mind of our beloved DA, once he got into court, that the prisoner had surrendered voluntarily.

"Okay, let's set up a place to meet," I said.

"Tomorrow night," he said. "It's Christmas Eve, they're having the big tree-lighting ceremony downtown. I'll meet you there—nine o'clock."

"We could miss each other, the streets will be packed."

"I *want* to do it in a crowd. That way the police won't try anything. You stand on the northeast corner of San Luis and Kit Carson, I'll find you there."

"As long as you're giving yourself up, why wait a whole day? We could meet tonight—"

"It can't be tonight," he said. "It's tomorrow night at nine, that's how long it's going to take me to get psyched up for this. Don't argue with me—please—or I could get cold feet and change my mind."

"All right, tomorrow night at nine. Mrs. Swenson and I will both be there."

"And listen—I don't think you should tell my parents about this. I know they must be worried, I'm really sorry about that. But it's only a little while longer, and they'd never be able to keep it to themselves."

"All right, we won't tell them."

I expected him to hang up now, but instead there was a pause. Then his tone of voice changed, suddenly he sounded a lot less urgent and anxious.

"There's something else I wanted to ask you about."

He stopped, and I guessed it was up to me to give him some encouragement. "Sure, anything at all."

"Well, once I get out of all this—if I do—I'll be graduating in June, and I don't want to go to grad school or anything. What I'm looking for is— Well, I want to start right out doing something practical, getting experience in the field. I mean, I think it's time I stopped just reading about criminology and really got in there and— Well, do you think there's a chance you'll be looking for an assistant?"

This one left me speechless for awhile. I've had dealings with a lot of accused killers through the years, but he was the first one that ever hit me for a job.

"I know this isn't exactly the perfect time to bring this up," he pushed into my silence hastily. "I don't expect an answer right away, I just want you to give it some thought, that's all. Everybody says you're short-handed in the public defender's office, you've got more work than you can handle, so if there was someone to take the routine stuff off your hands, to do the ordinary drudgery and leave you free for— And in the meantime, I'd be watching you and learning how it's really done. Well, I can't think of anything I'd rather do for the next few years."

"Sure, I could use some help. But you have to understand how these things work. We've got a budget, from the City Council. There's no money in it for assistant investigators."

My God, I thought, I'm talking to him as calmly and reasonably as if this conversation actually made sense!

"You wouldn't have to pay me a lot. I realize I'm completely inexperienced, I'd be more like an intern."

"We don't have intern money either. The truth is, we've got zilch."

A long pause, and then I heard myself saying, "Mrs. Swenson *has* been thinking of going to the City Council this spring, when the new budgets are due, and asking for a line item to beef up my side of the operation."

"If she did that, do you think I'd have a chance?"

"If the Council approved it. But don't get your hopes up. The City Council in this town is well-known for its stinginess with money, especially when it isn't for raising their own salaries. Also, the DA will probably recommend against it. His philosophy is, it's okay to increase *his* budget because he's out to take the criminals off the streets, but *we're* out to put them back on again."

Another pause, and then he said, "Well, whatever happens, I can't thank you enough for what you've done for me. And—well, I guess I'll be seeing you tomorrow night."

"Wait a minute. Can you tell me why you ran off like you did? And about the Reverend Candy's murder—"

"I didn't do it," he said. "That's all I want to say right now. When I think about it, I just feel so awful— Well, I don't want to go into it over the phone."

He hung up, and I thought for a moment what a nice kid he was. I became aware of the stiffness in my joints, the exhaustion filling my whole body, and I imagined what it might be like to have my own personal intern. An eager young man that I'd be molding and forming. My apprentice, you could call him. Like Michelangelo or one of those old furniture-makers.

And then I shook my head with exasperation. What kind of foolishness was this anyway? Making lovely plans for the future of a kid who was a fugitive from justice and could very well end up spending the rest of his life behind bars! Or worse.

I got on the phone to Ann at her home, and told her about Roger's offer to give himself up. I asked her if we had some legal obligation to report this to the district attorney.

I knew what her answer would be. It was her considered opinion that we were completely in our rights in keeping Roger's plans to ourselves. We were officers of the court. In a way, we *were* the police. Therefore, we were empowered to take fugitives into our custody.

As for tipping off the DA ahead of time—where in the city code did it say that the right hand must always let the left hand know what it's doing?

I didn't mention to Ann about Roger asking me for a job. To tell the truth, I wasn't sure she'd believe it.

FOUR

I LIKE TO SLEEP LATE on weekend mornings. I like to sleep late *every* morning, and I definitely will as soon as I find out how to provide for my food, clothing, and shelter without working for a living. Until then, weekend mornings are the only chance I get to be a vegetable.

So I can't say I didn't do some groaning and bitching when my alarm went off at eight on this particular Saturday morning, the day before Christmas. There was no way out of it though. I had to talk to the DA's witness, the crazy old prophet Luke Abernathy, and the only way to be sure of finding him was to get down to his usual beat by nine, which was when he put on his first show of the day.

I barely had time to slosh down my coffee and take a quick look at the front page of *The Republican-American*. The Candy murder was still being played up, with the DA dropping broad hints about a "secret witness" and the Chief of Police confiding to the world that "it was only a matter of time" before the fugitive killer would be caught and hauled off to jail.

A lot of people were in the downtown area when I arrived. I got out of my car, and felt a definite nip in the air. But that black-and-blue bruise wasn't in the sky anymore, dull gray was once more the general complexion of things. It looked as if we weren't going to have a white Christmas.

I went to the nearest corner where Abernathy usually made his rounds. No sign of him yet, so I lounged at a shop window—The British Tailor, Fine Clothes for Discriminating Men, the owner was on the board of the synagogue—and looked over the goods, preparing to wait for the mad prophet as long as it took.

While I waited, frantic signs of Christmas swirled around me. There were more Santa Clauses on the streets than there had been two days ago. Last-minute shoppers, loaded down with bundles and harried expressions, hurried past me. Children clinging to the hands of grown-ups stared up at the giant Christmas tree which had been put in place overnight. To me it looked dark and dense and foreboding, like a gigantic thick-witted thug blocking everybody's way.

Then I spotted the Prophet. He was coming through the crowds on my side of the street, heading straight towards me. In his shrill slurred voice, so that you could make out only half the words, he was delivering his usual warning to the world. "Egg-Eaters beware! The Lord has his eye on you!"

I moved forward and put myself in front of him. "I want to talk to you."

His red-blotched eyes widened.

"It's okay, you're not in trouble, I'm not a cop." I reached out for his arm, trying to make my grip gentle and unthreatening. "We can't talk out here," I said. "Did you have any breakfast yet? There's a little place down the street, they give you a good cup of coffee."

I started to ease him in the right direction, and I could feel his resistance ebbing away. A low moaning noise was coming out of him now. Was this how animals sounded when they were being led to the slaughter?

I reminded myself that he wasn't the one in danger of being slaughtered. The Meyer kid was, and this ancient wreck was cooperating with the slaughterers.

I got the old man into the coffee shop, the Java Hut. The terribly genteel hostess at the door gave us a look of mixed alarm and revulsion. She couldn't refuse to seat us though. We've got anti-discrimination laws nowadays. Affirmative action for broken-down old bums.

She led the Prophet and me to a booth, as far to the back of the place as possible, so that no prospective customer could see us through the window. I practically had to slide him into place and wondered if he'd be able to keep himself upright when I took the seat across the table from him.

He managed this feat somehow. He blinked at me for awhile, and something closer to the light of consciousness began to appear in his eyes. "Whatsa big idea?"

I told him who I was and that I wanted to ask him some questions about the Reverend Chuck Candy's murder.

"I don't know about that. Who says I know about that?"

"You're the prosecution's eyewitness, aren't you? You saw the Meyer kid go in and out of Candy's house."

"Who says so? Blasphemers! Told me nobody was going to know about me 'til the trial! They gave me their word! Fornicators!" He blinked a little more, and then produced a grin which almost had a touch of shrewdness in it. "You gonna buy me breakfast?"

"Positively. What do you like on this menu? Maybe a couple of fried—" I stopped myself just in time.

He didn't seem to notice. "Breakfast was never my big meal of the day," he said. "Whadda they got? They got doughnuts?"

"All kinds."

"I'll have a doughnut. A plain one, don't want all that powdered sugar falling over my shirt, those stains don't come out."

I took a look at his shirt and couldn't imagine where he supposed there was room for any more stains. But I called the waitress over and ordered coffee and a plain doughnut for both of us.

"Make that two doughnuts for me," he said. Then he gave me a quick anxious glance out of the corner of his eye. "Is that okay, two doughnuts?"

I told the waitress it was okay, and she went off.

"So let's have it," I said. "You were standing across the street from Candy's house yesterday afternoon—is that right?"

"Damn right it's right!" His fear seemed to have passed, and a kind of belligerence had moved into its place. "And don't you tell me I'm a liar!"

"Why should I tell you you're a liar?"

"*He* said you would. Fellow from the DA—little fellow with a lot of eyebrows. 'They'll tell you you're a liar,' he said, 'but you don't have to pay any attention to them. Nobody's going to pay any attention to them.' "

"You're right. Everbody'll be paying attention to you. That's what I'm doing now, paying attention to you."

"Yeah. Thass right. Thass what you're doing." A big wobbly smile came over his face.

"So give me something to keep up my interest," I said. "What were you doing outside that house yesterday?"

"Watching, whaddya think? Read about it in the papers. There's going to be lots of lights, there's going to be beautiful music, and cows, and baby Jesus. Like when I was a kiddie—like the Christmas tree at home. Said to myself, 'Thass something I got to see. Haven't seen something like that since I was a little kiddie, at home.' "

He ground to a stop, and I saw the faintest speck of a tear inching out of his red eyes, slowly sliding down his cheek.

"So when did you go to the house to look at all this?"

"Soon as I read about it. In the paper. I'm a big reader of the papers. Pick them up in the trashcans, people leave them there for me. Paper said the lights'd be lighting up at five, so I got there at five. Stood there all night, 'til the lights went out. Lots of people there, lots of cars, but nobody stood there as long as me."

"It must've been pretty cold for you, standing in front of that house all those hours. Didn't anybody invite you inside?"

"Invite me?" He scratched his head. "Nobody invites *me*. Don't get invited any more. Know a lot of people—everybody in town, I see them sooner or later, bringing them the Lord's message—but nobody invites me. Years ago maybe, when Sally was around."

"Sally was your wife?"

"Wife?" He shook his head, looking confused. "Whose wife? Who ever had any wife?"

My instinct told me I'd better get away from this subject. "The paper said the lights were turned on at five," I said. "But yesterday you were in front of that house earlier—by four o'clock at least—weren't you?"

"Was I?" He wrinkled up his forehead in thought. "Four, was it? Yeah, maybe so. Don't have any watch, you know. Used to have a watch—what happened to it anyway? Wanted to get there early, so I'd see the lights turned on. Be sure I wouldn't miss—" He gave a sigh, and a couple of tears began to form again. "Lights never did go on. Waited and waited, 'til the cops came up to me. Nobody ever turned them on."

"And while you waited, what did you see exactly?"

Again that little gleam of shrewdness came into his eyes. "What you wish I *didn't* see, thass what I saw. Saw this kid. Tall kid. Very dark hair. Wearing glasses. He came down the street—"

"From the house next door?"

"Didn't see that. Just saw him coming down the street. Went up the steps, went into the house—"

"Who opened the front door for him?"

"What?"

"He must've rung the doorbell, somebody must've opened the door to let him in."

He shook his head hard. "Didn't see that. Didn't see anything like that. He just went in. I kept watching. Didn't want to miss it when the lights went on. All of a sudden, door busts open, the kid comes out—he's running this time, running real hard. He runs up the street—"

"In the same direction he came from?"

"Thass right."

"Did you see what he did next? Did he go into the house next door, did he get into a car, or what?"

"Got into a car. Little car, old car. Drove away fast. Lot of screeching from the tires."

"How do you know it was Roger Meyer you saw? You'd never seen him before then, had you?"

"Saw his picture afterwards. Cops showed me his picture. Same fellow exactly."

"Come on, it gets dark early these days, by four-thirty or so it's dim already. So how could you recognize—"

"Not *that* dim." He grinned crookedly at me. "See—it's what they told me. You're going to say I'm a liar. They told me you would, and you did. But nobody's going to pay attention."

"Did you see anybody else go into that house while you were standing across the street watching?"

"Sure. Saw the woman."

My heart beat a little faster at this. "What woman?"

"Woman with the packages. Tall, skinny woman. Put her packages down on the front porch, opened the door, went inside. That was—that was after the young fellow left—long time after."

My heartbeat subsided.

"Saw the men too," Abernathy went on.

"What men?"

"Men with the siren. *Whee-whee-whee!* Big black car, lights flashing on top, then they went running up the steps, and the woman let them in—"

"You saw the police arrive, in other words?"

"Thass it. Then, awhile later, one of them comes up to me, asks me how long I been there, what I saw—"

"Did you know it was the police when they pulled up in their car?"

"Sure I knew. Don't you think I can recognize the cops? I had plenty experience with cops!"

"I don't suppose you like them very much, do you?"

"Hate em! All the time sticking their hands on you—"

"So when you saw the police car pull up in front of the house, how come you didn't get out of there before they could see you?"

"How come? They didn't turn on the lights yet. Didn't turn on the beautiful music. Thought maybe thass why they called the cops—to turn on the lights and the music."

"And who else did you see? Did anyone go into that house or come out of it *before* the police and the woman with the packages?"

"I told you. Kid. Dark hair, wearing glasses."

"Besides the kid?"

He shook his head. "Nobody. Nobody human."

"What do you mean by that? You saw an animal?"

He shook his head, and for some reason he looked frightened again. "The dark betrayer comes to that house."

"Who?"

"The fiend with the flat head. The Triangular Egg. Thass how I know he's cursed, the boy with the glasses."

"I don't get it. Why should the boy be cursed?"

"The fiend with the flat head follows him. He comes, he goes, he makes way for the dark betrayer."

"Do you mean the Devil?"

The old man stuffed the last of his second doughnut into his mouth and gulped it down with a swig of coffee. "Don't speak his name out loud! Ssh!" He jumped to his feet. "Got to go. Got to hurry." With surprising speed he ran to the door of the restaurant.

Instead of using my credit card I tossed some money down on the table—I could put it on my expense account later—and followed him out to the street. He was moving away from the Java Hut as fast as he could, though his legs didn't have much steam left in them.

"Wait a second," I said, catching up to him. "I want to thank you for your help." I pulled a ten-dollar bill out of my wallet and started to press it into his hand.

He pulled his hand away as if the bill were contaminated. I realized that it wasn't surprise or confusion he was showing; it was anger. "Don't need your money. Won't take any money."

His hand shot out suddenly, and his bony grip was on my arm. "Got to do something, got to see somebody. Don't like what I hear, maybe I'll talk to you instead. *Then* maybe I'll take your money."

"Sure, that would be fine."

"Lighting up the tree tonight." He waved in the direction of the giant Christmas tree a block or so away. It surprised me that he'd even noticed it, much less knew what it was all about. "You gonna be here for that?"

"Yes, I will. You too?"

"Lights! Love to see it when the lights go on! Just like it used to be at home—" There was a catch in his throat, I was afraid his tears might start flowing again. But they didn't.

He tightened his grip on my arm, and his voice was suddenly, surprisingly clear, almost commanding. "You be here tonight."

He let go of my arm, and hopped off across the street. Luckily the traffic light was with him. I don't think he even bothered to look.

I DROVE HOME and thought about going back to sleep and returning to the dream I'd been forced to interrupt this morning. In this dream I had reached out in the bed and felt something soft and smooth next to me, and realized it was that wonderful curve where Shirley's neck met her shoulder—

No chance though. The phone rang, and it was Ann.

"Cancel everything for this afternoon," she said. "We've got two appointments—at two o'clock and at four o'clock."

"Who with?"

"The Big Bad Wolves. You didn't know there were two of them, did you? And they both can't wait till they gobble us up. I'll come for you at twenty of."

She wouldn't tell me anything more. The mystery preyed on my mind, and sleep was now impossible. So I turned on the football game and watched it for the rest of the morning. It was a pretty good game, which meant I fixed myself a quick tuna sandwich and ate it on my feet in the doorway between the kitchen and the living room. Exactly the kind of eating that makes Mom shake her head and come out with gloomy predications about my stomach.

Ann pulled up in her car at exactly twenty of. As we drove, she told me we were going out to the Richelieu Hotel, but she still wouldn't tell me why. She wanted the impact to be fresh on me, she said.

We drove into that sweeping driveway, perfectly landscaped, always lined with fresh flowers, even in December. As usual, we had to cruise around for awhile before we could find a parking place. The Richelieu does good business in every season.

Somebody once said that you could settle into the Richelieu for months, in perfect comfort, without ever having to leave the premises. It's got outdoor and indoor swimming pools, tennis courts, an 18-hole golf course, its own movie theatre, stables for horseback riding, an artificial lake stocked with real ducks and swans, four different restaurants featuring four different styles of cuisine, a beauty salon, a day-and-night doctor, and a spectacular view of the mountains. People come to the Richelieu from all over the country, but it's especially popular with big spenders from Texas. On any typical day in the lobby you'll see a dozen ten-gallon hats and diamond rings as big as toadstools.

Ann and I went up the elevator to the second floor and down the corridor to one of the small conference rooms. There was a round oak table in the center, and a huge cut-glass chandelier hanging over it. Three men were sitting around this table, prosperous-looking figures with ties and expensively-cut suits.

Two of them I recognized immediately—the minister of the Episcopal Church, where all the wealthiest families in town worshipped; and Mayor Willard A. Butterfield himself. The third man I didn't recognize. He was small and wiry, in his sixties, with a fringe of gray hair ringing his baldness and a nose as sharp and craggy as an eagle's beak.

He introduced himself to us as Arthur T. Hatfield, owner and publisher of *The Republican-American*. I get around a good deal in Mesa Grande, there aren't too many public figures I haven't had contact with, but I had never seen the great Hatfield before; he kept his picture out of the papers, and hardly ever attended public functions. Some people said he was shy, and some people said he was such an arrogant bastard that he hated to put himself within smelling distance of ordinary human beings.

He turned out to be in charge of this meeting. He invited us to take a seat, in a voice that was soft and polite enough, but had a definitely dangerous rasp to it. "Glad you could make it," he said, with a nod at me. "Mrs. Swenson said she wouldn't talk business with us unless you were here too. Guess she was afraid of what we might put over on an unprotected lady."

Hatfield's thin mouth gave a small twist which was apparently meant to be a grin. Mayor Butterfield took this as a signal that a joke had been made and it was all right for him to enjoy it. He gave out his gravelly laugh, familiar to every citizen of Mesa Grande who had ever attended a Chamber of Commerce breakfast or the annual Fourth of July concert in the park.

Hatfield turned his eyes quickly and fixed them on the Mayor. The laugh choked off instantly.

Hatfield turned back to Ann. "I know you're a busy woman, Mrs. Swenson. We're all busy too. So I'll come straight to the point. We're concerned about this client of yours, this young fellow who killed the minister."

"Who *didn't* kill the minister," Ann said.

Hatfield gave a brisk nod. "I take your meaning. That's what an attorney's supposed to say about his client. Shows your professional integrity, and I commend you for it."

"Thank you," Ann said. You could search for irony in her face all day and you'd never find it.

"This is an informal occasion, though," Hatfield went on. "Everything we say here is off the record. Now just between us, Mrs. Swenson, there's not much chance the boy *didn't* do it, is there?"

"It's hard to give an intelligent answer to that question," Ann said, "since I haven't been able to consult with my client yet and hear his side of the story. I always think it's important to hear both sides of a story—don't you?"

Hatfield produced again that slight twist of the lips which seemed to be the closest he ever came to a smile. "There now," he said, "you've put your finger on one big part of your problem. The boy's not around to *tell* his side of the story. He's a fugitive. Makes it difficult to believe in his innocence. Leastways that's how it strikes *me*."

"That's how the law looks at it too," said the mayor. "I talked to the city attorney about it last night. Fleeing the scene of a crime, he says, is taken as presumptive evidence of guilt. The district attorney's within his rights to bring it up in court."

"If it *is* fleeing from the scene of a crime," Ann said. "There may be a perfectly innocent explanation why Roger Meyer hasn't come forward. He may not even know a crime's been committed."

"Assuming he doesn't read the papers," Hatfield said.

"There *are* people who don't read *The Republican-American,* Mr. Hatfield," Ann said. "Not many, I admit, since you have a monopoly in town—"

"Now, now, now, we're straying from the point, aren't we?" This from the Reverend Matthew T. Madison, our Episcopal minister. He was a short, round, reddish man who looked like a beardless Santa Claus and knew it; the perpetual twinkle in his eyes must have been the result of long practice in front of his bathroom mirror. "Mrs. Swenson, we've asked you and your associate to talk to us this afternoon because there's a serious situation afoot. It threatens the stability, the serenity, I might even go so far as to say the spiritual health of our community. We know you care for the welfare of Mesa Grande just as much as we do, and that's why we're asking you to help us."

"I'm not sure I know what situation you're referring to, Dr. Madison."

Hatfield took over again. "A prominent clergyman's been murdered, a man who in the eyes of many citizens represented the God-fearing Christian element in our town. His killer—all right, his accused killer—is a young man who, in the eyes of those same good citizens, might very well be seen to represent the element that stands against religion, the anti-Christian atheistic troublemaking element that's trying to bring in foreign influences and undermine—"

"Wait a second, wait a second," Ann said. "There's nothing foreign about Roger Meyer. He was born in the United States, he's as much of a citizen as any of you."

"Foreign to us," Hatfield said. "Foreign by Mesa Grande standards."

"I'm not sure I've ever seen those standards written down," Ann said. "When was the last time this town took a vote on them? And I don't understand your reference to atheism either. What do you know about Roger Meyer's religious beliefs?"

Hatfield gave a gentle snort. "We know where he goes to school, and what the prevalent attitudes towards religion are at that institution. We know about his hostility towards his neighbors, simply because they were engaged in the celebration of the most sacred Christian holiday. We know that the religious background of his family is far out of the mainstream—"

"I must be misunderstanding you, Mr. Hatfield. You can't be saying that Roger Meyer must be a murderer because he's Jewish."

"Mrs. Swenson, please, please," the Reverend Madison poured his benevolence over the flames again. "Nobody's saying anything of the sort. I assure you, I wouldn't be here this morning if I thought for one moment that even the slightest suspicion of anti-Semitism was animating anybody in this room. Indeed, the whole point of this meeting is that we're trying to head off any such feeling. We're trying to prevent the specter of anti-Semitism from rising up in our town."

"Just why should it do that?"

"When your client gets arrested," Hatfield said, "and I assume it's only a matter of time, a lot of people in this town are going to be violently antagonistic towards him. The way a lot of simple people are going to see it, he's a Jew who killed a saintly Christian minister because that minister was defending the celebration of Christmas."

"That's about the most absurd—"

"It may be absurd, but a lot of people are going to believe it. To them it won't be any different from the Jews killing Christ two thousand years ago."

"Such people are ignorant and narrow-minded, that goes without saying," said Madison. "Nobody deplores their prejudices more than I do, believe me. But Mr. Hatfield, I'm afraid, is being realistic. Terrible emotions will be unleashed by this case. And when the Meyer boy goes to trial, with all the incumbent publicity, stretching on for days and days, possibly weeks—"

"All right, so these emotions will be unleashed. So what? Accused murderers are never popular with the general public. Maybe I'll ask the judge for a change of venue. Anyway, the trial will run its course, I'm confident my client will be found not guilty, and sooner or later the whole thing will die down. People will find something else to get excited about."

"All very well for *you* to talk about sooner or later," Mayor Butterfield said. "Your whole income comes from the public payroll. You don't have a business to run."

"I don't see what your business has to do with Roger Meyer's trial."

"I'll tell you what. Sure, the hue and cry will die down eventually. But in the meantime, this is the sort of case that gets picked up by the media, the publicity won't just be limited to Mesa Grande. Newspapers around the state, around the whole region, will pick it up, TV stations— maybe even nationally, if it gets ugly enough—"

"You'd be surprised," Hatfield said, "how ugly the media can get if they smell a sensational story."

Wouldn't surprise *me,* I thought. I've read *The Republican-American.*

"Mesa Grande is growing," the mayor was going on, "this whole area is growing, we've got a good chance of attracting some important business interests—I'm getting feelers all the time—just the other day, for instance, I heard from one of the biggest computer companies in the country, they're looking to open up an office that'll cover the whole West and Southwest."

"And you think if there's an outburst of anti-Semitism over the next few months, they'll decide to pick some other town?"

"Anti-Semitism is the least of it. How're you going to defend this kid at the trial unless you throw mud at the deceased? Dig up a lot of rotten so-called scandals about him—I wouldn't blame you, I'd do it myself if I were you. Any of that mud sticks, what effect is that going to have on individuals and organizations that are looking for a decent, law-abiding religious community to settle in?''

"In other words," Ann said, "these business interests won't care if the town is anti-Semitic. They just want to be sure the Christians in it look good."

"You keep distorting things, Mrs. Swenson," said the Reverend Madison. "The business aspects of the matter mean very little to me. They're far less important than the question of Mesa Grande's spiritual health. You know the kind of world we're living in now. Faith is being weakened and undermined all around us—church attendance, the respect accorded to representatives of the ministry— I'm not in sympathy with the late Reverend Candy's religious views any more than you are. He stood for a brand of Christianity which, frankly, I've always found to be quite distasteful. But if there should be a public scandal involving a local minister, regardless of his sect or complexion, I shudder to think what the impact might be on religious faith in this community."

"All right, I get the idea." Ann looked around at them. "What I don't get is, what do you expect *me* to do about all this?"

"Get your client to plead guilty," Hatfield said. "Soon as he's caught, that same day or the next morning, he'll be brought up in front of a judge. He pleads guilty to second-degree murder, the judge gives him a reduced sentence—on account of mitigating circumstances, he was under unusual emotion pressure, he wasn't fully responsible, whatever. Your client gets fifteen years. With good behavior he's out in five years, maximum."

"And Mesa Grande doesn't get a black eye in full view of the rest of the nation," said the mayor.

"It's nice of you gentlemen to make this generous offer," Ann said. "But I'm not aware that any of you are moonlighting as judges or district attorneys."

"If that's what's worrying you." Hatfield leaned forward, his big beak quivering. "The district attorney will cooperate. So will the judge. You can take my word for it."

"You tell the district attorney and the judges what to do, Mr. Hatfield?"

"Certainly not. They're elected officials. Only the voters can tell them what to do. But I do happen to own a newspaper, and we do support and oppose candidates in elections, and the district attorney and those other fellows happen to be coming up for election next year."

There was a long silence. At last Ann spoke, very calmly and amiably. "Gentlemen, I appreciate what you're trying to do. And I agree that a full scale trial could be a terrible blot on the image of Mesa Grande. So let me make a counter-suggestion—an even better way to keep this scandal from erupting and spoiling everything for our town. When Roger Meyer gives himself up, have the district attorney announce that there's no evidence of his guilt. Drop all the charges against him."

She paused to let this sink in. Then, just as amiably, she went on, "It's the perfect solution, gentlemen. There won't *be* any trial. No outburst of anti-Semitism. No black eyes. No public scandals, real or so-called. Nothing to discourage outside business interests from locating in Mesa Grande. And best of all, Dr. Madison, the spiritual health of our community will be as safe as it's ever been."

Ann beamed around the table. Nobody beamed back at her.

At last Arthur T. Hatfield got to his feet. He wasn't very tall, but somehow he gave the impression of towering over everybody. "All right, Mrs. Swenson," he said, his raspy voice quiet and controlled. "Let me tell you what happens now. When your client goes on trial, the district attorney will demand the full penalty of the law—as you probably know, this state has just reinstated the death penalty—and every responsible person and institution in Mesa Grande will join the district attorney in this demand. Incidentally, you may be sure that will include *The Republican-American.* That's right, the full force and influence of my paper will be devoted to getting this vicious killer convicted and sent to the gas chamber."

Hatfield gave a nod at the rest of them, turned, and marched out of the room without another word.

The other two, though not quite so briskly and positively, got up, mumbled their goodbyes, and straggled after Hatfield.

Ann and I sat there for awhile. The big cut glass chandelier was catching the light and smearing it over the surface of the table. There was nothing for us to say.

IT WAS A LITTLE AFTER THREE, just time for us to grab a cup of coffee before our four o'clock appointment. We went to the Richelieu Coffee Shop, and while I toyed with a Danish, Ann told me about the second Big Bad Wolf.

We were on our way, she explained, to the Unitarian Church. Its pastor, Gene Morgan, had called her a few minutes after Hatfield and asked if she would be willing to meet with him for some further discussion of the matter they had discussed earlier. Ann told him she hadn't changed her mind, she still had no intention of withdrawing from Roger Meyer's defense and turning him over to the ACLU.

"I do understand that," Morgan had said, sounding nervous. "But the fact is, Mr. Kincaid is still in town—Victor Kincaid, the lawyer. Well, he'd very much like to talk to you himself. He thinks he can find an argument that might persuade you to reconsider your position."

"In other words," Ann said to me, "the great man figures he can bully this poor, small-town female shyster into knuckling under to him."

"But why are we meeting them at the church?" I asked. "Wouldn't it be better strategy if you made them come up to the office? To fight them on your home turf?"

"I considered that," Ann said. "But I decided there's one thing I can do on their turf that I couldn't do in my office."

"What's that?"

"I can make an indignant exit."

We finished our coffee and drove downtown again.

The Unitarian Church is an old stone building in a middle-level residential neighborhood, halfway between Mesa Grande College and the downtown shopping center. Its color is a mellow, somewhat mildewed brown, clumps of ivy cling to its walls, and it has a small belltower. In fact, this building has been through a lot of pious hands. A hundred years ago, shortly after Mesa Grande was founded, the Baptists built it; fifty years ago it belonged to the Methodists; a few years before I came to town, the Unitarians took it over.

On the front lawn was a signpost with the usual announcements that churches go in for, in dignified block letters, behind glass:

UNITARIAN CHURCH:
EUGENE GRANT MORGAN, PASTOR
CHRISTMAS MORNING SERVICES
PASTOR MORGAN WILL DISCUSS:
"IS CHRISTMAS OBSOLETE IN A
WORLD OF DIVERSITY?"

We went through the tall oaken doors into a vestibule with a wooden bench against the wall. On the wall were framed photographs. I didn't get a chance to examine them at leisure, but they seemed to show Morgan sitting at various tables gazing earnestly at celebrities; among these I recognized Senator Edward Kennedy, Shirley MacLaine, and Bishop Desmond Tutu.

A door opened from the vestibule, and Francesca Fleming emerged. "Thanks for coming!" she bawled at us. "You'll have to wait a minute or two, I'm afraid. Victor's on the phone, it's long distance to Washington, D.C. Actually I think it's somebody on the Supreme Court. Sit down, make yourselves comfortable."

She motioned at the bench, and Ann and I sat down.

Francesca stayed on her feet and went on talking. "Would you believe it, Christmas is on top of us once again! It seems like only a few days since we got over the last attack of it. You two doing anything special for Christmas Eve?"

"I thought I might take a look at the tree-lighting ceremony," Ann said.

"Really? That sort of thing amuses you, does it? Our beloved mayor spouting platitudes and all the yokels drinking it in and feeling like the Wise Men at the manger!" She laughed, but a little nervously, I thought. "Well, I shouldn't really be so snotty and superior. There are chinks in *my* armor too. I'll be glued to my TV tonight, watching *It's a Wonderful Life*. My yearly indulgence in slobbering sentimentality—"

She couldn't go on because Gene Morgan appeared at the door at that moment.

"Good of you to come," he said to Ann and me. "Mr. Kincaid is off the phone, he'd very much like to meet you."

Morgan ushered us into a small oak-lined room, with four or five armchairs in it. Sitting in one of them was a figure familiar to me from a hundred newspaper pictures and TV talk shows—the flaring nostrils, the deep burning eyes, the shock of thick white hair sweeping back from his forehead and down his neck, like snow on the ski slopes. That hair, I remembered, had been just as white when he was in his thirties as it was now in his fifties.

He jumped to his feet, strode up to us, and shook our hands briskly, applying a lot of pressure. Then he popped back into his chair, gesturing for the rest of us to do the same. Morgan was the last one down; it always took him awhile to fold his long loose body into a chair.

"Okay, let's get down to cases," Kincaid said. "Ms.— Swanson, is it?"

"Swenson. And it's Mrs."

"Mrs. Swenson, fine. I'll remember it from now on. Mrs. Swenson, the minister here and Ms. Fleming tell me a very strange thing. They tell me you turned them down flat when they offered to get me to defend your client on this murder charge. Frankly, I couldn't believe them. I figured there must be some failure in communication. So as long as I have to be here in Mesa Grande today anyway—on an entirely different matter—I figured the thing to do was talk to you face to face. I've got—" He looked at his watch "—half an hour or thereabouts before I have to get back to the hotel and start dressing for dinner. It's a vital meeting with some of the people I came out here to do business with. So that should give us plenty of time to clear up this whole misunderstanding."

He came to a stop, but he kept those intense eyes fixed hard on Ann's face. She managed to look right back at him without a blink. "No failure of communication, Mr. Kincaid. Mr. Morgan and Miss Fleming understood me perfectly."

Kincaid gave a low warm chuckle. "By God, that's what I was afraid of! I did a little research on you, before I came here. Talked to a lot of people who know you, either personally or by reputation. They all told me the same thing. She's a feisty lady, they said. She's got a mind of her own. And a strong will to match. And by God, they turned out to be right, didn't they?"

Ann lowered her eyes, her modest demure act. "It's nice of them to say so."

"Okay, you've proved your point," Kincaid said. "You're not some kind of wilting flower. You're somebody. You have to be reckoned with. Well, I respect that. Believe me I do. I'm going to try and talk you out of your decision—I don't believe in playing games, I'm laying my cards right on the table. I'm going to give you one powerful unanswerable reason why you should change your mind.

"Before I get to that, though, there's one thing we ought to establish from the start. It would be sheer madness if you and I didn't cooperate on this. We're on the same side, aren't we? We've got the same values. We hate the same people. These goddamned religious bigots, all that hellfire and brimstone crap, with people killing calves, and being dead and coming to life again, and feeling guilty because they slept with harlots, and God knows what else—playing on the superstitions of poor ignorant slobs—"

"I'm sorry, Victor, I just can't go along with you there," Morgan broke in. "I feel no impulse whatever to make fun of those people. Their religious orientation may not be mine—Christianity is above all the religion of reason, it's a distortion of the whole idea to reduce it to emotionalism—

but their religious *feelings* are just as genuine in their own way as yours or mine."

Kincaid laughed and lifted his hands. "Peace, Gene, peace. That's a beautiful ideal. Tolerance even for the intolerant. We can all learn from you, can't we?"

"Speak for yourself," said Francesca. "If I thought I had anything in common with those morons, I'd shoot myself. Such beautiful sincere Christian feelings! So they all bow down to a con man, a crook—"

"Be that as it may," Kincaid was turning smoothly back to Ann, "I'm confident you're going to see the validity of my argument, Mrs. Swenson. Since you're obviously a rational person, and a lawyer who puts her client's interests above her own ego—"

"How do you know I'm that?" Ann said, smiling gently. "Come again?"

"You don't know me, you've never set eyes on me before. Who says I put my client's interests above my own ego? Who says I'm a rational person? I might be a monster of egotism and irrationality. The fact is, you said all those things to me because you thought I'd be susceptible to flattery. And you know what, Mr. Kincaid? I'm not."

Ann sat back, her smile as gentle as ever. With her Vassar education and her Harvard law degree, nobody in town could give her lessons on how to be ladylike while kicking her opponent in the balls.

Kincaid, I could see, was still reeling from the shock. He tried his chuckle again, only it didn't come out quite as smoothly as before.

Francesca pushed in, making an effort to turn it all into a hilarious joke. "What did I tell you, Victor? You Easterners always underestimate us out here. You think we're a lot of yokels, with no sophistication, no knowledge of the world. You think everybody west of the Hudson prefers Coca Cola to Chardonnay and dirty pictures to Cézanne—"

She babbled on awhile, but her effort wasn't having much effect. Kincaid wasn't laughing; his face was gray, he looked as if somebody had slapped him.

Finally Francesca ran out of steam, gave a couple of little coughs, and became silent.

Ann spoke up again. "Now why don't we get back to the subject of this meeting, Mr. Kincaid. What's this one unanswerable reason you're going to give me?"

I could see Kincaid pulling himself together, putting on his smooth confident manner again. "First I'll tell you what it *isn't,* Mrs. Swenson. It isn't that I'm a better lawyer than you. I'm sure you could handle this defense just as effectively as I could, and I know you'll make a terrific impression on the jury. The reason also isn't that you haven't got the manpower or the resources to do a good job. From what I hear, your investigative staff is worth ten of the district attorney's." He gave a nod in my direction.

I kept a perfect deadpan. I'm pretty good at that.

He turned back to Ann, his fist pressed into the palm of his other hand. A gesture I was sure he used a lot in court. "The real question is, will that be enough? And the answer is, it won't. The forces of religious bigotry have the upper hand in this town. They're bound and determined to railroad this kid into the gas chamber. You don't stand a chance against them, no matter *how* well you perform in court."

"If that's so," Ann said, "I should think you'd be just as helpless as me to stop them."

"No. For one reason. It isn't anything I have any particular right to be proud of, it's really a kind of historical accident—but it's a fact, and you can't get around it. I'm a public figure. I'm a celebrity. What I do makes news. If I'm handling this kid's case, the establishment in this town won't be able to sweep their dirt under the carpet, to screw him with nobody noticing, with nobody crying out against them. The media will pay attention once I announce I'm defending him. There'll be a huge stink all over the country. Everybody will know what Mesa Grande is up to. Now that's my reason, and I don't think you can find an answer to it."

Ann lowered her head, and shaded her eyes with her hand. I recognized the gesture; she was thinking hard.

Finally she lifted her head and gave a nod. "You're right. Roger *will* have a better chance if there's a lot of publicity. It might even be enough to get him off."

Kincaid grinned broadly and sat back in his chair. "Well, that's it then."

Ann went on, "The only question is, would you want to get him off?"

Kincaid stiffened a little. Then he said slowly, "What the hell does that mean?"

"Why should you want to take over this case, Mr. Kincaid? What do you stand to gain by it? An obscure college kid, accused of killing a tenth-rate evangelist in a town that's in the middle of nowhere. Why should you even bother?"

"Because this isn't just an obscure college kid. He's a symbol. Of everybody who was ever persecuted by religious bigotry."

"Exactly. If you took over this case, you wouldn't be defending a boy. You'd be defending a symbol. And pardon me if I'm mistaken, but I think you wouldn't be shy about making the most out of that symbolism. Plenty of fireworks, angry speeches, interviews to the press, laughing at the judge's threats to hold you for contempt, insults hurled at the jury and the town—the whole three-ring circus that you've staged a hundred times already. And what happens to Roger? In the end he gets convicted, while the world cries out in horror. It's Sacco and Vanzetti all over again."

"Oh come on, Mrs. Swenson," Kincaid said. "You're overlooking some important differences. Among others, Sacco and Vanzetti were innocent."

"And Roger Meyer isn't?"

"Well, now—" Kincaid spread his hands before him "—I haven't had a chance to study the police records yet, but I've read the newspaper reports rather carefully. Once the fingerprint and shoeprint evidence is in, it's going to be an open-and-shut case."

"And you're willing to defend him even though you think he's guilty?"

"Of course I am. Every accused person is entitled to the best possible defense, regardless of guilt or innocence.

That's a fundamental principle. Don't they teach that in the law schools any more? Besides, our defense will be based on the contention that, in a deeper sense, the boy isn't guilty at all. He was provoked by the bigotry of the whole town, the political establishment, the Fascist-controlled newspaper.''

"You expect to get an acquittal with a line like that?''

"An acquittal?'' Kincaid's laugh was hearty. "You're living in a dream world, young woman! There isn't one chance in a million of getting an acquittal in this case. Our strategy has to be to keep making objections, come out with outrageous arguments, get the judge mad enough so he'll say things that'll give us grounds for a mistrial.''

"And what if that doesn't work?''

"First of all, it *will* work. I've always been able to make it work. Second of all, if it doesn't work, so what? The kid's guilty, for God's sake. He killed the guy. The worst that can happen is, one little hotheaded nobody rots in jail for awhile. He's a lot less important than the opportunity to make people aware of what a corrupt system we're living under.''

Ann sat for a moment, then she quietly rose to her feet. I picked up my cue: I rose to my feet too.

"Good afternoon,'' Ann said.

"Hey!'' Kincaid jumped up and started towards her. "You can't walk out on me!''

"I seem to be doing it,'' Ann said, and she kept on walking, without turning around to look at him.

"I'll be flying out of here first thing in the morning!'' Kincaid yelled after her. "But I can be back in a week, I expect you to change your mind by then!''

Ann was out of the room, and I was right behind her.

She was right, I was thinking. The exit couldn't have been improved on. And she never could've managed it if we'd been in her own office.

AT SIX O'CLOCK SHARP, Mom and I met in front of Rashomon's Japanese Steak House. We went inside, and the waiter showed us to a table.

"So what's this?" Mom said. "We're eating in the kitchen?"

I explained to her that that's how it was done in a Japanese steak house; there's a grill right in front of your place, and your waiter is also a chef who prepares your meat and vegetables for you while you watch.

"Maybe it's not such a bad idea," Mom said. "At least you can see if his hands are dirty and he sticks them into your food. Most of the restaurants I eat at, I'd rather not know what goes on in the kitchen."

We ordered our dinner from the waiter. The menu, I noticed, was specially decorated for Christmas, with little drawings of Christmas trees and Santa Claus faces. And Christmas music was being piped through the walls, instead of the Oriental music this place usually went in for.

We couldn't settle down to talking about the case until our waiter had performed his act, which he did with great flair and showmanship, flinging pieces of chicken and shrimp high in the air and tossing noddles from fork to fork like a circus juggler. Mom watched with a pleased smile on her face, and when he was finished she applauded.

She tasted what was put before her and gave a nod of approval. "Delicious," she said. "A little more salt, it would be perfect. So tell me everything that you did since yesterday."

I began chronologically, with Roger's call to me last night.

Mom listened carefully, and then she said, "So after he gives himself up to you, what next?"

"We'll have to turn him over to the police."

"But you'll talk to him first, you'll ask him what he knows about the murder?"

"Of course we will."

"So as soon as you're finished, you'll call me up and tell me what he said?"

"If you want me to. It might be pretty late though."

"I don't care how late. It's Christmas Eve, so I won't be getting to bed early."

"Since when do you celebrate Christmas Eve, Mom?"

"They're doing that old movie on television, it begins at nine o'clock. You know the movie I mean? With Jimmy Stewart, and he's thinking of killing himself but this old *meshuggenah* who's an angel talks him out of it. I like to look at that movie whenever I get a chance. It makes me cry like a baby."

"Do you know what else the Meyer kid said to me when he called last night?" I said. "He wants a career in criminology. He's been studying it in college, and when he graduates this year he wants to get a job that'll give him some practical experience at investigation. And he asked me if I'd hire him as my assistant."

Mom positively beamed at this; she doesn't do much beaming, but she's pretty good at it when she does. "That's nice. It shows how highly he thinks of you. An intelligent boy. And he'll make you a good assistant too."

"Mom, it's a hundred-to-one the City Council will never come through with the money to get me an assistant. And even if they do, who says this kid is going to be available? He does have certain problems hanging over him, like a possible conviction for first-degree murder."

Mom pushed that little problem aside with a gesture. "He didn't do any murders, did he? All right, so there won't be any convictions."

"I'm glad you're so sure about that. But even if he does come out of this all right, does that make him qualified for the job? For the same salary, if I did some advertising, I could find somebody with years of experience—"

"What's especially nice," Mom said, "he'll be able to live in the same city with his parents. It's a wonderful thing for old people, to have their children close by in their reclining years. And these days, with everybody moving around so much, it don't happen so often."

I knew there was no point going on with the argument. So I went back to the murder case. I told her in detail about my breakfast conversation with Luke Abernathy.

When I got to the end of it, I saw she was looking troubled. "I don't like it," she said, "when people that don't have any brains think they're smart."

"What do you mean exactly?"

"This crazy old man. God knows what type life he's been leading, but one thing is for sure, after all these years leading it, he's got a mind like chopped liver. To take a simple logical step from A to B is impossible for him by this time. People like this are dangerous."

"You don't think *he's* the killer, do you?"

"When did I say such a thing?"

"But why not, when you come right down to it? He admits himself that he was at Candy's house at the time of the murder. He said he was watching from across the street, but we've only got his word for that."

"And what was his motive already?"

"He's a religious nut. Maybe he's decided to eliminate all the false preachers in town who are leading people astray by giving them eggs to eat."

"And how did he get into this Candy's house, into his living room, so he could grab hold of his gun and kill him?"

"He rang the doorbell and Candy let him in, I suppose."

"Did you get a good look at him this morning? You told me they didn't want to let him into the coffee shop where you took him for breakfast. Even though you were with him. So Candy was alone in the house, he must've answered the doorbell himself, and what does he see on his front porch? A drunken old bum with his hair looking like an earthquake hit it! And Candy says, 'Come in, come in, I'm glad to see you!' and invites him politely into his living room?

"Also, after the old man commits the murder, how come he waits around in front of the house till the police get there, so they can see him at the scene of the crime?"

"All right, I admit it doesn't seem likely. But what did you mean then, when you said he's dangerous?"

"To himself I meant. There's a cloud inside his head, a big black cloud, and it keeps him from seeing things like they really are. You said it yourself, he crossed the street without bothering to look if the light was green or red. There's another street he's crossing now, and I'd be surprised if he's looking at the light."

"What street, Mom?"

"Who knows? If I could tell you the answer, it wouldn't be so dangerous anymore. The big thing that's worrying me, where is he getting money?"

"He *hasn't* got any money. Except for what you found out, that his daughter pays his rent. But she sends her check directly to his hotel, everything else he gets from begging."

"The begging business must be doing pretty good lately. You made him an offer of a ten-dollar bill. You had it in your hand and held it out to him. And he wouldn't take it. Why not?"

"Some kind of misplaced pride?"

"He takes his rent from his daughter, he gets his food from the Salvation Army, he picks up newspapers from the trashcans, he begs on the street for money to buy his liquor. Some pride!"

"I give up then. Why did he refuse the money?"

"Because today is no ordinary day for him. Because he can *afford* to be proud today. If he could refuse your ten dollars, it has to be because he's getting money from somebody else. And what I'm asking is, who?"

"Have you got any answers?"

"Not yet. I'll think it over for awhile."

Mom had a forkful of shrimp on the way to her mouth, when suddenly she did something I couldn't remember ever seeing her do before. She stopped the fork in mid-air, her hand shaking.

"Are you okay?" I said.

"I'm fine." The shaking stopped, and her fork finished its trip to her mouth. After chewing the shrimp for a few seconds, she looked up at me. "Excuse me. This feeling came over me that he was close to me."

"Who was close to you?"

"The fanatic. The one I can smell in this murder. Somewhere he's hiding, any minute he could come jumping out."

"But you still don't know who it is?"

"All I know is, he's getting closer. If I shut my eyes, I can almost see his face." She shut her eyes, and I held my breath. But then she opened her eyes again and sighed. "It's gone." She gave a shake of her head, and then smiled. "So has anything else come up about this case?"

I told her about our two meetings this afternoon—with Hatfield and later with Kincaid. Mom laughed when she heard what Ann had said to them.

"A lovely person, your boss. When are you going to invite her over for dinner?"

"You know she's got a perfectly good husband. He's an ear-nose-and-throat specialist so he makes a good living—"

"Naturally I know it. What do you think I am, the type that's always trying to fix people up with people? You'll invite the husband too, and also some nice unattached woman of your acquaintance. And maybe I'll invite a man for me."

The prospect of this delightful social occasion didn't do my stomach any good. I hurried to change the subject. I asked her if she'd like to come to the Christmas tree-lighting ceremony tonight and be present when Roger gave himself up.

"It's nice you should ask me," she said, "but I don't think so, I'll enjoy it more on the television news."

Ten minutes later we left the restaurant. It was almost eight o'clock, dark already, with a chill in the air. There were more people on the streets than usual at this time of night.

A Santa Claus came up to us, holding out a box and asking for money for "the poor children's fund."

"What poor children?" Mom said. "You ask my opinion, it's your own children we're talking about. And since you've been on this corner for the last three weeks, by this time you can afford to send them for the holidays to Miami Beach, Florida. All right, here's a five-dollar bill for you. But you should get it in your head, you're not fooling me for a minute."

She turned her back on Santa Claus and strode over to her little red car. "No matter how late!" she snapped at me over her shoulder, and then she went driving off.

FIVE

Christmas Eve

ANN AND I HAD ARRANGED to meet at the giant Christmas tree at a quarter to nine. Our plan was to stand together at the fringes of the crowd, on the corner of San Luis and Kit Carson, and presumably, while the ceremony was in progress, Roger Meyer would appear and put himself in our custody.

I still had forty-five minutes, so I killed it by strolling around in the downtown area. The shop windows were all lighted up, and some of the stores were still open. It's not the usual practice in Mesa Grande for stores to stay open at night, but the promise of last-minute Christmas business was evidently too much to resist.

As I moved from window to window, a heavy depressed feeling began to settle over me. It didn't matter what each store was selling—clothes or hardware, hunting rifles or liquor—the same message was being blared out. *Our merchandise is better than anybody else's.* 'Tis the season to be cutthroat.

At a quarter to nine I drifted to the block where the ceremony was going to take place. It had been closed off to traffic, and a fairly large crowd was already gathered in front of the giant Christmas tree. There was a raised platform with a standing microphone; the mayor would be making a speech before he pressed the button.

The crowd was growing, and I let the newcomers slip in front of me. Then I felt a hand on my arm, and there was Ann, wearing a red coat and a fur hat, and looking pale and anxious. "If he doesn't show—" she said.

"He'll show, he'll show," I said, realizing how much I was sounding like Mom. As a little kid, whenever I needed

reassuring, Mom's standard technique was to say everything twice. ("They'll like you, they'll like you!"—"You'll
get there on time, you'll get there on time!")

I wished my feelings were as optimistic as my words. It
had been in my mind off and on all day that Roger would
get cold feet. What would I do in his position? Reading the
newspaper, seeing how the mob was being whipped up to
pounce on the mad Christ-killer and tear him to pieces?
Even if I was innocent—

Squawking noises were coming from the public address
system, breaking in on the noise of the crowd. "Ladies and
gentlemen! Ladies and gentlemen!"

A little man in a huge overcoat was standing on the dais,
shouting into the microphone. The crowd quieted somewhat, and the little man said, "It gives me great pleasure,
ladies and gentlemen, to introduce our mayor, the Honorable Willard A. Butterfield, who has a few words for you
before this year's municipal Christmas tree is officially il-
luminated!"

I was sure the crowd had no idea who the little man was,
but they applauded him anyway, as he blushed and stumbled off the platform. He was replaced by the mayor, towards whom the crowd was much less enthusiastic.
Somebody even yelled out, "Sit down, Butterball!" Nevertheless, the mayor lifted his arms in the air and said,
"Thank you, thank you," and took a long time to get
started, as if he was being drowned out by the applause.

"Ladies and gentlemen," he finally said, "Christmas
comes but once a year—"

I won't repeat the full text of the mayor's speech. To tell
the truth, I didn't pay much attention. I was looking around
at the crowd, and over my shoulders at the shop windows
and the dark alleys, wondering where and how and when
Roger Meyer would materialize. I glimpsed a lot of familiar faces in that crowd. Near the front was the Reverend
Eugene Grant Morgan. At the other side, also near the
front, was Dwayne McKee, the real estate man. A little bit
behind him, surrounded by thick earlaps and a heavy scarf,
was the pudgy, anxious face of Gabriel Candy.

"And so, as I light this splendid Christmas tree," the mayor was saying, "with the hope and belief that the lights of peace and prosperity will be lighted up all over the world and bring light to all its peoples, let me add just one brief prayer of my own—in the immortal words of the Bard, 'God bless us, every one!'"

He had a switch in his hands, and he pushed the button on it. Then there was a moment when every eye was on that Christmas tree and every heart, I suspect, was yearning that the damn lights wouldn't work.

But the moment passed, everything worked fine, the sky was a blaze of red and green and yellow, and a tremendous roar went up from the crowd.

That was the moment when Ann tugged at my sleeve and pointed behind her. In a doorway a few feet away from us, with his collar pulled up to cover his chin and his hands shoved deep into his coat pockets, was Roger Meyer.

We went up to him, trying to hurry but at the same time not be conspicuous.

"I'm sorry," he said, sounding out of breath. "I was here at nine, I tried to attract your attention. But I didn't want anybody to see me."

"Never mind that," Ann said. "My car's parked a block away, we'll get you to police headquarters."

She took him by one arm, and I took him by the other. Flanking him in this way, trying to block him from view, we started down the street. The crowd had its back to us, most people were still oohing and aahing at the lights of the tree. In a couple of minutes we'd be safe in Ann's car, and on the way to headquarters we could hear the kid's story, and maybe something encouraging would come out of that—

"Hey! Where the hell are you going?"

It was a cop, a beefy young guy in uniform, and he was standing on the corner, five or six feet away from us, looking right at us.

"That's the Meyer kid!" he was shouting. "I *thought* I recognized— Hey, that's the kid that killed—"

Ann stepped forward quickly, her hand still locked on Roger's arm, and spoke up loud and firm, "Officer, I'm the public defender, and this is Roger Meyer. He just learned that a warrant is out for his arrest, and he's voluntarily given himself up to me, so that I can turn him over to the proper authorities."

"I'm Mrs. Swenson's investigative assistant," I said, stepping forward too, "and I want to confirm what she just told you. Roger Meyer voluntarily gave himself up to Mrs. Swenson's custody, and we are now officially turning him over—"

But by this time the cop was blowing his whistle and yelling, "It's the Meyer kid! I've caught the Meyer kid!"

The disturbance was attracting attention. More and more people in the crowd were turning to see what was up. Then they started moving towards us. Then a few more cops appeared, and they were yelling at Roger too. "Okay, don't make a move, put your hands up behind your head—"

"This defendant is in my custody," Ann was saying, but the noise around her was drowning her out.

And then who should pop into the picture but assistant district attorney George Wolkowicz, with a big grin on his ugly face. "Good work, officer," he was saying, "looks like you've got the man we've been looking for!"

"This defendant surrendered himself voluntarily," Ann said, pushing Roger and herself towards Wolkowicz. "I am now turning him over to you—"

"Wait a second, wait a second," Wolkowicz said. "This officer here has arrested this man. He's a fugitive, you can't come along and pretend—"

"He was going voluntarily to headquarters," Ann said, "but since you happen to be here, he can save himself the trip."

The crowd was pressing in, getting more interested. I could hear people murmuring behind me: "Is that the kid who killed that minister?" "Why don't they put handcuffs on the son of a bitch?"

"Goddamn it, George," Ann raised her voice, "you know damn well we wouldn't be out here with this boy, in the middle of the street, if he wasn't giving himself up!" She turned to the crowd and raised her voice even more. "You can see this boy isn't resisting arrest! You can see we were bringing him in peacefully, only these policemen are trying to grandstand—"

"You better let that officer put the cuffs on him, Ann," Wolkowicz said, trying to equal her loudness, "or you'll be guilty of obstruction of justice! I'd hate to have to run you in too!"

"I'm not obstructing anything! I'm trying to see that justice is done! Do you know what the word means, justice? Ever heard of it before?"

Their voices were mingling in anger, and the crowd was joining in now, cheering on one side or the other, like spectators at a football game.

And then, suddenly, a small figure in a tight-fitting gray overcoat, with the usual strip of black cloth on the top of his head, came pushing out of the crowd and bustled right up to Wolkowicz.

"Excuse me," Rabbi Loewenstein said, "but I saw the whole thing. I saw this young man walk up to these two people. I heard him say, 'I want to give myself up.' I heard them say, 'We'll take you to the nearest policeman.' And as soon as they saw this officer here, this young woman said, 'This is Roger Meyer, officer, and he's giving himself up.' There's no doubt about it, and if necessary I'll be glad to testify under oath."

He was the shortest adult in the whole crowd, yet the way he faced up to Wolkowicz and the police officers he might have been taller than any of them. And his voice carried over everybody else's too—on my rare appearances at synagogue I had never thought he was much of a speaker, but obviously that pulpit training was good for something.

Wolkowicz had been staring at the rabbi in astonishment, now he finally found his voice. "Who the hell are you?"

"I'm Eli Loewenstein. I happen to be the rabbi at Temple Beth-el here in this city. You're assistant district attorney Wolkowicz, aren't you? We were introduced a year ago, at a Chamber of Commerce breakfast. I believe I was the guest speaker."

Wolkowicz opened his mouth, but for a few moments no words came out. It wasn't hard to imagine his thoughts. Who was a jury going to believe, this beefy cop who looked as if he had the IQ of a ten-year old, or this quiet confident little man of the cloth who spoke at Chamber of Commerce breakfasts?

The rabbi just stood there, smiling brightly, waiting for the inevitable.

"All right, all right," Wolkowicz said, "let the record show that the suspect surrendered voluntarily to the authorities." He turned to the cops next to him. "Put the cuffs on him. Read him his rights. Take him to headquarters."

"And we'll go with him," Ann said.

"The hell you will," Wolkowicz said. "Nobody travels in an official car when an arrest's been made, except the prisoner and the arresting officers."

"We'll be right behind you then," Ann said. "So we can talk to the prisoner just as soon as you've booked him."

Roger was handcuffed now. I caught a glimpse of his white scared face as the cops hustled him off, away from the crowd. Wolkowicz hung back just a second, and spoke straight into Ann's face. "This won't do you any good in court," he said. "Fugitive or no fugitive, we've got this bastard dead to rights."

Then Wolkowicz went after the cops, and Ann turned to Rabbi Loewenstein. "We appreciate it, rabbi," she said.

He gave a little shrug. "Seemed like the thing to do," he said. "Well, I must be off now. Somebody has to get to that poor boy's parents. I wouldn't want them to hear about this on the television." He sighed. "And maybe, with luck, I'll be home tonight in time to see the last part of *It's a Wonderful Life*. My family and I always watch it on Christmas Eve."

WHEN THE NEW courthouse and jail were built a few years back—two handsome brownish-red buildings, attached by an underground passage, and looking so much alike from the outside that you couldn't tell which one was for the lawyers and which one was for the crooks—a new police headquarters was supposed to be part of the package. But the city ran out of money, and so the police department had to make do with its old building across the street. It was squat, gray, and ugly, the plumbing constantly breaking down, and there was no air conditioning. The chief of police never tired of expressing his annoyance about this, in newspaper interviews and on TV: "It's undignified. The jailbirds have better living conditions than we do."

It was nearly ten when Ann and I got to police headquarters. We had to cool our heels in the waiting room for half an hour, and then one of the uniformed flunkies told us that Roger wasn't there. He had already been booked and sent across the street to occupy a cell. If we wanted more information, we had to get in touch with assistant district attorney Wolkowicz.

Ann called his office from police headquarters, and the night switchboard operator told her he had gone home. Swearing softly under her breath, Ann called Wolkowicz's home. With some irritation, he told her he was trying to settle down with his family to look at *It's a Wonderful Life* on TV. It had begun at nine, so he'd already missed half of it.

"And I wouldn't want you to miss another heartwarming moment," Ann said. "Just call the jail and tell them I'll be there in two minutes and they should let me talk to my client."

"Sure, why not?" I could hear Wolkowicz saying.

"And while I've got you," Ann said, "we might discuss the question of bail."

"The DA's office is totally opposed to bail," Wolkowicz said. "It's a capital crime, and your client has already been a fugitive."

"He gave himself up voluntarily, remember? So I hope you're not going to try that fugitive line in front of a judge."

"Nobody'll be trying anything in front of a judge for a few days. Tomorrow's Christmas, and Monday's an official non-working day too. Most of the judges in town will be holed up in their homes or their mountain cabins, not answering their phones."

"I can ring a phone pretty loud," Ann said. "Meanwhile, you'll call the jail, won't you? Two minutes."

In the jail building there's a small, soundproof room where attorneys can talk to their incarcerated clients. It has a table, a few chairs, and an iron door with a barred window, outside of which sits a uniformed guard wearing a conspicuous gun. In another half-hour, Ann and I were sitting in this room with Roger Meyer.

His face was very white except for the dark blotches around his eyes. He looked as if he hadn't slept for days. He was wearing the same jeans he had been wearing when he gave himself up—in fact, he had been wearing them on Thursday, when he disappeared—and he was in his stockinged feet. "They took away my shoes," he said. "They said they were evidence."

On account of the bloody shoeprints on the floor of Candy's hallway, I thought. But naturally nobody had explained it to Roger. Once you cross to the wrong side of the bars, you discover you're in a world that sees you as a lower species of animal life; your peace of mind no longer has to to be considered. I had noticed this plenty of times when I was on the police force back in New York. It had never much bothered me then.

"How are my folks?" Roger asked. "Will they get to visit me here?"

"They're doing as well as can be expected," Ann said. "You've put them through a terrible two days."

He lowered his head, like a little boy caught doing something naughty. For some reason, haggard and rumpled and sitting in this crummy room, he looked even younger than he had looked a few days ago. "I know that. I'm sorry. But I just couldn't think of anything else to do. *Will* I get to see them?"

"We'll fix it up," Ann said. "Now I know you're not feeling so great, but you have to forget about that, you have to get yourself together and answer my questions. Clear, complete answers—a lot may depend on it. Do you think you can do that?"

He wet his lips. "Okay. I'll do my best. I'll sort of pretend that it's only a movie—I'm this character in a movie who's falsely accused of a crime. And there's really nothing to worry about, because everybody knows he'll be cleared by the end of the picture. Like Paul Muni in *I Am a Fugitive from a Chain Gang*."

I remembered that movie. What I didn't point out to him was that Paul Muni never *does* get cleared.

"*Are* you falsely accused?" Ann said, with no change in her flat matter-of-fact tone of voice. "You didn't kill the Reverend Chuck Candy?"

"No! I swear I didn't!"

"You know what the District Attorney's case is?"

"They told me a little when they arrested me. Somebody saw me go into that house."

"*Did* you go into that house?"

"No, I never—" He lowered his eyes again. "All right, I did. But I didn't kill him! I never even touched him! He was dead when I—"

"Start from the beginning," Ann cut in. "What made you go into his house in the first place?"

"He called me on the phone. He asked me to come over there."

"You're saying Candy himself invited you over?"

"I guess it sounds crazy, but it's true. I was at my parents' house, around four-thirty or so. I got this phone call. Didn't they tell you I got a phone call? It was Mr. Candy. He said he was sorry for everything he'd been doing. For the way he'd been treating my parents, and pulling that gun on me, and lying about it to the police. He asked me could I come over so he could apologize and then he'd call the police and fix things up about the charges against me."

"Did he say *why* he had this sudden change of heart?"

"He said it was Christmas-time, and people are supposed to show kindness and good will at Christmas-time. Oh, and he told me not to tell my parents or anybody where I was going, because he wanted to be sure first that everything was all settled about the trial."

"And that's what you meant by that remark you made to your parents—'If Christians can do it at this time of year, Jews ought to be able to do it too'?"

"I guess I did say something like that."

"So you left your parents' house and went down the street to Candy's house," Ann said. "Then what?"

"I rang the doorbell a few times. He didn't answer the door. But then I noticed it wasn't shut all the way, it was open a few inches. I figured he'd left the door open for me, so I went in. I stood in the hall for a couple of seconds—the same hall where I had my trouble with him before—and I called out his name. When he didn't answer, I went down the hall to this archway that opened into the living room— anyway, I guess it was the living room. I went through this archway, and I saw the Christmas tree, all decorated with lights and that silver stuff. And there were packages under it, and then I saw—"

He stopped, pressed his lips together, then made himself talk again. "At first I thought it was another package under the Christmas tree. A pretty big package. And then I realized it was him—well, a person, I didn't know who right away—he was lying there, with his legs bunched up and his arms sticking out. I thought maybe there was something I could do for him, so I kneeled down by him, and that's when I knew who it was, and I knew he was dead."

"How did you know?" Ann said. "Did you feel his pulse? Put your ear up against his heart?"

"No, I could never have—I just knew. It's the way his head was sort of twisted and all that blood coming out of him. And the gun was there too—"

"Where? Close to the body?"

"No, it was halfway across the room. On the carpet, I saw it there."

"You didn't go up to it, did you? Pick it up or anything?"

"No. I just saw it, and then I stood up. And then I started thinking. I was supposed to go on trial for trying to shoot him. With that gun. So wouldn't it look as if I busted into his house and tried it again, and this time I succeeded? Then

I saw this picture of Jesus over the fireplace, and it reminded me I'm a Jew—which, to tell you the truth, isn't something I think about very often—so nobody in this town was going to believe my story. So I ran out of the house!''

"Did you shut the front door behind you?"

"I don't know. I don't think so."

"Where did you go after that?"

"Down the street. To my parents' house. I didn't go in. My car was parked in front, so I got in it and took off."

"When Candy called you on the phone, how did you know it was him?"

"He told me who it was."

Ann leaned forward a little. "But how could you be sure it wasn't someone else using his name? How many times have you ever heard his voice?"

"Well, only once actually. When I went to talk to him about what he was doing to my parents—and he pulled that gun on me."

"At which time, you weren't listening carefully because you were excited and he wasn't talking clearly because he was excited too. So how did his voice sound to you over the phone? Did he seem to be talking naturally and easily, the way people talk in ordinary conversation?"

"Now that you mention it, his voice was pretty low, almost a whisper. Like he was under a strain, forcing himself. I thought that was because it wasn't easy for him, apologizing and admitting he was wrong and all."

"Did you see that message he wrote on the carpet before he died, those words in red crayon?"

"I read about that in the paper. But I didn't see anything written on the carpet. I just didn't notice it, I guess. I must've been too scared and in shock and all. I've never actually seen a dead body before. All I could look at was his head, and all that blood."

A look of skepticism appeared on Ann's face. "If he'd scrawled only a word or two, you might have overlooked it. But he wrote four words. 'Gold, frankincense, and myrrh.' They took up a lot of space. Don't you think it's strange you didn't see them there?"

"I don't know why I didn't. I just didn't, that's all I can say. Why would I lie about it?"

Ann made the little clicking noise that she makes with her tongue whenever she's skeptical or suspicious about something. "After you drove away from your parents' house, where did you go? Where have you been these last two days?"

"Nowhere in particular. I've just been wandering around."

"Where did you sleep? What did you do about eating?"

"I—I got a room in a motel. I brought food in from a 7-Eleven."

"What motel? What 7-Eleven? Let's have names and locations."

"I don't see why it matters."

"Because the people there must've seen you. They might've noticed your manner, how you behaved, whether you acted like somebody with a murder on his conscience."

"I just don't remember where those places were. I was feeling so scared and mixed up—"

His voice trailed off. Don't you ever play poker, kid, I was thinking. Somebody could get rich off you.

"I'm your attorney," Ann said. "Everything you say to me is strictly confidential. It would be illegal for me to tell the police about it even if I wanted to. You won't get anybody into trouble, believe me."

"There *is* nobody for me to get into trouble," Roger said, but his eyes were all over the place.

I decided it was time for me to put my oar in. "What's the point of beating around the bush?" I said. "We know where you went. You've been hiding out for the last two days with Rabbi Loewenstein."

Roger's eyes widened. Ann flashed me an astonished look. It isn't every day I can produce such a spectacular reaction, and I admit it gave me a certain pleasure. I could understand what Mom feels.

"It's pretty obvious actually," I said. "What was the rabbi doing downtown tonight? He said he always stays home with his family on Christmas Eve and looks at *It's a*

Wonderful Life. Which began at nine o'clock on TV. He wasn't going to deprive himself of that treat just to watch the mayor switch on some lights and say that Christmas comes but once a year. So he was downtown because he expected something special to happen, something he had a personal interest in, and he wanted to be sure it turned out all right."

Roger was on the point of tears. "He's not going to get in any trouble for this, is he? Can you guarantee—"

"Not from us he won't," Ann said. "That much I can guarantee. If the DA finds out from somebody else, though—"

"You went straight to the rabbi," I said, "after you found Candy's body?"

"Yes, I did. He was the only person I could think of. He'd been so nice to my parents and me while I was waiting for the trial." He reddened suddenly. "I mean, you two were nice to us too—but I didn't think—I mean, you being representatives of the law and all—"

"Did you go to the rabbi's house?" Ann said.

"No, I didn't want to drag his family into it. I went to the synagogue. I didn't know if he'd be there or not, but I thought I could wait for him if he wasn't, and if anybody saw me there, they'd think I was praying. But the rabbi was in his study, and luckily there was nobody else around."

"And where did he hide you out?" I asked.

"There's a little room in the basement. They use it as a storeroom, mostly for stuff they only need on special occasions—the *shofar* for the High Holidays, and the fancy Torah, stuff like that. He told me I could sleep in there, and he'd keep the door locked so the janitor wouldn't barge in on me. And he brought me my meals himself. Mostly sandwiches and cookies. It was like Sir Cedric Hardwicke and Frederick March—that old movie, where Hardwicke is the bishop and March is this escaped convict—"

A look of alarm came into Roger's eyes. "I don't want you to get the wrong idea! The first thing he said to me, after I told him what had happened, he said I should give myself up to the police. He said the same thing every time he saw me in the last couple of days. That's why I finally called you, because the rabbi talked me into it, he made me see that the longer I hid out, the worse it would be for me. You're *sure* he won't get into any—''

Ann gave him her promise all over again, and we couldn't think of any other questions for him, so the interview came to an end. The uniformed guard led Roger out, and from the look on the kid's face he thought he was going straight from that room to the gas chamber.

Ann and I went up to the main reception room of the jail, and found Roger's parents sitting there. Rabbi Loewenstein was with them.

The Meyers rushed up to us, throwing questions at us, asking if Roger was all right, and could they see him, and was there any chance of his being released on bail? Ann answered all their questions as clearly and patiently as she could, then she went to the desk and asked the officer on duty there to arrange for Roger's parents to see him right away. Before the officer could say no—it's the nature of bureaucrats to say no, even when they have no idea what you want—Ann said, "assistant district attorney George Wolkowicz says it's all right. So let these people see the boy, or do you want me to call Wolkowicz right now and tell him you're responsible for disturbing him on Christmas Eve?''

The officer agreed to let the Meyers talk to Roger.

All through this fuss, the rabbi had been standing at the side with a polite look on his face. As soon as I could, I edged up to him and spoke in a low voice. "I'm afraid you're going to miss *It's a Wonderful Life,* rabbi.''

He shrugged. "I know how it comes out.''

"That's the movie about the young fellow who's in trouble, isn't it?" I said. "But luckily he's got a guardian angel who looks after him and keeps him out of trouble?''

"That's the story.''

"Strictly a fairy tale, wouldn't you agree? In the real world, what can a guardian angel do for somebody? Except maybe give him sandwiches and cookies and a little bit of moral support?''

The rabbi didn't say a word. He went on smiling softly.

IT WAS AFTER ELEVEN-THIRTY when I got out of the jail building. Ann was exhausted and headed straight home. I had a strong inclination to do likewise, but something was nagging at me; it had been kicking around in the back of my mind for hours. Something that had happened tonight.

No, that wasn't accurate. What worried me was something that *hadn't* happened tonight. Old Abernathy, that crazy prophet on the street corner, didn't he tell me, when I gave him breakfast this morning, that he'd be in touch with me tonight? Didn't he say he'd find me in the crowd, while the Christmas tree was being lit up, and talk to me some more about what he knew?

So where was he? Why *didn't* he talk to me tonight? Why didn't I even catch a glimpse of him in the crowd, during the tree-lighting ceremony?

I could think of a lot of perfectly plausible answers. He could've been blind drunk in his hotel room. He could've forgot about me completely. He was such a nut, how could you expect him to follow through on *anything* he said he'd do? Even so, I knew I couldn't go home yet, not until I'd been to see that crazy old man.

I went faster than the speed limit, which was very odd since I kept telling myself there was nothing to be anxious about. Three blocks from the hotel, I found myself behind a big moving van that was inching along but was so wide you couldn't get around it.

On its bumper was a familiar sticker: "Honk Twice if You Love Jesus."

I honked four or five times, and as angrily as I could.

A large hand appeared from the driver's window of the van. Its middle finger was raised in a classic gesture which has pretty much the same meaning all over the Western world. That meaning is *not* "Merry Christmas."

Finally I got to the Hotel Cochran, a five-story building across the street from the seedy little downtown park, Manitou Park, which is built around the statue of General William Henry Harrison Wagner on horseback; the general was the founder of Mesa Grande, near the end of the nineteenth century. It's hard to imagine what the General would have thought if he'd known about the drug-dealing and other nefarious activities that went on at his horse's feet a hundred years later.

I parked in front of the hotel, with its neon sign letting the world know that this was "HO EL COC RA." It's been a fleabag for as long as I've lived in Mesa Grande, though I've heard that it once saw better days. The stone steps leading up to the front door were chipped in many places, a definite safety hazard in the dark. The light bulb over the front doorway didn't help much; it was so low in wattage that it hardly managed to illuminate more than itself.

Inside was what the management hopefully called the "lobby," a dark, musty-smelling little room with a couple of chairs at one end and a dingy desk at the other end. The old clerk behind the desk looked like one of the victims in a Dracula movie. Having sucked all the blood they could out of him, the vampires had apparently, in a paroxysm of desperate hunger, started in on the lobby chairs; there were deep rips in the arms of both of them, and the stuffing was coming out.

I went up to the desk and asked the clerk if Mr. Abernathy was in.

"Old Man Jesus?" said the clerk, his voice so hoarse and depleted that it might have been coming from the next room. "Ain't seen him tonight."

"He hasn't come in yet?"

"Never went out. Went up to his room around four in the afternoon, been there ever since."

"He didn't go out for dinner?"

"Nothing peculiar about that. Lots of nights he don't have dinner. Drinks his dinner up there, if you know what I mean. Room is a damn pigsty too!"

"Call up and tell him I want to see him," I said.

"You think we got phones in the rooms? You think this is the Richelieu?" A dry grating chuckle came out of him. "I'll go up and knock on his door."

"I can do that myself. What's his room number?"

For a second the clerk looked as if he wasn't going to tell me. Vague thoughts about the dignity of the establishment and the privacy of its clientele might have been chasing through his head. Before he could commit himself to such delusions of grandeur, I flashed my badge at him. Yes, I have a badge, and it gives me the right to go anywhere that the regular police can go. That was part of the arrangement when the City Council established a public defender's office.

So the clerk took a quick look at it now and muttered, "Room twenty-three, second floor at the head of the stairs."

I climbed the stairs, the elevator in the Hotel Cochran having been out of order since the end of World War II. I found myself in a hallway that was even dimmer than the lobby. It had a sweet pungent smell to it, like the stuff you kill mosquitoes with. They sprayed these halls with it every few weeks, I supposed, on the theory that it was cheaper than actually vacuuming the carpets, giving the walls a new paint job, and evicting all guests who refused to get deloused.

I knocked on the door of room twenty-three. I got no answer. Somewhere halfway between my conscious and subconscious mind, I think I didn't expect to.

I tried the door. It wasn't locked, which didn't surprise me either. I pushed the door, and it creaked open slowly. I took a couple of steps into the room. The ceiling light was on—the bulb shone palely through a fly-specked glass globe—and some streaks of moonlight filtered through the only window. It was enough to show me three or four piles of newspapers on the floor and a bundle of rags on the bed.

Then I moved closer and saw that the bundle of rags was Luke Abernathy, and the chances were he wouldn't be getting up again.

I heard the faintest rustling sound behind me, and before I could turn around the entire weight of the world's woes and mankind's suffering crashed down on top of my head.

I wasn't knocked unconscious. In spite of what you see on television and read in private-eye books, it's not so easy to get knocked unconscious. I fell down, I was on my knees, but I wasn't out like a light, as the saying goes. In fact, what I was mainly aware of was too damn much light, flickering at me from all directions, especially from inside my head. And also dizziness, everything spinning around, giving me a powerful urge to throw up. It took me awhile to get that urge under control. When I did, the lights stopped bombarding me, the spinning in my head slowed up, and finally I recognized the ceiling I was staring up at.

The crack on my head may not have knocked me unconscious, but it served its purpose just as efficiently as if it had. By the time I staggered to my feet and out to the hall, nobody was in sight and no sounds of receding footsteps could be heard. I propped myself up against the railing on the stairs and yelled my lungs out for the clerk.

The first yell or two came out as squeaks, but pretty soon my voice got back its old resonance. The clerk came running up the stairs.

"Who just left?" I cried at him, maybe even grabbing him by the shoulders.

"Nobody! I didn't see nobody!" His face was contorted with fear. Of me, I realized. I must have looked like hell.

"Is there any way out of here except through the lobby?"

"The fire escape. There's a window at the end of every hall, and there's a fire escape out there."

I ran down the hall to the window, knowing perfectly well what I was going to find. The window was open, and big surprise, the fire escape was empty. And nothing in the alley below.

By the time I got back to the clerk, he had seen what was to be seen through the doorway of room twenty-three.

"He's dead, ain't he? He finally did it. They all do it sooner or later. Good riddance is what I say. The world's better off without them. They're better off without themselves."

His gabbling went on, while I stepped back into the room and up to the bed to take a closer look at the body. The bloodshot old eyes were wide open, staring, and the mouth was twisted. The bony wrist felt cold and stiff. On the rickety bed table was a glass with a few mouthfuls of pale yellowish liquid in it. On the floor was a wine bottle.

I told the clerk to go downstairs and call the cops from his switchboard, and then to come right up again. While he was out of the room, I took out my handkerchief and used it to pick up the glass. I sniffed at it. I recognized that smell right away. Then, bending down, I did the same with the bottle. It was still half full of liquid, and that smell was even stronger. The label said "Chablis," from some vineyard in California. Reasonably expensive stuff.

The clerk came back but still didn't walk through the door. I was in no mood to torture people, so I went to him out in the hallway. "Anybody else living on this floor?" I said.

"Three, four other fellows."

"Any of them in their rooms now?"

"They all went out. I seen them all go, earlier tonight. Different times."

"Where'd they go, do you know?"

He shrugged. "Couple of them has families somewheres. Couple of them went out drinking. It's Christmas Eve, Saturday night, lots of places going to be open late."

I jerked my thumb at the bed. "Anybody come to see him tonight?"

"Only you."

"How long you been on duty at the desk?"

"Since three o'clock. I saw him come in, nobody come to see him. You want to call me a liar?"

He didn't say this angrily or even defensively. It was more or less a simple statement of fact, something that happened to him so often he had come to take it for granted.

"When he came in—around four, you said? Did you happen to notice, was he carrying a bottle with him?"

"Mighta been," he said. "He was carrying a white paper bag. Yeah, from the shape of it, a bottle coulda been in it."

"If somebody got out by the fire escape, could somebody get in that way too?"

"There's inside locks on the windows, they're supposed to keep people out. It's a long time since they worked though. Mostly they're rusted and you can't keep them closed."

I returned to the room and looked around more carefully than before. I walked the whole length and width of the floor, peered under the bed, poked at the piles of old newspapers, checked in the tiny closet, looked inside the wastebasket. I saw nothing that struck me as out of the ordinary, that I could possibly connect with the murder.

I heard sirens coming down the street and took another quick look around the room; this would be my last chance before the buffalo herd descended. Still nothing that caught my attention. I heard loud clumpings from the stairs. I was out in the hall again, humming to myself idly, when they arrived.

The rest was routine stuff. I was hustled downstairs to the lobby, and a lot of questions were thrown at me, and I answered them all three or four times. The last time from assistant DA George Wolkowicz, looking bleary-eyed and mad as hell because he'd been pulled out of his Christmas sleep. But the word had gone out that the dead man was his chief witness in the Meyer case, so how could he roll over in bed and tell them it could wait until morning?

"So what do you think happened here?" Wolkowicz finally bothered to notice me.

"You smelled the glass and the bottle? Don't quote me on it, but your Medical Examiner is going to turn up a first-class case of cyanide poisoning."

"And there's a million ways for people to get hold of the stuff. It's used for gardening, photography, printing, killing mice—" He peered at the bottle. "This doesn't look like the usual cheap rotgut these rummies go in for."

"Maybe somebody gave it to him for a Christmas present."

"We'll send it down to the lab, there might be fingerprints. Not much chance though. The killer must've wiped it clean before he gave it to the old man."

Then Wolkowicz's face hardened up. "Very convenient him dying like this. Seeing as he was our main witness against your client for the Candy murder." He narrowed his eyes. "What the hell are *you* doing here anyway? We didn't make it public yet, who our witness was."

"Things get around," I said.

"If there's some kind of leak in my office—"

Wolkowicz's eyebrows were beginning to look vicious, so I quickly changed the subject. "Our client couldn't have done this, he's been in jail all night. Unless he slipped out while your guards weren't looking."

"Your client's whereabouts are unknown till nine P.M. The old man brought this bottle back to the hotel with him at four."

"And our client was keeping out of the way of the cops all day. You think he went into a liquor store and picked up a bottle of wine? And took the chance of being recognized?"

"Maybe your client isn't too bright," Wolkowicz said. "The Ivy Leagues are full of brilliant geniuses who have trouble balancing their bank accounts and remembering their shoe sizes. Besides, even if nobody identifies him, it doesn't mean a thing. There are hundreds of liquor stores in this town, and a lot of them do big business, and lots of wine gets bought the day before Christmas, so what's the chance the clerk will remember one customer? Also, he could've bought that bottle a long time ago, he could've brought it with him from the East when he started his vacation, his folks could've had it sitting around the house."

"And what about Abernathy—you think he just accepted a bottle from the man he's testifying against in a murder trial? Whoever gave him that stuff, it had to be somebody he thought he could trust."

"He was an old rummy. Anybody who gave him free booze he'd trust them."

"Then what about the character who slugged me?" I said. "*That* wasn't Roger Meyer, you have to give me *that*."

"I'm giving it to you," Wolkowicz said. "Roger Meyer definitely didn't slug you." He paused and I didn't like his grin one bit. "If anybody did."

Shortly afterwards he let me go. On the way home my head began to ache in a big way. I had been holding that particular pain at bay for the last hour or so, I realized, because I had to keep my mind on more urgent matters. But now it engulfed me, and I practically couldn't see straight as I stumbled through the front door of my house.

My last thought, as I threw myself on my bed, was that Mom was going to be mad because I hadn't called her.

SIX

Christmas Day

CHRISTMAS MORNING dawned bright and clear. I didn't see it dawning, as a matter of fact, but I heard about it on the radio news at ten o'clock or thereabouts. That's when I was awakened by two phone calls, one right after the other, so if there were still any shreds of sleep left in me after the first one, the second one took care of them neatly.

The first call was from Ann. "What's this I read in the paper about you finding bodies? And the bodies of prosecution witnesses at that? Don't you believe in sharing these exciting experiences with the folks at your office?"

"I finished having this exciting experience around two in the morning," I said. "Did you want me to call you then? I'll keep that in mind for the future."

"Sorry, I didn't mean to come on as the heavy boss. It's something of a shock, though, to wake up on Christmas morning and see your client's name in the headlines, with strong hints that he might be charged with a second murder. Not exactly what I'm used to finding in my stocking."

I filled her in as best I could and asked her if she wanted to get together with me today. She said it wouldn't be necessary. She had intended to spend this glorious Christmas day scrounging around for a judge who might hear her request for Roger Meyer's bail. The most recent murder didn't give her much hope though. "Check in around six," she said, "I'll be home or in the office. I'll let you know if anything has to be done."

I had just barely hung up on Ann when the phone rang again. I wasn't surprised to hear Mom's voice, sounding concerned and motherly.

"You shouldn't blame yourself, darling," she said. "According to the paper he was dead before the tree-lighting ceremony last night. So there's nothing you could've done for him, even if you'd thought about it sooner."

"I wasn't letting it worry me, Mom," I said.

And I wasn't. I long ago stopped feeling guilty about the crimes I might've prevented if I had happened to get to the scene sooner. What I always tell myself is, it's the criminals who commit the crimes, not me. Without such an attitude, how could I have survived in my line of work all these years?

"So good," Mom said. "As long as it's not weighing on your mind, why don't you tell me exactly what happened to you? And incidentally, before you get started, didn't you promise you'd call me up last night no matter how late?"

"I knew you didn't want me to wake you up at two in the morning, Mom."

"Now he decides for people what they want and what they don't! All right, I'm a mother, I forgive. So about last night please?"

I went through it for her in detail. When I got to the part about being hit on the head, she broke in, "You're all right? You went to the doctor? He took some X-rays?"

"It wasn't that bad," I said. "I hardly even feel it this morning. I don't need any doctor or X-rays."

"This is what you always say. Always you have to prove what a tough guy you are! Since you were a little boy, I couldn't get you to put on your rubbers in the rain—'

"Let me go on with what happened, Mom." I hurried on with my story.

At the end of it, after a long pause, she said, "So I'm sure you're noticing what's peculiar about all this?"

"The old man getting killed? But the reason for that is pretty clear, isn't it? He saw something outside Candy's house which he didn't tell the DA or me about. Maybe he saw somebody besides Roger go in and out the front door, and maybe he was trying a little blackmail on that person— you *said* he was getting money from somewhere. So he tried to get some more last night, and this person decided to pay him off for good, by giving him a Christmas bottle of wine."

"Absolutely, this is clear. But there's one thing that isn't so clear."

"Which is?"

"Why did you get hit on the head?"

"I don't see what's so peculiar about that. I stumbled in on the murderer—"

"All right, I'm only asking the question. So tell me about earlier last night. I saw the boy getting arrested on the television news. He didn't look so happy."

I told her about the arrest in detail, and then I repeated the talk Ann and I had had with Roger at the jail. Mom listened intently, but her only comment came when I described Rabbi Loewenstein's part in rescuing Roger from the police and in hiding him out earlier.

"The rabbi yet!" I could hear the pleasure and surprise in Mom's voice. "It goes to show, you shouldn't jump at conclusions with anybody in this world. Even a rabbi can turn out to be a *mensch!*"

"But what are your thoughts about the murder, Mom?"

"There's too many different things to think about," she said. "I don't have the time to sort them out right now. In ten minutes I'm expected at the YMCA, they're having a Christmas party for the poor kiddies, and I'm Santa Claus."

An incredible image came into my mind. "Mom, you don't mean you're putting on a long white beard and stuffing a pillow in your coat—"

"You think I'm *meshuggenah?* I'm bringing some food and toys over to the party. So are plenty other people. This is what I mean by Santa Claus. I'll tell you what. We'll meet this afternoon, we'll go together to the Nutcracker, by that time maybe I'll have some thoughts in my head."

"What nutcracker?"

"The Nutcracker Ballet. From Tchaikovsky. With the little children and the snowflakes? They do a matinee of it every Christmas Day in this town. It's a tradition, you didn't know that? I've got a couple tickets, it begins at two o'clock but you'll meet me at a quarter of so there's time for us to settle down in our seats and read the story in the program."

"What are you doing with an extra ticket?"

"Mrs. Archuleta from the house next door was supposed to go with me, but I got a call from her early this morning, she's sick with the flu so she's spending Christmas eating aspirin and breathing steam. I was going to sell the ticket at the box office, but who wants to sit next to a stranger? Maybe it'll be a heavy breather, or somebody who fans himself with his program. It'll be much nicer sitting next to you, my son who hasn't got any bad habits."

"To tell you the truth, I wasn't planning to take in the Nutcracker Ballet this afternoon. There's a football game on television."

"You prefer a football game to an inspiring cultural experience? All right, all right, it's your choice. If you'll enjoy more watching a bunch of apes kicking out each other's teeth instead of listening to beautiful music and looking at beautiful dancing with your mother, and afterwards maybe talking over your murder case with her! This murder case, if I understand you, that you and your boss don't have any idea what you can do to help your client."

"You can tell us what to do?"

"The ballet, a quarter of two," Mom said, and she hung up the phone.

So I read the morning paper, grinding my teeth over the latest Hatfield editorial. He commended the police department for apprehending a dangerous fugitive, then he hinted broadly—but didn't quite say it in so many words—that it was too bad they hadn't caught him a little sooner, before he managed to strike again.

I realized I was in no mood for the football game. Something else was on my mind, something I wanted to do. It was ten-thirty, I still had time to get there.

HALF AN HOUR LATER, at eleven o'clock on Christmas morning, I sat in the back row of the Church of the Effulgent Apostles and watched and listened while Saint Chuck Candy was given his send-off to heaven.

His funeral would be held Monday morning, a private family affair, but this memorial service was open to the public, and it looked as if a large segment of the public had accepted the invitation. Candy's congregation was there in full force, of course, and so were plenty of others, drawn by religious fervor or maybe lowdown curiosity. How can you tell the difference? The people who gather around a bleeding accident victim on the street, are they filled with the compassionate urge to give the poor fellow moral support, or do they get turned on by the sight of blood and the sound of groans? Chances are they don't even know which themselves.

Anyway, the Church of the Effulgent Apostles had never had such a crowd in its history. It was a big barn of a room, inelegant, and somehow going to seed, though the building had been put up less than ten years before; but every seat was taken, with a lot of squeezing going on. There were dozens of standing room customers in the back, and the side aisles were packed too.

I craned my neck while the service was going on, trying to see who was there. Most of the faces in the crowd were the gaunt, sagging, woebegone type that was a specialty in this section of the country: thin-lipped, narrow-eyed people who looked as if all the juice had been squeezed out of them somewhere along the way. There were old ones and young ones, and a lot of babies in arms or toddlers in hand, but somehow they all looked to be the same age. Or maybe what I mean is that the age had been squeezed out of them too. And the effect was reinforced by what everybody was wearing—dark suits and dresses mostly, too tight or too loose because they hadn't been put on for years. Everybody was fidgeting and looked out of place, and the men were especially uncomfortable, tugging at their neckties as if they were nooses.

The show didn't have any more life in it than the audience. There was a small choir of twelve elderly ladies and three elderly gentlemen, and they hardly even made the pretense of singing the same notes at the same time. In the audience nobody did what audiences always do at revival meetings in the movies. Nobody screamed or had fits, nobody jumped into the aisles or up to the altar to writhe.

Gabriel Candy was a disappointment too. He lifted his arms in the air and invoked his father's name as if he fully expected this death to be followed by a Second Coming. He shouted "Hallelujah!" and "Jesus loves us!," and the congregation dutifully shouted after him. But much of this was spoiled by the unfortunate tendency of Gabe's voice to turn into a squeak at the top of his crescendos. And though he called on the crowd for all the appropriate emotions, nobody seemed to have their heart in them very much.

He delivered his father's sermon, pretty much as I had read it in his office a few days ago. I didn't notice it galvanizing anybody to more than a few perfunctory "Amens."

Then he delivered his own sermon. It began with him whooping it up for the deceased, letting God and Jesus know how lucky they were to be joined by the new arrival, who no doubt would soon be turning the Trinity into Quadruplets. Then he lowered his voice and said he wanted to express "some personal feelings on this tragic occasion."

The personal feelings stretched into a rambling reminiscence of the first time his father made him get on his knees to pray. "And in my innocent five-year-old heart, I knew at that moment—friends and brothers and sisters, at that moment I *knew*—that God was with me! His right hand was touching me on the shoulder, and his left hand was on the top of my head, and he was loving me and I was loving him, and Daddy was loving us both, and we were loving—"

I tuned out for the rest of this orgy.

It ended eventually with Gabe crying out, "God bless you at this holy Christmas season, my mother and I are grateful to you for coming, love Jesus, and we'll see you in church next Sunday!"

But he wouldn't be seeing as many of them, I thought, as his father had seen.

I moved through the front door with the rest of the congregation and found a long line forming on the porch. This line was filing slowly past Gabe Candy and his mother, standing next to him and half a head taller. Each departing mourner got a handshake from Gabe and a nod from Mrs. Candy, though her face was covered with a black veil so there was no way of seeing her expression. Every once in a while Gabe clasped a particular hand longer than he had clasped the others.

Ahead of me in the line I saw Mrs. Connelly. She wore a black dress, and her blonde hair was reined in by a gray bandanna. Her face was red; I was sure it was from crying.

Finally I got to the front of the line. It seemed to me that Gabe gave a little start when he saw me, and said some words under his breath to his mother. But he shook my hand without giving out anything more than his standard polite murmur.

I went down the front steps of the church and started across the lawn, when I heard a voice calling out to me. It was Gabe; he had left his post among the mourners to run after me.

"Just want to tell you something," he said, a little out of breath as he stopped in front of me. "It's nice of you to come pay your respects to Daddy. You didn't have to do that. I truly appreciate the kind gesture."

I muttered something, fidgeting. The fact is, I didn't have the slightest idea why I had come. Vulgar curiosity more than anything else, I suspected.

"And I—" Gabe hesitated, and I saw he was blushing a little. "I—I wanted to ask you something. Your opinion. I figure you don't go to too many occasions like this one. So I figure you can give me an impartial opinion. What'd you think of the service? Tell me honestly."

"I was very moved," I said. "It was very sincere."

"Well, *that's* true enough. I made it as sincere as I could." He was smiling, but then his smile wavered. "The trouble is, they didn't want what I gave them."

I was beginning to feel embarrassed. I couldn't think of a damn thing to say.

"The thing about Daddy—he wasn't an educated man. He had to quit school at age thirteen, he was needed to work the farm. He never finished high school. It's a lucky thing the Bible College didn't have a high school degree for one of its requirements. But one thing you could always say about him—he gave the people what they wanted. He just knew what it was, every time. Without any book-learning or anything like that.''

He made an effort and firmed up his wavering smile. "I'm going to learn how to do that. That's the big challenge I'm facing. In my ministry. That's what I have to learn.''

After an even more tremendous effort, he managed to bring out a laugh. Joyous and confident. "And I'm going to do it. Christ is with me. How can I fail?''

He stood there smiling a little longer, and then he turned sharply and headed back to the porch and the mourners who were waiting to shake the hand of his father's son.

I GOT HOME a little after twelve and watched the first quarter of the football game, while I munched a baloney sandwich for lunch. Mom would've been horrified, so I wouldn't upset her by telling her. I washed it down with a glass of beer, and then it was time to go to the ballet.

Every middle-sized town across the United States does the Nutcracker Ballet during the Christmas season, so there's no point retelling the plot or describing what happens on the stage. In our town the performance—one matinee on Christmas day, and always sold out—was sponsored by the local Symphony Guild, with the City Council letting them have the auditorium for nothing. This was the auditorium of General Wagner High School, a huge barn of a room with mediocre acoustics and sightlines, but there was nowhere else for the performance to take place; the voters keep turning down all proposals to build an up-to-date performing arts center with taxpayer money.

In the pit would be the Mesa Grande Symphony Orchestra, conducted by Maestro Ludwig Mandelbaum, who was starting a promising career as a young conductor in Austria when the Nazis chased him out in 1937. On the stage would be a platoon of local dancers, led by the chairman of the dance department at Mesa Grande College and his wife, who also taught at the college; they had once been second-string soloists with the Ballet Theatre. Also on the stage would be a dozen devastatingly cute child dancers, chosen after a series of viciously competitive auditions which every year created everlasting bitterness among mothers all over town.

I got to the high school exactly on time, but naturally Mom was in the lobby already, pacing up and down and looking at her watch. I knew I wasn't late—so why did I *feel* late?

"Any brilliant thoughts?" I said, as I walked up to her and kissed her.

"I'm getting closer," she said. "There's only one little bit I can't fit it in yet. I'll make my mind a blank, I'll look at the ballet dancing, and maybe it'll sneak up on me. Some things, Davie, they only come to you when you aren't looking."

I had to be satisfied with this, so I opened my program and read the story of the ballet—which doesn't make much sense, but who goes to ballets for sense?—and began to look forward to the performance. Shirley used to drag me to this sort of thing back in New York, and I always complained bitterly; it was a matter of self-respect that the guys in Homicide should never find out I was developing a taste for the stuff.

Maestro Mandelbaum appeared, a wrinkled hunched-over figure with wispy gray hair, but he moved to the front of his orchestra with the springing step of a young man. The prospect of making music seemed to invigorate him, and the sight of him invigorated everybody else. We gave him a round of applause, which he cut off by lifting his baton and shooting a stern look at those who were still applauding. Then he tapped the music stand in front of him, lifted his baton again, and the overture to The Nutcracker began.

Since I'm far from being an expert on ballet, I won't give you a play-by-play report on the performance. I'll only say that the production may have had a certain tackiness to it, the combined result of lack of funds and lack of profes-sional talent, but somehow I found it enjoyable. The way a

baseball game between a couple of kids' teams can sometimes be more exciting than a pro game, not in spite of but
because of the enthusiastic errors that everybody makes.

One example of the amateurishness of this Nutcracker
production: The old toymaker who gives the magic nutcracker to the little girl was played by a local insurance man
who had been doing the part for the last ten years. The
character was supposed to wear a skullcap, in the nine-
teenth-century bourgeois style, but the inept lighting blot-
ted it out from the audience's sight completely and, to the
accompaniment of irreverent giggles, made the old toymaker look as if the top of his head had been sliced clean
off.

Another example: one of the little boys attending the first-
act Christmas party in nineteenth century St. Petersburg was
chewing gum all the time he was on stage, and on several
occasions large pink bubbles emerged from his mouth. The
gigglers loved this touch too.

And then, about twenty minutes into the first act, came
the scene where there was a big Christmas tree on stage, and
the little girl stood in front of it and lifted up on her toes,
and an ecstatic look appeared on her face, and the lighted-
up Christmas tree started getting bigger and bigger. And the
music built up to a crescendo the climax of which was—a
sudden explosion coming out of Mom. "Oy!"

Everybody around us turned to look at her. She blushed
and lowered her head.

The act ended half an hour later, and Mom and I went out
to the lobby for intermission.

"Are you all right?" I asked her. "For a few minutes
there you seemed to be having some sort of fit."

All Mom answered was, "Didn't I tell you it would be an
inspiration, this ballet? That Tchaikovsky, what a genius!
A hundred years he's been dead already, and out of his grave
comes the truth!"

"The truth about what?" I said.

"We'll see the rest of the ballet," Mom said. "We still
have to get to the sugar plums. And after it's over, you'll

come home with me, and I'll give you a nice cup of coffee and a schnecken, and we'll decide who's doing all these killings.''

SEVEN

Christmas Night

THREE HOURS LATER, at eight o'clock on Christmas night, Ann and I got together in her office, and I gave her the benefit of Mom's chain of reasoning.

I didn't exactly tell her who that chain came from. Mom always makes me promise I won't; she says that people don't believe things if old ladies say them, and I'm afraid she's got a point there. On the other hand, I didn't take credit where I hadn't earned it. I never once claimed, either directly or by hints, that this chain of reasoning originated with me. If Ann assumed that it did, it was positively no fault of mine.

I also gave her Mom's suggestion as to how we should handle things with Francesca Fleming tonight. The suggestion made sense to Ann, and we agreed that's how we would proceed.

Ann called Francesca at Fleming's Flake and told her we wanted to see her. Francesca said she was much too busy, there was nothing that couldn't wait until after the holidays, she positively refused to submit to this bureaucratic harassment. Ann just kept repeating her request; she comes from this section of the world, and there's a good deal of the bronco-buster in her. Eventually Francesca told us to come along.

Fleming's Flake was packed. People who can afford to eat out don't like to stay home and cook on Christmas night. We maneuvered ourselves through the crowd, weaving in and out of the tables, ducking waiters, getting sawdust in our shoes. Finally we went through the swinging doors in back and knocked on the door of Francesca's office. She shouted for us to come in.

She was sitting behind her desk, and the first thing I noticed was her clothes. No Indian headbands or trailing shawls, nothing exotic at all. Jeans and a plain yellow jumper, and a pair of pale-rimmed glasses tilted forward on her nose. During business hours, it seemed, she dressed for business.

She didn't ask us to sit down, but Ann plumped herself down in a chair anyway. Then, as matter-of-factly as if she were making a remark about the weather, she said, "We know who killed Chuck Candy."

"Who doesn't?" Francesca said. "Your client killed him."

"Our client was framed for killing him. That's all come apart now. There really isn't any point in going on with it."

"I'm sure," Francesca said, meeting Ann's eyes with perfect steadiness, "that I haven't the slightest idea what you're talking about."

"I'll let Dave tell you. He's the one who worked it out."

So I told her. I went through the whole thing, step by step, just the way Mom had gone through it with me a few hours earlier....

...IT WAS a little after five when Mom and I settled down in her living room, each of us getting comfortable in one of her old twin easychairs.

These chairs had come to the Rocky Mountains from Mom's apartment in New York. She had sold off most of her furniture before she left—"I've been looking at these old sticks for forty years, let me give my eyes a rest already! I'm starting up my life again in a new place, don't I have the right to sit on some new things?" But I remembered these two easychairs from when I was a little boy, I had seen my father sitting every night in one of them while he read his *New York Daily News*. So I did a lot of begging and pleading, and Mom finally agreed to bring the chairs to Mesa Grande with her.

We sat in them now and drank coffee and ate Mom's schnecken, that delicious concoction of cinnamon, nuts, raisins, and calories, while I waited for Mom to do some of her inimitable unraveling. Other women knit; Mom's specialty is taking apart other people's knitting.

"So you're interested maybe in who killed this Candy?" she said. "I could tell you straight out, but you'll believe me better and agree with me more if I go through the thinking with you the way I went through it with myself, in my mind.

"The first thing that popped into my mind was a coincidence. Coincidences happen, naturally. Like your Aunt Selma, a long time ago when she was visiting her sister in St. Louis, Missouri, she suddenly got a vision of your Uncle Max, my brother who got rich, may he rest in peace, sitting at a table in the Stork Club buying dinner for a blonde. And sure enough, when Selma called the Stork Club long distance and asked for Max, the waiter brought him to the phone. And was Max a surprised man!

"But when you look closer at this coincidence, it isn't so peculiar any more. For years before she took her trip to St. Louis, Selma was saying to Max, 'Why don't you take me out for dinner and dancing to the Stork Club one of these nights? Or do you take your blonde secretary there when you tell me you're working late, and you don't want to take me because you're afraid the waiters will say something and give away your secret?' And then she'd give a laugh, ha ha!, to show she was only making a joke. Some joke! It wasn't so funny in her mind, and who can say she didn't put it in Max's mind too?"

"Mom, has this got anything to do with the murder?"

"What it's got to do is, I always look close at coincidences. This woman who was Candy's secretary, this Mrs. Connelly, she used to have an affair with him, he took her into his office for dictation, he locked the door and what he dictated wasn't letters. Why did he have to do it that way? Love on an office couch, is this anybody's idea of being comfortable? Especially a man in middle age, when the bones aren't so flexible like they used to be?

"But the point is, he didn't have any choice. He was a minister, he preached how you have to be pure and upright and you don't fool around if you're married or even if you're not. So at night he had to stay home with his wife, he didn't go off on trips or to play cards with the boys at his club. And he couldn't say he was working late at the office, like my poor brother Max, because the office was the church, and it stayed open late at night with people coming in and out to pray. And in the daytime Candy also had to be in the church, so when could his secretary and him do their dictation except in office hours behind a locked door?

"Which makes me ask myself—after he stopped his affair with the secretary and took up with some other woman, he still had to be home every night, didn't he? And in the church every day, including Sunday? And what was worse for him, he couldn't use his office any more. From then on what he had to dictate in there *was* letters. So if this new affair was going to be carried on anywhere except in his head, when did he have any free time for it?"

"Maybe he got together with this new woman when he went out to lunch."

"The secretary, Connelly, told you he had lunch every day at the Italian restaurant, in the mall near the church. And he came back from lunch every day smelling from garlic on his breath. So take my word for it, he wasn't spending his lunchtime in bed making love to a woman. Unless they were maybe eating garlic together in the bed, which to me sounds like a very peculiar idea. Even nowadays, with all the peculiar things people do in bed.

"All right then—there's only one time Candy could possibly be meeting this new woman and having his hanky-panky. On Thursday afternoons. When he went home to write his Sunday sermon, and he left word he shouldn't be disturbed till dinnertime, nobody should come to see him, he wouldn't even answer the phone. His sermons were strictly from notes, he didn't even write them out word for word, so why did he need a whole afternoon, without interruptions, to work on them? Thursday afternoons—it's the only time he *could* be seeing his new woman.

"Thursday afternoon, Thursday afternoon—it went spinning around in my mind—what was there about Thursday? And finally it came to me. Thursday was the day, the only day in the week, that the Francesca Fleming woman, the one that owns a restaurant and belongs to the Union from Civil Liberties, wasn't actually working at her restaurant with a lot of people seeing her there all day long. Thursday was the day she drove out to the country and visited the farms and the smalltown markets and ordered fresh vegetables. She told you about this when you talked to her the night before the murder—you remember, naturally?''

I didn't remember, until Mom reminded me. Mom remembers everything, of course. No detail, no matter how trivial, ever escapes from that rat-trap memory of hers; this was one of the chief reasons for her popularity among the gossiping women in her old neighborhood in the Bronx.

"And I'm also asking myself," Mom went on, "was this a job that had to take up her whole day? You could do your shopping for vegetables in the morning, couldn't you? How long does it take to look at a cauliflower and decide if it's any good? It takes me half an hour to pick out at the supermarket all my vegetables for a week. So you do that before lunch, and after lunch you drive back to town and park your car around the corner from Candy's house—"

"You're saying Francesca Fleming was Candy's latest girlfriend? I'm sorry, you'll need a lot more evidence to convince me of that! There must be thousands of women in this town who are free on Thursday afternoons!"

"Did I say this was evidence? I only said this was a coincidence, and I like to give a close-up look at coincidences. Which I did, and pretty soon I started noticing other peculiar things. For instance, you read to me Candy's last sermon, the one he jotted down on Thursday just before he was killed. About the prodigal son that had an affair with the scarlet woman. She played her little games with him, and tempted him he should go to bed with her, and dragged him into the mud, but finally he broke it off with her and came crawling back to his father, with rags on his back, asking for forgiveness.

"So I'm saying to myself, it's obvious he wrote this sermon because his own personal problem was on his mind, and it filled him up with guilt, and in his sermon he could get it out of his chest. He was the prodigal son, and his new girlfriend was—''

''Hold on, Mom. There's no reason to believe he was talking about himself. If every minister who tells a Bible story from the pulpit had to be talking about himself—''

''There's two reasons to believe it in Candy's case. First of all, this wasn't like his usual sermon. You noticed this yourself, and his son admitted it too. Usually his sermons were full of optimism, and they told people how all their troubles would be over if they just believed in God. But this last sermon of his was full of gloominess and bitterness and completely down in the mouth. Why such a big change in his style? Can you think of any other reason except this sermon meant more to him than the others, it came from out of his heart, it expressed something from his personal life?

''And there's a second reason. The story he told in this sermon is from the Bible. It's a story Jesus tells in the New Testament. Only Candy didn't tell it the way the Bible does. In the Bible the prodigal son leaves home and loses all his money, and he's starving so he goes back to his father. In the Bible there's no scarlet woman. Candy invented her for his sermon. Why? Because she was real, she was somebody he actually had an affair with and he felt guilty about it and he dumped her to go back to his father—meaning God maybe, and his church and his married life.''

''All right, it sounds plausible, Mom. I didn't know you were so familiar with the New Testament.''

''Why wouldn't I be? I got plenty *goyische* friends, isn't it natural I should take a look at what they're reading? Also, if you liked the original, wouldn't you also want to read the sequel?'' She gave a little shrug. ''It isn't bad, incidentally. Not so good as the first part, but what sequel is? The only thing I couldn't figure out, why do they have to tell the same story four different times? Did they pad it out so people would think they were getting their money's worth?''

Mom as Biblical scholar did have a certain fascination for me, but I was more immediately interested in the murder. ''All right, so Candy was referring to himself and his new girlfriend in the sermon. But how does that prove she was Francesca Fleming?'

"This is easy. Only pay attention to the words he used. 'The scarlet woman' is what he calls her. Meaning what?"

"It's just a phrase. It means any woman who's unusually sinful."

"Naturally. But there's plenty of different phrases for such women. In his sermon Candy didn't use any of them. He just kept calling her 'the scarlet woman.' Why do you think? Maybe it's because this is exactly how he saw her. This is a description of how she looks. She's a redhead."

Thinking this one over kept me quiet for a few seconds. Then I said, "All right, I see the point you're making. But it's still hard for me to believe that Francesca did this killing. I could swear it's not in her character."

"It's in everybody's character to commit a murder," Mom said. "How many times I felt like doing it myself! The difference between most of us and official murderers is, their opportunities were better."

"Maybe so, but I just can't see Francesca loving a man, any man, so passionately that she'd kill him for walking out on her. And a man like Chuck Candy, for God's sake! Physically he wasn't particularly attractive, and intellectually, emotionally, *politically* he was at opposite poles from her."

"As far as that goes," Mom said, "people at opposite poles are always getting together in this world. Short ones marry tall ones, beautiful ones marry homely ones, Democrats marry Republicans, devout Catholics marry devout atheists."

"What are you saying, Mom, that Francesca is the fanatic you've been hunting for all this time? The fanatical atheist as counterpart to the fanatical fundamentalist?"

"I thought about that," Mom said. "In my head I played around with this idea. But I saw pretty quick it wasn't so. Francesca Fleming's reason for killing Candy didn't have much to do with being an atheist or a rejected lover or anything that's got any passion in it. You remember another thing she said to you the night before the murder? She said

Candy had a reputation for being honest, there weren't even any rumors he was stealing money."

"What does that prove?"

"Yesterday, when you had your meeting at the Unitarian Church, she said Candy was a con man and a crook. How come she contradicted what she told you two days before? It's because two days before she was telling the truth, Candy *didn't* have a reputation as a crook. But two days later she made a slip from the tongue, it came out of her he *was* a crook. How could she know such a thing about him? Only if she was in on his crooked deal with him.

"You see what the answer is? She's the one that knew about the Eastern company building a shopping mall in the Fairhaven neighborhood. She's the one that put Candy up to making an offer to buy the Meyer house. And she's the one, when the offer was turned down, that was behind Candy's dirty trick to force the Meyers to sell."

"I'm confused," I said. "Are you saying now that Francesca *didn't* have an affair with Candy?"

"I'm saying both things. When she found about this shopping mall—incidentally, my theory is she heard about it from Victor Kincaid, didn't he mention to you that he's representing some big Eastern firm that wants to make investments in the Southwest?—she decided to take advantage of the information by buying up property in the neighborhood.

"But she needed somebody to be—what's the expression?—her 'frontpiece,' and Candy looked like a good candidate. He was so different from her that nobody could suspect there was any connection between them. Maybe she met him somewhere while she was doing her research on local churches for the Civil Liberties, and she looked him over very careful and came to the conclusion he wanted money bad.

"So she got herself introduced to him, and she blinked her eyelashes at him and let him know how attractive he was by her, and pretty soon he was eating her hand, she was twisting her little finger around him. When she finally brought up what she wanted him to do for her in this real estate deal, how was he going to say no? Could he resist her body, if along with it came also a nice financial profit?

"So he bought up property in the neighborhood, and when the Meyers wouldn't sell he put up his Christmas nightmare to drive them away, and all the time Francesca Fleming was pulling on his strings and keeping him happy with their Thursday afternoons in bed. Until they went too far, with this assault charge against Roger Meyer, and suddenly you and Ann Swenson were making an investigation.

"With this development Candy wasn't so happy any more. In fact, he got worried what it would be like to stand up in court and testify under oath. He worried what he'd say if Ann Swenson asked him embarrassing questions about the Meyer boy's so-called assault against him. Most of all he worried the public defender should find out about the real estate deal. And then, on Thursday afternoon, maybe while Candy was waiting in his house for Francesca Fleming's weekly massage, he got a call from the real estate agent you talked to, from Dwayne McKee. McKee told him the public defender's investigator was just in his office, he asked about the offer to buy the Meyer house, and McKee gave him the right answer.

"For Candy this was positively the final blow. The public defender knew all about the shady real estate deal, and there wasn't any doubt she'd bring it up in public at the Meyer boy's trial. He decided he had to save his skin, even if it meant burning somebody else's. So when Francesca Fleming got there for the afternoon, he told her the hankypanky between them was over, and what's more he intended to go to the district attorney and tell the truth, that the assault charges against Roger Meyer were a fake, that the Christmas display in front of his house was a plot to drive the Meyers out of the neighborhood, and that Francesca Fleming was the one who's responsible for all the trouble. By confessing it all, he said, he could maybe save some of his reputation—Christians are supposed to confess their sins, God has mercy on them for this. And if she lost *her* reputation, and even possibly went to jail, that's too bad, he'd pray for her.

"Naturally Francesca Fleming wasn't so pleased to hear this. Her reputation was as important to her as Candy's was to him. If he made a big *mishegass* in public, everybody would find out how she, the big liberal, the big fighter for noble causes, was actually cheating people out of their houses so a big corporation could put up a shopping mall. Such a phony she'd look like! And what's more, with the bad publicity, that Eastern company could decide to build their mall someplace else, and she'd be stuck with a lot of property that wasn't worth so much. So she answered Candy back by taking his gun from the hall table and shooting him.

"Then she decided maybe she could get away with it if she made everybody think somebody else killed him. So she called up Roger Meyer on the phone—she knew he was in his parents' house because she saw his car parked out front. She put on a deep voice, talked with a whisper so he wouldn't realize it was a woman, and she told him she was Candy and asked him to come over right away. The idea was, he should find the body, and maybe get some blood on him, and with luck he'd be blamed for the murder, since already he had a first-class motive. This was why she left the front door unlocked when she walked out of the house herself. Only it didn't work out exactly like she hoped. One thing happened that she never expected."

"Abernathy?"

"Who else? The crazy old man was standing across the street, behind a bush, watching the Candy house. He saw Francesca Fleming leave the house, maybe he even saw her go into it earlier. He saw her leaving *before* Roger got there. But he didn't tell anybody what he saw. Instead, he got in touch with her and started asking her for money. She gave him a couple handouts, but when he set up a meeting on the day before Christmas and asked her to bring the biggest amount yet, she decided she wouldn't ever be free from him again unless she killed him.

"So she met him early that afternoon—maybe at her house, maybe at the park near his hotel—but instead of bringing the money she made some sort of excuse to him. She told him she didn't have that much on her right now, but she'd get it to him in a day or two. Meanwhile, to show him her heart was in the right place, she gave him a Christmas present, this nice bottle of wine—it was easy for her to get hold of it because she runs a restaurant, and in the cellar she's got plenty of bottles with wine in them. Ahead of time she's already put enough cyanide in it to kill twenty old religious maniacs. So he takes it from her, and she goes to her meeting with you at the Unitarian Church, and then she goes home for the night to watch Jimmy Stewart on television.

"And that should've been it, the whole *schmeer*. But here comes another peculiar thing. Since she expected the old man to drink the poison in the privacy of his hotel room, wouldn't you think she'd sit home quietly that night, watching television and waiting for the news that somebody's found the body? This would be sensible and reasonable, but what did she do instead? Late on Christmas Eve, around eleven-thirty or so, she left her nice comfortable house, went to the old man's hotel, sneaked up the fireplace, and slipped into his room. Such a chance she was taking! Somebody could see her, she could get caught at the scene of the crime! As a matter of fact, it almost happened. *You* got to the room while she was still in it, so she had to hit you over the head.

"But *why*, I'm asking myself, should she run for herself such an unnecessary risk? Only one possible reason comes into my mind. Late that night, sitting in front of her television watching Jimmy Stewart, it suddenly came to her that there was something in the old man's room which could maybe prove she killed him. Something she didn't want the police to find. And if the body wasn't discovered yet, maybe there was still a chance she could get into the old man's room and pick up this something before the police got there. Anyway, even if she failed, it was important enough so she had to give it a try.

"What is this something? This is the question I'm asking myself over and over. And also, did she get what she was looking for? It seems like she did, because the police *didn't* find anything in that room, any clue that could lead them to her, and you didn't find such a clue either. If she got it, the next question is obvious? What's missing from that room?"

"You can't possibly answer that one. If it's something whose existence nobody even knows about—"

"Davie, Davie, there *was* something missing from that room, and we *do* know about its existence. The wine bottle that had the poison in it—how did the old man carry it through the streets and up to his room? He carried it in a white paper bag. The hotel clerk told you that's what the bottle was in when Abernathy walked through the lobby at four o'clock. So what happened to that white paper bag? You looked at every inch of the floor, you looked under the bed, you looked in the closet, you looked all over the place—and isn't it true you didn't run across that paper bag?"

I gulped a little at this. It was obvious now that Mom pointed it out to me, but to tell the truth it hadn't occurred to me earlier. "All right, the bag was missing. But why would she want to take such a big risk for *that?*"

"Because when she got that bottle from her restaurant in the first place, she thought this was a completely safe thing to do. The police could go around to liquor stores for the next ten years, she thought, and no clerk was going to identify her. But late that night she suddenly remembered something. How did *she* carry the bottle from the restaurant to her meeting place with old Abernathy? She carried it in that white paper bag, one of the doggie bags she kept around her restaurant. She gave it to Abernathy in this bag, and this was the bag Abernathy brought back with him to his hotel room. And don't you remember, Davie? All of these doggie bags, like the napkins and the tablecloths and the windows and the doors, had that little monogram on them, FF, with the Fs tangled up with each other so they looked like a couple making love.

"You see what this suddenly meant to her? When the police found the paper bag that the bottle came in, they'd be able to tell by the FF that it was from Francesca Fleming's restaurant. They'd know there was a connection between her and the dead man, and how long would it take them after that to figure out what it was? So she had to go back to that room and get hold of that paper bag.''

I was getting excited now, I have to admit it. There's something about the way Mom piles the details up to make a case. Before I could say anything, though, she said, ''And now we'll go back to Candy's murder, so we can see where the fanatic comes in.''

''The fanatic?''

''When Francesca Fleming ran out of Candy's house, she didn't realize he wasn't dead yet. He had in him enough life still to tear open a box of crayons that was under the Christmas tree and write a message on his carpet. What he wrote, in capital letters, was 'GOLD, FRANKINCENSE, AND MYRRH.' Now why should he use his last ounces of life to write on the carpet?

''This had to be because he was trying to tell the police who killed him. It had to be—but what I couldn't see was how this message he wrote told the police anything. What was the connection between Francesca Fleming and the Three Wise Men? I gave myself pains in the neck trying to figure this out. Until I noticed another peculiar thing about this message.

''What I noticed was, Candy couldn't have written it. First of all, it would be too hard for a dying man to put down so many words, and especially in such a short period of time. Remember, he had to do it *after* Francesca ran out of the house but *before* Roger got there and found him dead—which wasn't more than a few minutes later.

''And the second reason why he couldn't have written this message—Candy was a terrible speller. You saw it for yourself in the posters he put up at the church and in the sermon he wrote. So does it make sense to you that he could spell 'frankincense' and 'myrrh' absolutely without any mistakes? With no chance to look them up in the dictionary?''

''You're confusing me again. One minute you say he wrote the message to name his killer. The next minute you say he *didn't* write the message.''

"Part of it he wrote, most of it he didn't. What he wrote was only four letters, that's all he could manage before he died. But those four letters were enough so the police would understand who killed him. F-R-A-N. The beginning of the name Francesca."

"But what I saw on that carpet was a lot longer than—"

"At five-thirty, his wife came home from her shopping. She found her husband's body, she called the police, they got there in fifteen minutes. She told you she spent those fifteen minutes sitting in the room across the hall. But the mystery of this message clears up once you catch on she spent that time in a more creative way.

"She saw what Candy wrote on the carpet, and she understood what those four letters meant. She wanted to erase them, only she couldn't, because the crayons were indelible, it would take turpentine and cold water and a lot of time to make them invisible. All she could do was try to disguise their meaning, by adding on to them, by turning her husband's short message into a longer one, by hiding the capital letters that really meant something in a larger collection of capital letters that *seemed* to mean something but actually didn't. So she turned FRAN into FRANKINCENSE, and she tacked GOLD on to the front of the word and AND MYRRH on to the end of the word. Right away we've got the Three Wise Men, only their main purpose in life is to make the rest of us stupid."

"But why did Mrs. Candy do it? You'd think she'd *want* her husband's murderer to get caught."

"There's something she wanted a lot more. She knew her husband was having an affair, maybe she even knew it was with Francesca Fleming. Either way, she realized when she saw those letters on the carpet what would happen if Francesca got charged with her husband's murder. All the dirty details of their affair would come out into the open. The whole world would find out her husband was a lecherer, an adulterer, a breaker of two or three commandments, and a dirty old man. And for Mrs. Candy, like you noticed yourself when you talked to mom, the most important thing in her life is keeping up the appearance what a holy virtuous man her husband was. He was a saint, and she wants the world to go on thinking so. Maybe *she* still thinks so, maybe she's managed to convince herself that the evidence of her own eyes was false. This is what religious faith is, isn't it? Ignoring the evidence of your own eyes?"

"Then Mrs. Candy is the fanatic you've been looking for all this time?"

"Who can doubt it? She'll never admit it though. Under torture, in my opinion, you couldn't get her to confess that she changed that message on the carpet or to say what the original message was. Luckily, your case against Francesca Fleming is strong enough so you won't have to bring in Candy's dying accusation. Once you have her arrested, you'll maybe find powder burns on her fingers—didn't you tell me once they last for a week or more, after somebody fires a gun? And I'll make a bet, if the police go over Candy's living room carefully, they'll find some of Francesca Fleming's fingerprints there. And somewhere there must be signed agreements between her and Candy so she could take over ownership of those houses he bought. All this is just routine details, it doesn't interest me."

And Mom poured out another cup of coffee for herself and disguised her self-satisfaction for the next few seconds by gulping it down noisily....

...THOUGH FRANCESCA HAD no coffee cup to use as a prop, she remained as cool and unruffled as she had been from the start. No way around it, I just had to admire her.

She said nothing for awhile, and then she said, "It wouldn't do any good, I suppose, if I denied the whole thing?"

"*Do* you?" Ann said.

Francesca laughed. "As a matter of fact, I don't. You've hit a lot of nails on the head. I must admit it never occurred to me that either of you was capable of this much sheer brainpower. Yes, I did have a little private real estate deal with Chuck Candy. And the idea of getting the Meyer couple out of their house by dressing up Chuck's house for

Christmas was entirely mine. Pretty imaginative, wasn't it? And appropriate for the season too.

"One little bit you've got completely wrong, though. I'm not a murderer. As it happens, I didn't kill Chuck Candy or anybody else."

This was what I'd been waiting for. Nice work, Mom, I said silently.

Out loud I said to Francesca, "But you know who did, don't you?"

For just a second her gaze flickered away. It was enough to tell me that Mom was right.

"I can't imagine," she said, meeting my eyes steadily again. "As far as I know, none of my friends are murderers. Some of them, I grant you, are asking to *be* murdered—"

"It's all right," I said, "you don't have to tell me who it is. I'll tell *you,* okay? And then you can say if I'm right...."

... MOM GULPED DOWN some more of her coffee, and I got up and gave her a kiss. On my face was that look of awe that's been there countless times since my boyhood. "I believe you've done it again, Mom."

"I'm glad you believe it. Because you shouldn't sit here on your backside one minute more. You should call up Ann Swenson and tell her about this, and tonight the two of you should go to Francesca Fleming and tell *her*—and it's very important she should believe that you believe it."

"Why *shouldn't* she believe we believe it? She knows better than anybody that it's true."

"Excuse me," Mom said, "but what she knows better than anybody is that it *isn't* true."

I stared at her.

She laughed and said, "Close your mouth, and I'll tell you what I left out the first time around.

"Like I told you already, Francesca found out from Victor Kincaid about the company from the East that's building the mall. It's natural he should know about it because he's the lawyer for this company. But there's something else Kincaid knew which isn't so natural.

"In the meeting you had with him yesterday, he made a remark about the type sermons that preachers like Candy give. He said such sermons are all about 'people killing calves, and being dead and coming to life again, and feeling guilty because they slept with harlots.' You know what all these items come from? They're all mentioned in the story of the prodigal son, which Candy quoted in his sermon."

"Well, he *did* quote those things, didn't he?" I said. "So how was Kincaid wrong?"

"He wasn't. He was right. This is the point. How should Kincaid, when he wanted to give an example how ridiculous sermons are, come up with exactly the sermon that Candy just got finished writing? It's another coincidence, and this one is so big even Jonah and the whale would choke on it.

"Now you see what's not natural, don't you, Davie? Candy wrote that sermon on Thursday afternoon, just before he got killed. Nobody saw it afterwards, except his son and you. His son didn't deliver it in public 'til this morning. So how did Kincaid know what was in it? He could know this in only one way—if he was in Candy's house on Thursday afternoon.

"And here's another thing you should notice. Luke Abernathy, the old prophet, saw the murderer coming out of Candy's house, recognized this person, and eventually got killed because he went in for blackmail. But *how* did Abernathy recognize the murderer? Abernathy wasn't what you'd call a social butterfly. He wasn't welcome in any circle of Mesa Grande society. If Francesca was the murderer, and Abernathy saw *her* leaving Candy's house, he wouldn't know who she was so he'd be able to contact her later on and blackmail her. It isn't likely Abernathy ever saw her or knew her by name before or since.

"But with Kincaid it's different. Kincaid is a celebrity, a well-known face. In Wednesday morning's paper was a big picture of him, how he just came to town on business. And the paper not only gave his name and his face, it also mentioned he was staying at the Richelieu. Abernathy read the paper regularly—he picked it up out of trashcans—so it's a sure thing he saw Kincaid's picture on Wednesday. And recognized that face when he saw it coming out of Candy's house on Thursday afternoon.

"And finally, there's the wine bottle with the poison in it. This bottle came from Francesca Fleming's restaurant, this we can be sure of. And Kincaid had lunch with her in that restaurant on Saturday, she mentioned it to you yourself. Did she give him a bottle of wine for a Christmas present? This is what I think. And did she put it in one of the restaurant's white bags so he could take it away with him? So he took it all right, put the poison in it, and gave it to Abernathy a little later in the afternoon when the old man came to him for money. And naturally it was still in the same white paper bag—why should Kincaid bother to switch it to a different one?

"But an hour or so after that, when he was with you at the Unitarian Church, Francesca Fleming said something which to Kincaid was like getting a kick in the stomach. She made her little speech how Easterners always underestimate Westerners. They think Westerners prefer Coca Cola to fancy wines with French names and dirty pictures to paintings by French painters. It was a combination of these two items that suddenly made Kincaid realize what he did. He gave Abernathy a bottle of French wine from Francesca Fleming's restaurant, and he put that bottle inside a paper-bag with one of her monograms on it—the FF monogram which, let's face it, is practically a dirty picture. You noticed it yourself, didn't you, how awful Kincaid looked after Francesca Fleming made this remark?

"And the worst part of it was, he couldn't do anything about it right then. He had a business dinner that he couldn't get out of. In my opinion, he didn't enjoy the food very much at that dinner. But as soon as he could break free from it, around eleven-thirty, he went to Abernathy's hotel to get his hands on that paper-bag.

"The point is, Francesca Fleming could never make such a mistake. She could never put the murder weapon in one of her own paper bags and leave it at the scene of the crime.

She'd realize right away, maybe even without thinking about it, that the bag could be traced back to her from the monogram. Kincaid, though, could make such a mistake easy. He knew about her special FF monograms, because she tells everybody about them, but they weren't on his mind."

"But what was his motive for killing Candy?" I asked.

"The same motive that I accused Francesca of having, only with Kincaid it goes double. He found out about the Eastern company's plans for a mall, he got in touch with her because she's right here in Mesa Grande, on the spot, and she agreed to handle the arrangements. She reported to him regularly. On Thursday, when she got to his house for her weekly date, Candy told her to go away. He told her he was ending the affair and blowing the whistle on the real estate deal.

"After she left his house, the first thing she did was to call her partner at the Richelieu. Kincaid was even more upset about this development than she was. He stood to lose a lot of money, and his reputation is all over the country, he's built his career on being this unselfish fighter for human rights. If it ever gets out he's mixed up in a sleazy real estate business, his whole career flushes down the toilet. So he told Francesca Fleming to sit tight and keep her mouth shut, and he'd take care of the situation."

"What about Candy's dying message? He wrote the letters FRAN on the carpet, and his wife changed them to—"

"He didn't write FRAN on the carpet. What he wrote was KINC. He was accusing Kincaid, only he died before he could finish writing his name. It's KINC that Mrs. Candy changed to FRANKINCENSE. She knew her husband was in this shady real estate deal with Kincaid. She did it to protect her husband's reputation, like I said before—only not from a sex scandal, from a money scandal."

Mom finished her cup of coffee with a loud satisfied slurp....

...I FINISHED MY CHAIN of reasoning and waited for Francesca to make a comment.

After a moment she shrugged. "You don't really think that case is strong enough for you to get a conviction. Victor's an awfully good lawyer, you know."

"You're right," Ann said. "We probably couldn't make it stick in court. Unless we could find a witness to strengthen it. Somebody who could testify to Kincaid's part in the real estate deal. And somebody who knows he intended to visit Candy that afternoon."

Francesca's eyebrows lifted slightly. "You surely aren't referring to *me*. What on earth makes you think I'd testify against my dear old friend?"

"I didn't think so actually. I was just hoping. I always prefer it if the guilty party gets punished rather than an innocent party."

"Your client?" Francesca gave a splendidly contemptuous shrug. "I can't imagine how that concerns *me*."

"I didn't mean our client. He's out of it. The evidence clears him completely, the DA will have to let him go. No, I was referring to *you*, Francesca. Our case against *you* is more than strong enough."

Francesca gave one of her loud laughs. "But you *know* I didn't do it! You'd charge me with murder even though you know I'm innocent?"

Ann produced a beautiful duplicate of Francesca's contemptuous shrug. "What else could I do? My duty is to get my client off. I'd be neglecting my duty if I didn't do everything in my power to achieve that goal. Even if it means sending somebody else to the gas chamber in his place."

"But I didn't *do* it!"

Ann smiled gently. "I can't imagine how that concerns *me*."

There was a long silence. I could see from the way Francesca's eyes were scrunched up that she was thinking hard. The trick was to keep quiet and give her thoughts a chance to percolate and come boiling out.

Finally they boiled. "I didn't have anything to do with any killings," she said. "And I didn't know Victor had killed anybody. I may have had my suspicions, but there was nothing I could take to the police. I want that clearly understood.''

"All right, that's understood," Ann said.

"So I can't help you by telling the police that I saw any murders being committed, or anything like that. All I can testify to is that I called Victor on Thursday and told him that Chuck was turning against us and Victor said he'd take care of him. I can testify that I gave Victor a bottle of white wine at lunch the day before Christmas, and I might be able to identify the bottle too. And I can testify about that real estate deal, and Victor being the one behind it—he would've got the biggest cut for himself, I'll be happy to testify to *that*."

"You're willing to say all this under oath?"

"Oh that'll be easy. I'll take as many oaths as you please, I'm very good at oaths."

Ann looked at her a moment and said, "It doesn't bother you a bit, does it?"

"What doesn't bother me, dear?"

"Well, for openers, what you did to that old couple?"

"What *did* I do to them, for Heaven's sake? It was a simple business deal. They had something we wanted, we tried to buy it for the lowest possible price. That's what makes our country strong and free."

Francesca laughed. "Chuck *was* bothered by that part of it, I have to admit. He worried about what this deal would do to his relationship with God. He finally had to square his conscience by telling himself the money was for his church, not for himself.

"And Victor too. That's really rather funny, when you come right down to it. Victor had to square his conscience too. He told himself that *he* couldn't be discredited, *he* couldn't lose his career, *he* had a right to get away with murder, because if anything happened to him the forces of injustice would triumph. They're very much alike really, Chuck and Victor.

"I'm luckier than either of them. I don't believe in God, and I know there's no such thing as justice. I can sleep soundly at night, without any pangs of conscience.'' She gave her head a shake. "Now if I testify to all this, you're sure it'll get me off the hook for the murders?"

"I'm not the district attorney," Ann said. "But I wouldn't be at all surprised. Suppose we drive over to George Wolkowicz's house right now, and we can thrash the whole thing out."

Francesca looked at her for a moment, and then her cool crumpled all at once. A long sigh came out of her, like a death rattle. "It's all so fucking ironic, really. You know why I got into this deal in the first place? Because I'm an idealist. I've always been one. I've always made sure my friends were idealists too. That's where I learned all I know about greed and materialism. Watching my dear high-minded liberal friends march against the Vietnam War and fight to save the whales and sign petitions for everybody to divest their holdings in South Africa—and in between they're taking their long trips to Europe and trading in their old Maserati for a new Porsche and clipping the coupons from *their* investments. I got sick of it, can you understand that? I wanted some of the gravy for myself."

She broke off, took a few deep breaths, and then looked up at us again with one of her old sarcastic grins. "Little Francesca's been screwed again, hasn't she? I should've known it would turn out this way. Whenever I try to get out of this crummy hole—"

She broke off with a quick bark of a laugh. Then she took out her mascara and started to repair her face.

I CALLED George Wolkowicz's house from the phone on Francesca's desk. He wasn't pleased to hear my voice, and even less pleased when I told him Ann and I wanted to come over right away to tell him about some new developments in the case.

He couldn't exactly turn us down, though, so he gave one of his unpleasant chuckles and said, "I've got some new developments for you too, counselor. Like the reports are back on those fingerprints from the murder gun. And the lab has compared the kid's shoes with the shoeprints in

Candy's hallway. None of it looks good for your client, I'm sorry to say."

"Well, we're in for a terrific evening," I said. "Exchanging good news with each other."

Ann and Francesca left a few minutes later in Ann's car, and I followed them in mine. As I drove along, something odd began to stir in me. Deep down, like a vague tickle at first. A few minutes passed before I recognized what it was.

I was feeling happy. Happy didn't do it credit. Try elated, ecstatic, jubilant. I wanted to stick my head out the car window and give a yell to the world. It was Christmas. Only a few hours left of it, but Christmas it unquestionably was. And suddenly I was in favor of the whole thing.

I didn't give the yell though. Instead I turned on my car radio, and as if this was a movie with exactly the right music rising up exactly when you want it, about a million voices came blasting into my ears in the Hallelujah Chorus. Wonderful! Dear God, how wonderful! If You could create something like that—or to be accurate, if You could create the mind that could create something like that—You can't really be all bad.

And He answered me. He acknowledged my compliment. Because at that moment something landed on the windshield of my car. A snowflake! And another one followed it, and another one. And looking out the side, I could see that the snow was coming down. Slowly, not so thickly, but it was definitely snow. We were going to have a white Christmas after all! All right, semi-white. Which is better than nothing, right?

That's the secret of dealing with God, I decided. Very seldom does he give you what you want. But a lot of the time what he gives you is better than nothing. Settle for better than nothing, and life can be a reasonably enjoyable experience.

In front of me I saw a car with this bumper sticker: "Honk If You Hate People Who Honk If They Love Jesus."

I honked joyously, feeling like Ebenezer Scrooge in the last chapter. In the words of our esteemed Mayor Willard A. Butterfield, God bless us, every one.

EIGHT

After Christmas

AT THE END of a story, I always want to read a chapter where the author winds everything up. You find out what happens to all the people, you get the answers to all the unanswered questions. So this is what I'm going to do now, as briefly as possible.

First of all, there's Christmas. Whatever you may think about it, it's always over eventually. It reaches its climax in a great big New Year's Eve bash, and from January first it's strictly recovering from the hangover.

Here in Mesa Grande—in most towns like ours, I suppose—the hangover took the form of debris on the street. The giant Christmas tree got hauled away pretty fast, but it took much longer for the pine needles to disappear. Well through the end of January, you could still find yourself crunching a cluster of them underfoot, you could still see them mixed up with the garbage that clogged the drainage holes at the curbs. The remnants of Christmas posters, paper frost, glass bells, and so forth could be seen in store windows or flapping from the sides of buildings; Santa Clauses with half their faces torn off took their good time about disappearing from sight.

The churches, from the first days of January, started advertising a whole new line of sermons; "the spirit of the New Year" replaced "the spirit of Christmas" as a hot topic for our local clergy. The restaurants got rid of their menus with sleighbells decorating the margins, and started featuring special Presidential Birthday dinners.

And January also brought us a lot of snow. Heavy but intermittent, bitter cold days alternating with days that were so mild you could go out in a light coat. That's how it usually happens out here. The local saying is, "If you don't like the weather, be patient for an hour or two; it'll change."

Victor Kincaid was in California the day after Christmas, when the Mesa Grande district attorney's office requested the Los Angeles district attorney's office to arrest him and hold him for extradition. Immediately he launched a series of legal obstruction tactics, fighting the extradition, questioning the legality of the grand jury, petitioning for a change of venue, casting doubts on the integrity and impartiality of the judge, and issuing sizzling statements to interviewers that he was being framed by the establishment on account of his political opinions. Nevertheless he was held in our city jail without bail, his trial was scheduled for early February, and Francesca Fleming was summoned to be one of the leading witnesses against him.

Then, practically on the eve of the trial, he surprised everybody by going to the district attorney with the offer of a plea bargain. The result was that he pleaded guilty to second-degree murder in the death of the Reverend Chuck Candy and received a sentence of fifteen years, with eligibility for parole in five. The death of Luke Abernathy, late Prophet of the Cult of the Egg, wasn't mentioned either in the courtroom or the media.

Because there was no trial, Francesca didn't have her day in the witness box. But she'd already made her deal with the district attorney, and there was nothing he could do but stick to it. She pleaded guilty to charges of harassment and commercial fraud in connection with her attempt to get hold of the Meyers' property, she was sentenced to a year and a half in prison, and the sentence was suspended on condition she went into psychological therapy.

The day this sentence was announced, Francesca invited all her friends and acquaintances to a celebration dinner at her restaurant. A hundred people showed up, including most of the stars of the artistic, musical, theatrical and left-wing political world of Mesa Grande. The Reverend Eugene Grant Morgan was there, representing the ACLU, which had been prepared to take up the cudgels for Francesca's civil rights in the event that the judge had decided to send her to jail. He left the party early, however, before one of Francesca's friends made a little speech praising her as a heroine who had fortunately escaped martyrdom at the hands of the forces of oppression who controlled this fascistic town.

The Republican-American described this party in a scathing editorial the next morning: unsigned, but everybody recognized Arther T. Hatfield's style. To give one sample that will convey the flavor of the whole, the first sentence began: "Not since the most degenerate and disgusting orgies of imperial Rome...."

The Church of the Effulgent Apostles of Christ announced at the end of March that it was closing its doors and filing for bankruptcy. Attendance had fallen off sharply right after Christmas, but the death blow was the discovery, when auditors were brought in as a routine aftermath of Candy's death, that the capital surplus which the church was supposed to have in the bank was nonexistent and in fact there were fifty thousand dollars worth of debts. Mrs. Candy broke down and admitted that her late husband had been raiding the surplus for years, not for his own personal gain—this was obvious from the modest way he lived: no gold-plated foreign limousines or Shangri-la palaces, like certain other more highly-publicized evangelists—but to pay the mortgage on the building and to meet the monthly payroll, heating bills, phone bills, and costs of the video tapes in the lobby.

Shortly after the closing of the church, Gabriel Candy got a job selling real estate with Dwayne McKee's firm. If he was like most of the real estate salesmen in town, he worked strictly on commission.

In April, Chuck Candy's widow went back to New Mexico. Rumor had it that she moved in with her unmarried sister on the ranch where she was born.

Cutting back to December—the day the charges were officially dropped against Roger Meyer his parents had a modest luncheon celebration. Ann and I were invited, along with the rabbi, another elderly couple from the synagogue, and two or three young people who were Roger's friends. After the meal, Roger took me aside and asked me if I'd given any consideration to what he had discussed with me a few days ago. About his becoming my apprentice, or intern, or gofer, or whatever I wanted to call it, after his graduation from Yale in June.

"I feel I can be even more helpful to you," he said, "now that I've seen the other side. I mean, I've actually *been* in jail, I know what it feels like, I know the living conditions in there, and don't you think it's important for us to empathize with the people we're trying to help? It's like Joel McCrea in *Sullivan's Travels,* where he's this movie director who wants to make a movie about the poor and the bums and all, but he doesn't really know what their lives are like until he gets locked up in this chain gang—"

I told him again that I'd certainly take his offer into consideration, but I didn't think there was much chance of getting the money from the City Council. Privately I was thinking that it might not be a bad idea to have somebody to take some of the drudgery, the routine legwork, the filling out of forms off my back. The kid was bright, and he was definitely motivated.

If I'd ever had a son, I thought, he might be about Roger's age.

I talked to Ann about it after we left the Meyer's house, and her reaction was what I expected. "If you want somebody, Dave, you should have somebody. The problem is, how are we going to squeeze his salary out of the powers-that-be? And you know DA McBride'll be fighting us all the way."

But the solution to this problem dropped in our lap—the way the plums of life occasionally do—without any particular effort on our part. A few days later *The Republican-American* ran an editorial in which—if you can believe it—the public defender's office was praised for the good work it did in bringing the murderer of the Reverend Chuck Candy to justice. We could not be commended too much for the service we had done to the community by exposing the true nature of the radical left in its never-ending conspiracy to subvert America's cherished religious traditions—

Ann's first reaction to this editorial was to pull at her hair, like some Old Testament prophet bewailing the sins of his people. The next step would be sackcloth and ashes. It was almost too much for her, the idea that the hard work of her office should be used by these lunatics to push their crazy political philosophy. But after awhile she calmed down and decided we might as well pay the lunatics back in kind. Since they were using us for their purposes, why shouldn't we use them for ours? By this means some good could come out of the evil.

So she asked for an appointment with Arthur T. Hatfield and put it to the old scoundrel that the public defender's office, which he was so kind as to praise in his recent editorial, needed an increased budget if it was to go on operating effectively. Specifically, we needed money for an investigative assistant to take some of the burden off our overworked and undermanned investigatory staff (me). Would the newspaper be willing to put its weight and influence behind our effort to persuade the City Council to increase our budget so we could hire this extra person?

Hatfield implied he was willing. In Ann's opinion, which she expressed to me when she got back from her meeting, Hatfield was feeling a little guilty about the attempt he had made to railroad an innocent man into the gas chamber. He wanted to do something to erase that error from his conscience. "He *has* a conscience," Ann said. "You wouldn't think it from looking at him or reading his paper. But somewhere, deep inside there, hidden under those layers of steel plate, it's alive and occasionally fluttering."

The very next day *The Republican-American*'s editorial came out with the suggestion that it would benefit the crime-stopping capacities of the city if the public defender's investigatory staff were expanded. And the day after that, Ann made a formal proposal to the budget committee of the City Council. It took another month or so for the allocation of funds to go through, but during that time not a word of protest was heard from District Attorney Marvin McBride. Elected officials—even those like McBride who operate most of the time in a pleasant alcoholic haze—will seldom go out of their way to antagonize the only newspaper in town.

I had dinner with Mom the night of the City Council meeting. She was delighted with the news. "What a wonderful thing you're doing for his mother and father!" she said. "They suffered enough already, it's about time they got a little pleasure from life."

I tried to convince her that giving pleasure to Roger's mother and father had absolutely nothing to do with my decision, but she didn't seem to hear what I was saying.

And at that moment, for some reason, a question which had been kicking around in the back of my head since Christmas decided to come to the front. What was there in the Nutcracker Ballet which had given Mom her clue to the solution of the murder?

I asked her about it now.

She frowned and shook her head. "What was it, what was it?" she said. "It must've been something, but to tell you the truth, it's slipped out of my mind completely."

I felt a twinge of suspicion. Nothing ever slips out of Mom's mind. And when she begins a statement with "To tell you the truth," this usually means she's about to tell me a lie. But I couldn't see how it mattered, so I felt no urge to push Mom any further.

And just then my phone rang, and I forgot all about the Nutcracker Ballet and the Candy murder because I heard the voice of this woman I had met the other day at a Chamber of Commerce luncheon. She was the editor of the Woman's Page in *The Republican-American,* but from a few oblique remarks she dropped it had become clear that she had the same opinion as me about the paper and its policies. So I had asked her out to dinner this coming Saturday, and she was calling me back to say she had cleared her calender and she could make it.

I didn't talk to her long—Mom was in the room, sitting a few feet away from me. Sure enough, after I hung up, Mom said, in an airy voice, as if she hardly had her mind on what she was saying, "So who was that? A friend of yours? The voice sounded nice and cultured. A woman's voice, or am I mistaken?''

As a matter of fact, Saturday turned out to be a great evening. I found out, over spaghetti, that we shared exactly the same taste in movies. After dinner we went up to her place and watched *His Girl Friday* on her VCR. Cary Grant and Rosalind Russell exchanged cynical wisecracks, and my hostess and I laughed our heads off, and an hour or two later I found myself wondering if I might not believe in God after all.

EPILOGUE
Mom Praying

Dear God,

All right, You're probably surprised to see me here. I know I'm not the type that spends a lot of time in this place. I wouldn't be here in the middle of a weekday when there's nobody else around, if it wasn't a matter of importance.

It's about this murder, naturally. All right, the murder is ancient history, it was all solved and wrapped up and put away in the closet a couple of months ago, on Christmas day, and since then everybody is telling my son Davie what a fine job he did and how smart he is, which I'm certainly not unhappy to hear. But what You know is that the whole truth and nothing but didn't come out yet. And you know that I know it too.

Which is why I'm here, why I'm talking to You now. Dear God, am I wrong to keep my mouth shut about this? Am I doing a terrible thing which forever into eternity You'll be angry at me for doing? I did it only because I thought it was for the best, I didn't mean to do something wrong. How could I lie to You about that? All these years You've been acquainted with me, how could I expect to fool You about my feelings and my motives and so on? But even so, maybe I'm wrong, and I should open my mouth and come out with the truth.

In other words, dear God, I'm full of doubts. I'll tell You the whole story—which naturally, You know already, but I have to tell it anyway—and then I'm hoping You'll give me Your honest opinion....

Besides, it isn't as if I let a murderer go free. This Victor Kincaid, I proved he was guilty, and that's what he was, guilty. This You know, and I'm sure You'll take it into con-

sideration. *If I happened to do a little deceiving, a little covering up, and let's face it a little outright lying, it wasn't so the murderer would get away with his crimes, it was strictly to keep other things, important things, from coming out.*

For instance, all that business about the message that the murdered man wrote on his carpet in crayon. "GOLD, FRANKINCENSE, AND MYRRH"—we both know this had nothing to do with Victor Kincaid or with Francesca Fleming. We both know he didn't write FRAN on the carpet, and he didn't write KINC either. I made that up so Davie and Ann Swenson and everybody else would be thrown off the track.

And we both know that Mrs. Candy wasn't the one who saw those letters on the carpet and stretched them out into GOLD, et cetera. Who could believe that she, any more than her husband, could spell those long peculiar words correctly? All right, she had a better education than him, but I noticed right away that when she copied her husband's posters for the church, she never corrected any of the spelling mistakes.

So Mrs. Candy isn't the fanatic that I smelled from the beginning in the woodpile. I told a slander about her, and for this I apologize, though she never knew I told it, it was never brought out in public, so it didn't actually hurt her, did it? This You have to admit.

What I had to hide from everybody, naturally, was that the letters Candy wrote on the carpet before he died weren't FRAN or KINC but MYR. Which, with his terrible spelling, was the best he could do to write MEYER. In other words, it was Roger Meyer he was trying to blame for his murder, with his last ounce of energy.

And how do I know this? Because of the way those letters were placed on the carpet. Smack up against the left-hand edge came GOLD, FRANKINCENSE, AND, after which, right underneath them, also smack against the left hand edge, came MYRRH. What a peculiar arrangement, if the person who added on to Candy's message started off with FRAN or KINC. Why not write MYRRH on the same line with GOLD, FRANKINCENSE, AND? Why carry it over into another line all by itself? It's obvious why. The M in MYRRH was already up against the lefthand edge, this is where Candy put it. There was no room to put GOLD, FRANKINCENSE, AND to the left of it, so they had to go above it.

So who made these additions? The first answer that came into my head was that Roger Meyer made them himself. He really did kill Candy, and he started to leave the house, and maybe he heard Candy groaning from the living room, so he went back there, and saw that Candy, who was now dead, had written MYR on the carpet. So Roger knew he had to add the other letters, or he'd be arrested for the crime.

But pretty soon I realized this couldn't be the explanation. First of all, I already proved, with pure logic, that the murderer was Victor Kincaid. (And later on, as You know, he confessed to the murder and right now he's in prison, organizing protests against the lousy food.)

Second of all, if Roger was the guilty party, look at all the things that must have happened while he was in Candy's house—Candy lets him into the house, they have an argument, he kills Candy, he starts to leave, Candy tears open the crayon box, he writes a short message on the carpet, Roger comes back in, he changes Candy's short message to a long one, he goes out again. But he wasn't inside that house more than five minutes, according to old Luke Abernathy, the witness who was stan.'ing across the street. It isn't possible all those things should happen in only five minutes.

Third of all, when Roger was arrested and admitted he saw Candy's body in the living room, he said he didn't see any red-crayon message on the carpet. If Roger was the one that wrote the message, with the idea of hiding what Candy really wrote, wouldn't he have said he saw it there when he was standing over Candy's body? Wouldn't he have to say this so we'd believe it was written there before he got to the scene of the crime?

The reason Roger said he didn't see that long message was because it wasn't written yet when he found the body. If it *had been there, he would've noticed it. But it was easy for a scared, mixed-up boy to overlook what actually was there, just those three letters MYR.*

Incidentally, along with the question who wrote that long message, I had to ask myself why did Candy write the short message? Why did he try to accuse Roger Meyer of killing him when he must've known that Roger didn't do it, that it was Victor Kincaid who killed him? The answer to this I didn't like very much, but there wasn't any way to get around it. Candy wasn't interested in exposing his real killer. It didn't matter to him Victor Kincaid should go to jail for his murder. Candy wanted the police, the whole world, to think he was killed by Roger Meyer.

The reason was, if the real killer got caught, then the truth about Candy's real estate deal would also come out. And that would be the end of his reputation. The saint would look like a sinner, and for Candy this was the worst thing that could happen. In his opinion, it was necessary that people should go on thinking how holy he was. He was God's missionary on earth—real estate swindle or not—and if people lost faith in him, they'd lose faith in God.

You notice, when I'm talking about God in connection with this Candy, I don't say "You."

And what would be the harm, he asked himself, if Roger Meyer was punished for the murder? Meyer the Jew. Wouldn't it be a good thing that everybody should think the Jews killed this saintly Christian minister, just like they killed Jesus Christ? So he wrote MYR on the carpet, and then, with a little bit of life he still had in him, he pulled the phone down on the floor, dialed the Meyers' number, and asked to speak to Roger. His voice was weak, practically a whisper—like Roger and his father both said—but this wasn't because somebody was trying to disguise the voice, it was because Candy was close to dying.

So when Roger got on the line, Candy told him to come over right away. Maybe he knew the front door would be open because, when Kincaid ran out of the house, Candy never heard him slam the door behind him.

There's the hidden fanatic, dear God. The dead man himself. Nobody took him serious, because he sounded like a used-car salesman instead of a Nazi from the movies. Everybody automatically said, 'He's a hypocrite, he don't really believe what he's preaching.' Only he did believe. He was such a genuine believer he died telling a lie in God's name. A fanatic, what else?

Also a schmuck.

Still, this don't explain yet how those letters he wrote, MYR, got changed to GOLD, FRANKINCENSE, AND MYRRH. Between the time Roger ran away, which was around four-thirty, and the time Mrs. Candy got home from her shopping, which was around five-thirty, somebody came to the Candy house. This somebody found the front door open—Roger, when he ran out, forgot to slam it behind him, just like Kincaid forgot when he ran out earlier. So this somebody walked into the living room and saw the letters MYR on the carpet. Realizing right away that Candy was accusing Roger of murder, and wanting to cover up the accusation, this somebody changed the short message to the long one. And this somebody, in leaving the house, did slam the door, which is why Mrs. Candy found it locked when she got home.

So who could this somebody be? It couldn't be Roger's parents, because at the time of Candy's murder they were on the phone talking long distance to their daughter in Los Angeles. Also, Abernathy would've seen one or the other or both of them entering and leaving the house, but he didn't mention anything about them.

Another thing about this somebody. Isn't it peculiar he, or maybe she, was in the house at that particular time? Who could it be, finding the front door of a house unlocked, is going to walk right in and wander into the living room, and after seeing a dead body there is going to walk out again without calling the police? To me it could only be somebody who knew ahead of time the body was going to be there. Maybe even somebody who came to that house because the body would be there.

So who could have told this somebody? Not the murderer, Kincaid, who certainly didn't want that anybody should know he knew about the body. So who else knew about the body? Nobody except Roger Meyer—and the person he told all about it ten or fifteen minutes after he ran away. The person he ran to, so he could hide out.

Don't go so fast, I told myself. You're forgetting about Abernathy. He was standing outside Candy's house until the police came. Didn't he see this somebody come in and out? So explain why he never mentioned it.

Quick as a flash, I answered myself: Abernathy did mention it. Only in his crazy way, with maybe a little too much alcohol in him. He said to Davie he saw "the dark betrayer" go into Candy's house. He also said he saw "the fiend with the flat head" and "the Triangular Egg." Who was "the dark betrayer"? To Abernathy, this religious maniac, what he saw was the representative, the symbol, of the biggest betrayers of all, the betrayers who killed Jesus Christ. And why did this fiend, in his eyes, have a "flat head"? Because the light wasn't so good at five o'clock or so, and to Abernathy it looked like the top of this visitor's head was sliced off. Instead of being shaped like an egg— which most heads are, more or less—this head was flat at the top, turning it into a triangle. A triangular egg.

How could such an effect be produced?

Didn't I see it being produced on Christmas day, when Davie and I went to the Nutcracker Ballet? Didn't the bad lighting make the old toymaker's head look like the top of it was sliced off? Why? Because he was wearing a black skullcap. A yarmulke.

And finally, there's a clue which nobody remembers except me. And You, naturally.

When Davie and Mrs. Swenson examined the scene of the murder, they noticed there was a picture of Jesus Christ over the fireplace, only its face was turned to the wall. Why would such a thing be done? Obviously because the person who did it was feeling guilty about something he or she was doing in the room and didn't want Jesus to watch it happening. But what type person would this be?

It couldn't be any of the people we know were in the house that afternoon. Mrs. Candy, if she had actually changed FRAN or KINC to FRANKINCENSE, wouldn't have felt guilty about it. She would've felt she was doing it as her religious duty, she would've been proud for Jesus to watch her do it. Same thing for Candy himself, writing MYR on the carpet to bear false witness against Roger Meyer. In Candy's opinion this was an act that Jesus could only approve of.

On the other hand, it couldn't be Victor Kincaid, feeling guilty about committing a murder. Kincaid is a big atheist, he announces it in public, it's part of his reputation that he don't believe in You or in Jesus. He wouldn't give two thoughts about killing somebody while Jesus was looking on.

Besides, whoever did this, it was somebody who got to the house after the murder was over and after Roger Meyer ran away. How do I know this? Because Roger, when he told his story about finding the dead body, said that he saw Jesus Christ's picture on the wall and it made him nervous because it reminded him he was Jewish. So the picture wasn't turned to the wall yet when Roger was in the house.

So who's left? The person who came to the house and changed MYR to MYRRH and so on.

This is when I remembered something that happened to my late cousin Sadie years ago when she was a young girl. She told her parents she was spending the weekend with friends of hers in the country, but actually she was spending it in one of those country inns with her boyfriend Irving. They checked into a room together, and they got all ready to have a little fun in the bed—You'll excuse me mentioning these things so openly, but after all, if You don't know about them, who does?—when suddenly Sadie noticed, hanging from a hook on the wall of the room, a cross. And hanging from the cross was Jesus Christ, carved up in wood. The people that owned this inn were Catholics, and every one of the rooms had such a cross in it. So anyway, Sadie couldn't go on with what she was doing until first she made Irving get up, stand on a chair, take the cross off the wall, and put it away in the bottom drawer of the dresser. It wasn't logical, it didn't make sense, and what's more Sadie knew it. But she had to do it anyway.

Incidentally, Sadie and Irving got married a few months later, and lived together fifty-two years, with three children, so the story has a happy ending.

But the point is, it was the same thing with this person who turned Candy's picture of Jesus to face the wall. This person knew he was doing something in that room that wasn't exactly right. This wouldn't stop him from doing it— in fact, he came to the house especially to make sure there wouldn't be any evidence to connect Roger Meyer with the murder—but still in his heart he knew he was breaking the law. And who is it, when he's doing something definitely not kosher—or even when he isn't—feels nervous that Jesus Christ should be looking at him all the time? It isn't a Christian, it's a Jew.

Not only that, it's a religious Jew. The more religious he is, the more self-conscious he feels about Jesus, the more he worries about doing something wrong with Jesus himself, the biggest Christian of all, as a witness. And particularly it's so at this time of the year, at Christmastime, when for Jews it seems like everywhere they go they can't get out from under Jesus Christ's eye.

All right, dear Lord, so now it was pretty clear to me who the somebody was—but maybe what You want to know is, why I've been keeping quiet about these deductions, why I never even told them to my own son. Well, this is exactly what's bothering me now and why I'm here in the synagogue asking You for Your advice. I did keep quiet, I'm still keeping quiet even though Roger Meyer is in the clear and the real killer has already been found guilty and sent to jail, because how would it look, in this town that's full of Christians who don't much like Jews, if the most prominent local Jew, the man that represents his people in everybody's eyes, is accused of tampering with evidence in a murder case? It certainly wouldn't be good for the Jews.

And incidentally, I've got a good idea this is exactly why the rabbi—all right, what's the point saying "somebody" when we both know who I'm talking about?—did the tampering in the first place? Part of it maybe because he thought Roger Meyer was innocent and didn't want him falsely accused of the murder, but most of it, in my opinion, because it wouldn't be good for the Jews.

Even so, dear Lord, I'm not sure it's right for me to go on keeping quiet. What happens when I finally meet You in the eternal life after the Messiah comes? Will You hold this lie against me already, even though I only told it with the best intentions, which I'm sure You know from looking into my heart? Because I was trying to protect my people, who are also Your people, does this make me in my own way another fanatic? Please God, do me a big favor, give me some guidance on this question....

... That's it?

All right, yes, I think I see the point. It isn't being a fanatic if You're trying to protect others against fanatics? Doesn't the Talmud itself say it's permissible to fight fire with fire? I'm positive that's in the Talmud somewhere.

Also, God, You love Your creations, You don't go around getting mad at them for this or that little thing, unless it happens that they broke one of Your Commandments. And in all honesty, who can say I've done that? Show me where there's a commandment against lying. Against bearing false witness, yes. A person definitely shouldn't bear false witness against the neighbors or anybody else. But tell me please, what neighbor or other innocent party has been hurt by the lie I told? So what's stopping You from forgiving me? Nothing.

One more question I'd like to ask You. If I don't make the truth public, shouldn't I at least go to the rabbi privately and tell him what I figured out about him? Is it justice that he should think he got away scotch free with what he did?...

... That's Your answer, God?

All right, all right, the truth is I knew this answer even before I asked the question. If I go to the rabbi and tell him from my deductions, my reason wouldn't have anything to do with justice. My real reason—and I know You know it, and You know I know it—would be that I couldn't resist the *temptation to show the rabbi I'm smarter than he is. So I'm sorry, dear God. I withdraw my suggestion, and I hope You'll excuse me that I ever came up with it in the first place.*

Now it's time for me to go home. Davie's coming to dinner, and also I've invited that nice Meyer boy, and some girl he's going out with, so I have to put my pot roast in the oven.

Goodbye for now, dear God.

And I nearly forgot. Amen.

THE MAN IN THE GREEN CHEVY

THE HOMICIDE UNIT CONSISTED OF ME AND ANYBODY WHO WASN'T BUSY THAT I COULD BORROW...

Chief deputy Milt Kovak of Prophesy County, Oklahoma Sheriff's Department had a rapist and murderer on his hands. To make the whole thing really stink, the victims were little old ladies, the nice cookie-baking, sweater-knitting kind.

His prime witness is Mrs. Laura Johnson—about thirty-five, three kids, an absentee husband—the sexiest woman Milt has ever seen. She's identified a man in a green Chevy emerging from the murder scene. Find that man, he figured, find the killer....

SUSAN ROGERS COOPER

MYSTERY WRITERS OF AMERICA GRAND MASTER

HUGH PENTECOST

A PIERRE CHAMBRUN MYSTERY

MURDER IN LUXURY

First Time in Paperback

CHECKOUT TIME

Rich, beautiful, lonely and in trouble, Valerie Summers arrived at New York's luxurious Hotel Beaumont dragging a trail of murder that baffled even the Beaumont's legendary manager, Pierre Chambrun.

First, her mother; then, a man she had a crush on; then, her husband; then, her best friend; then, a punk in her apartment—and now, a dead cop in her hotel room. Was she the terrified victim of a killer with a grudge . . . or a monster hidden behind a lovely face?

Everbody is playing wild guessing games, but it's clear there's a killer out there, mad as a hatter, deadly as a cobra, circulating in Chambrun's world—watching . . . and waiting.

MIL

ATTRACTIVE, SPACE SAVING BOOK RACK

Display your most prized novels on this handsome and sturdy book rack. The hand-rubbed walnut finish will blend into your library decor with quiet elegance, providing a practical organizer for your favorite hard- or soft-covered books.

Only $9.95

Approximately 16" x 8" when assembled

Assembles in seconds!

To order, rush your name, address and zip code, along with a check or money order for $10.70* ($9.95 plus 75¢ delivery) payable to *The Mystery Library Reader Service*:

Mystery Library Reader Service
Book Rack Offer
3010 Walden Avenue
P.O. Box 1396
Buffalo, NY 14269-1396

Offer not available in Canada.

BKR-MLR

*New York residents add appropriate sales tax.